I0587414

The Last Griffin

Cadillac Press

Cadillac Press
185 Drummond St. Rd
Drummond, NB E3Y 1V9
Canada

Copyright © 2016 Wendy L. Koenig
All rights reserved
Printed in the United States of America

This book, or parts thereof, may not be reproduced in any form without permission. The scanning, uploading, and distribution of this book via the Internet or via any other means without the permission of the publisher is illegal and punishable by law.

Cover image by Lynn Perkins

2 4 6 8 10 9 7 5 3 1
FIRST EDITION THIS PUBLISHER

For Vince.

The Last Griffin

Wendy L. Koenig

Chapter 1

The silence of the attack surprised Olivia Bonaparte. She wasn't sure what she thought that kind of thing should have sounded like, but silence hadn't been it.

It was eleven p.m. on Christmas Eve in Boulder, Colorado, and the whole night had been quiet. As she walked home from her job as a bartender at Q's, a local bistro at the open air Pearl Street Mall, snow fell in thick wet flakes, hiding the sky and anything more than a few feet away. It muffled the night sounds: car engines, horns, voices, and shouts. She didn't see the dark shapes skulking behind her, nor did she hear their footsteps.

She had no reason to worry. The way home to her Spruce Street apartment was well lit and usually busy with other pedestrians, though she hadn't seen many that night. The peace of the season surrounded her. Even her normally raucous neighbors were silent. No televisions or radios invaded the building with carols or commercials. From a few doors down came the soft strains of laughter. Had all but one family gone away for the holidays?

As she opened the door to her home, something heavy landed between her shoulder blades, knocking her to the floor. Two intruders barreled into the apartment. The ricocheting door trapped a third attacker outside and he pulled it off its hinges, splintering the wood. The sound echoed loudly in the quiet entryway. She'd never forget it. Her neighbors must have heard it. Help would come soon.

Though she only saw the three attackers, she almost felt the presence of more waiting not far away. Of course, that could have been her imagination. Like cowards, her muggers wore red-brown bear costumes and flanked her as she struggled to her feet. In Miss Atwood's self-defense class, she'd learned a wide, defensive stance and she took that now, rolling her hands into loose fists. Specific moves eluded her; she just hoped instinct would take over. The yell that bubbled in her throat died away as the bear-men attacked, quiet as grave-robbers.

Desperate, Olivia fought, connecting her boots to shin bones and knees, and her fists to everything she could reach. Still, the men threw her to the hard linoleum like a rag doll. On the floor, she continued to kick, connecting more than once with rigid bone. She wrapped her hands around legs and bit. She thought there'd be some screams or shouts at least. But the only sounds were grunts, growls, and deep raspy breaths. The sounds scored across her mind, and she knew she'd remember them forever.

Her ribs snapped under one kick and another brought an ache deep in her back where she figured her right kidney was located. Then all fight fled her and she huddled as tightly as she could into a ball. This would ruin the holiday for her neighbors. Bright wrapping paper and ribbons would have a darkened hue, hymn singers would be a tad more somber and everyone would be dressed in black. No longer would she be thought of as the plain girl down the hall. She would be remembered as the girl who ruined Christmas. Would anyone tell Miss Atwood at the orphanage? Or would the elderly woman learn of her death from the newspaper? Olivia was pretty sure the final blow would come soon, but suddenly the brutes scattered.

It was silent for only a moment, and then footsteps pounded outside and across the floor. Unable to see the door from her position near the opposite end of her couch, she called, "Who is it?"

When no answer came, she turned her head in a small movement. White-hot pain in her back penalized her, but she could see a tall, clean-shaven man with curly brown hair approaching. Police? So quickly? Apparently, her neighbors had heard. He squatted beside her, his knees popping at the effort. His nose looked like it had been broken once or twice, the bump exaggerated and slightly skewed off-center.

His brow was furrowed with … what? Confusion? Concern? His rich, brown eyes stayed focused on hers. It felt as if something tangible passed between them. He frowned as if he felt it too, and it worried him. He took her hand with a gentle touch. "Medical help is coming. Hang on."

She squeezed her fingers around his, and he rubbed his thumb across the back of her fist. He said, "I'm Brian Merullo. What's your name?"

"Olivia Bonaparte."

"While we wait for the ambulance, tell me a little about yourself, Olivia."

11

"I'm twenty-three, and I work Q's as a bartender. There's not much else to tell."

He asked a few more questions. Her answers were basically all the same:

"No, I didn't see their faces."

"No, I don't know of any enemies."

"No, nothing out of the ordinary happened the past few weeks, or month even, except this attack."

Olivia opened her mouth to say more, but crisp wind blew through her ruined door. Shivers from cold or shock rippled through her. Reaching across her body, he pulled a couch blanket to cover her. Close to her face, like he was, the scent of snow and mud from his street clothes filled her nostrils. He held her chilled hands in his warm ones and talked to her about anything that seemed to cross his mind. She was glad to have something to take her thoughts off the pain and terror she felt shaking inside her skin. His dialogue was as gentle as his voice, and she found it easy to listen, though wave after wave of nausea and deep-dwelling pain rolled over her.

At last, she heard the cry of a couple sirens entering the parking lot. At the same time, a black-haired man arrived. He spoke to Brian in a voice as smooth as ice. "They're gone."

Brian's gaze locked with Olivia's, and she again felt that connection pass between them. What was that? Her brown-haired knight loosened his grip on her hand. "I'm going to find the men who hurt you. Just hang on, okay?"

She wanted to hold him back, to say, "Wait! No! I need you here." Anything to keep him from leaving. She clenched his hand as hard as she could. She needed his strength; it would keep her safe. He smiled an apology, worked his hand out of her grasp and left as ambulance workers in bright coats and white pants entered. The paramedics gently probed her body, sending Olivia into spasms every time one of them touched the small of her back. It seemed like forever, but at last they decided she was stable enough to transport to the hospital.

Uniformed cops arrived. She asked one, "Where are the men who rescued me? I want to thank them."

She looked for Brian, the man with the mesmerizing brown eyes, but she didn't see him anywhere. He'd probably gone to interview neighbors. He was on the job, after all. Still, she felt the keen edge of disappointment.

Olivia was lifted onto the transport gurney. The harsh bite of pain enveloped her completely, and she lost consciousness.

Chapter 2

Brian waited in Tony's navy blue Escalade at the edge of the apartment parking lot. Two fire trucks, an ambulance and three police cruisers stood at odd angles to each other, crisscrossing the parking lines, with the ambulance closest to the door of Olivia's apartment. Emergency lights flashed in the dark, adding more gaudiness to the twinkling Christmas decorations and plastic snowmen up and down the block.

He couldn't get the picture of her out of his head. Her fighter's stance said she'd had some kind of training, but he didn't think it was much. Still, outnumbered and outsized, she stood up to her attackers, giving almost as good as she got. Even when they finally got her down, she continued to fight. She was a tough one. He hoped she'd make it.

Tony crossed the lot, avoiding the arriving Channel 4 news van, and slid into the driver's seat. The brilliance of the flashing lights strobed across his face, turning it red, then blue, then purple. They sat for a moment, watching the tableau until the stretcher came out and the paramedics loaded Olivia into the ambulance.

"Do you think she'll survive?" Brian held his breath. For some reason, it mattered. He wasn't sure why, and frankly, it unnerved him. He could still smell the copper-base-salt of her blood on his hands. It had been all over her apartment, all over her.

"Yep." Tony looked at him. The headlights from the leaving ambulance lit his face then, and Brian saw his friend's eyebrows hard knit into a frown. "All I found were footprints: bare human feet. But, it was Carl Hall. I'm sure of it."

Brian nodded by means of an answer. He wished they'd arrived sooner, then Olivia wouldn't have been attacked at all. "We need to verify that."

Neither said anything for a few moments. Then Tony spoke again. "If it was them, my source is valid. He said Hall and his buddies were on the prowl for something."

"I didn't see anything in her apartment to tell us why they attacked, and she didn't know either."

Again, they were silent. Brian's thoughts returned to Olivia. He tasted the name in his mouth, rolling the sound of it around and around. He liked it. He wondered about that snare of a connection he'd felt when he'd met her gaze. What was that? He'd never experienced anything like it before. It felt as if their future had tied together in that brief meeting. It was no mere attraction. Strangely, it felt like he was falling in love. He shook his head. No. It couldn't be. He'd been with her for only a few short minutes. Besides, love wasn't for the likes of him.

He again saw her fighting in his mind. Saw her honey-colored hair swing as she whirled to block one of her attackers. In the few seconds he'd watched her fight, he'd glimpsed her fierceness and determination. It

15

impressed him that she didn't go down easily. He'd seen her attackers' surprise in the way they had moved, but they had been equally determined and aimed their blows to inflict maximum injury. "They'll be back to finish."

"We'll need to interview her tomorrow, find out what insights she has on this after she's got some distance from it. You're right; though, it didn't look like a scare tactic to me. They wanted her dead. We need to find out everything about her that we can."

"I'll stay with her tonight. You talk to your sources again."

"You don't like babysitting."

Brian stared at his friend's silhouette in the dark. He shrugged. "She needs protection. That's either you or me, and your contacts won't talk to me."

The parking lot was dark and bare now, except for a lone police cruiser. Tony turned to regard him full on. He said nothing for a few beats. Then, "Don't get involved with her. It'll end badly. It always does."

Brian had offered Tony a valid reason for staying with Olivia, yet his friend had jumped to the opposite conclusion. He narrowed his eyes and glared at the man beside him, knowing Tony could see it. "What the hell are you talking about? I'm not interested in getting involved with anyone. You don't know anything about what I'm thinking."

"I do know it. And so do you. It's all over your face. It won't last long and you'll be alone again in the end. Just don't do it."

Brian turned away from the conversation. He didn't want to hear any more of Tony's logic. Of course, his friend was right. He often was. In his mind, he again saw Olivia bleeding out on the floor of her destroyed apartment. Something deep inside him twisted and tore. He couldn't let anyone hurt her again. He'd stay by her night and day. If necessary, he'd give his life to protect her. But he'd keep his distance. He wanted nothing to do with romantic entanglements. He jutted his chin toward the road. "Let's get going."

Tony started the car and turned it in the direction the ambulance had taken.

Chapter 3

Olivia woke late afternoon in the hospital on Christmas day. Gaudy red and green streamers twisted from the top of the wall-mounted TV to the corner of the closet door frame. Gold garland draped the window in the door. Somewhere, elevator music played a sappy instrumental of "White Christmas." The usual hospital smell of cleaning solution and medicine rounded out the festivities of the season.

A dark-haired man in jeans and a leather jacket stared at her from the easy chair in the corner of the room. Deep brown eyes met hers frankly. It took her a moment to remember what had happened and who he was: her rescuing knight.

He stood and walked to the bed. He was tall. A lot taller than Olivia remembered, though from her position on the floor of her apartment, anyone would look tall. He stood at least six and a half feet. When he spoke, though, there was no intimidation in his voice. It was strong, yet gentle. Calming. Like it had been last night. "Do you remember me? I'm Brian Merullo. I sat with you in your apartment before the ambulance came. My friend, Tony, wants to speak with you. He'll be here in a few minutes. He's chatting up a nurse down the hall. Do you remember us?"

Chatting up…? This did not instill confidence. Nor did Brian seem to approve of it; his voice had been laced with criticism. "You were the two cops from last night." Olivia's voice sounded like a scratchy LP record. She didn't even want to know what she looked like.

Brian shook his head, brow furrowed. "We're —"

"Good. I see you're awake." As if speaking of the second hero summoned him, the silky voice she'd heard while curled up on the floor of her apartment interrupted from the doorway. She turned her head and met the startling blue gaze of Brian's partner. He held out a long fingered hand that was as finely groomed as his jet black hair. He was almost as tall as Brian. "I'm Tony Silver." His voice was smooth like his name. She felt no empathy with him, no connection and one word came to mind: slick.

Olivia couldn't help herself. She asked, "Tony Silver? What kind of a name is that?"

"It's Italian. It's really Antonio Silvani." He smiled and winked. "Don't tell anyone. How are you feeling?"

She wasn't sure about trusting him, but Brian obviously did. Since she trusted Brian, she decided to trust Tony, too. She answered honestly. "Woozy. Sore. Have a headache."

Olivia moved a hand to where her kidney had hurt the previous night and found gauze. It stretched high on her back and all the way around her chest. Broken rib? Great. What other injuries did she have from the previous night's escapades?

Tony said, "I'm going to get your take on what happened and let you return to healing. That good with you?" He sat on the edge of the bed and Brian returned

19

to his chair in the corner. The chair was low and his knees rose high in front of him. He crossed his right ankle over his left knee, exposing Nike running shoes and white gym socks. He picked up and began reading a celebrity magazine from the stack on the small table beside him. The cover depicted one of the Kardashian women with big words: "She's done it again!"

Olivia said to Tony. "I don't really know any more than last night."

He pursed his lips, hesitated, and then said, "Close your eyes."

She glanced again at Brian, but he appeared not to have heard: he was engrossed in his magazine, and she wondered if he was really reading it or pretending. Obediently, she lowered her eyelids.

Tony's voice led her back to her memories of the evening before. "Don't be afraid. I'm here with you. What do you smell?"

Smell? Her mind jumped to the whirlwind of the attack for a brief second before it recoiled. She didn't get anything and tried again, leading with her nose. She remembered the smell of the city walking home: snow on the wind, exhaust, food. She did her best to blacken the images and focus on the smell. "Snow. Sweat. Musk. Mud." Why mud?

"Good. That's great. Do you hear anything? Did they speak?" His voice held her in the scene.

Again, Olivia tried to blacken the images, but this time it didn't work. She heard the brute attackers in her head. Saw the swinging legs and fists. She wanted to leave the memories far behind and open her eyes to broad daylight. Instead, she squeezed them shut tighter and twisted the hem of her blanket, wrapping it around and around her finger, using the pain to keep her from falling into the nightmare. "No. There was nothing except the occasional grunt and growl. They were breathing hard." She then became conscious of her own deep breaths at that memory.

Tony asked, "What about before they broke in? Did you hear voices in the hall?"

"Nothing. I'm sorry." In the small hospital room, Olivia heard a noise from the chair in the corner that sounded like a cross between a sharp inhale and a throat clearing. What was that about? She opened her eyes and glanced at Brian. His magazine was laying on his lap, open to some gaudy page or other. His legs were stretched straight out in front of him, but his gaze was on her, eyes sparkling. He shook his head and closed his dark brown eyes pointedly.

She unwrapped her now purple finger from the blanket and shut her eyes again.

Tony coached her, "Tell me about their footsteps when they broke in."

Footsteps. Okay. She wasn't in the apartment, getting the crap beat out of her. She was here, in the hospital. Two cops in the room with her. Safe. She could do this. She replayed the moment she first was knocked to the floor to the point where they surrounded her. It was hard to notice the feet, when the memory of the attack was still so vivid. She wrapped her finger again. "They were mostly quiet, I think. A few scuffs, but no hard heels or anything."

"And when they kicked you? What did you feel? Were the shoes pointed or round? This is a hard question, I'm sorry."

She swallowed her rising panic, licked her lips, and tried to follow the action in her mind. She was knocked to the ground. She got up and tried to fight. They surrounded her. Again, Olivia felt the angry kicks meet her own and her arms bruise from their heavy blows. Panic edged into her, overwhelming her memories and her mind veered away. She stopped, took a deep breath

21

and focused again. She'd fought them and held them off. She'd survived. She went back to the memory where she'd left off: on the floor, fighting. "No, definitely not pointed, but not quite round either. It was like they had hard ridges on the front of them. You know, like some of those Wellies."

"So, they had Wellington boots. All of them?"

"The ones that kicked me, anyway."

Brian's voice asked the next question from beside the bed now. "Were their shoes hard or soft?" Olivia started at the nearness of his voice even though she kept her eyes shut; she hadn't heard him leave his chair, and she thought she should have, given his size. A big man like that should have made some noise.

Tony whispered, "Sit down. Let me handle this."

Brian's voice was subdued when he asked, "What? It's important." But his voice had already receded to the far corner of the room again.

Perversely, she decided to answer Brian's question. "The ridges were hard, but I think the shoes themselves must have been soft because they had to keep changing the angle of the kick, as if their feet got sore. If that makes sense." She opened her eyes as Brian gave Tony the "see!" gesture of open hands toward her.

Tony waved him away and addressed her. "Last question. What were they wearing on their bodies?"

She kept her eyes open, but pictured it in her mind again, feeling the fists and the feet. She'd reached out and grabbed legs, bitten them. She could still taste the warm, salty blood of her attackers. "Fur. They were wearing full costumes."

Tony glanced at Brian who raised his eyebrows in return.

With a forced smile that Olivia thought was supposed to be reassuring, Tony turned back to her and said, "Well, that's all for now. You've given us

22

something to pursue. I have a few ideas, and I'm going to start on them tonight. Tomorrow morning will probably be the soonest I can return to see you. Brian's going to stay with you again tonight, just to make sure you're safe. Okay?" Without waiting for an answer, Antonio "Smooth" Silvani left, his gaze snapping up and down the hallway. Though a poser on several levels, he had proven he was skillful at interviewing. He had driven right to the heart of what he wanted to know.

She looked back at Brian who watched Tony leave with a worried expression. His elbows rested on his knees, and his hands were clasped loosely together. Snow and sleet pelted down outside the window behind him. The weather added to Brian's gloomy frown. When he saw her observing him, he mimicked his friend's smile, leaned back and concentrated on his magazine again.

They knew something. Olivia was sure of it.

Chapter 4

Brian picked up his magazine and chose an article at random, determined to focus on the words written there. He hated celebrity magazines, but all those in the waiting room had been the same. His fingers itched to draw, but he hadn't brought his sketch pad.

He felt Olivia staring at him, her gaze burning into his forehead. More than anything, he wanted to tell her the truth about the attack. It bubbled to his lips, wanting to pour out.

A movement on the periphery of his vision caught his attention. Tony beckoned to him from the hall, beyond the edge of the window. With relief, Brian set down the magazine and escaped from the room, Olivia's gaze following every step he made.

The sting of antiseptic and medicine pinched his nose the moment he entered the hallway. In the room, it had been noticeable, but out here, it lay like a heavy fog on his senses. It echoed from the sparsely decorated white walls, the white tile floor and the white desk covered with charts and books. The nurses and doctors all reeked of it. He smelled something else on them, too. Decaying flesh. The sick, the wounded, the dying. In the distance, a dinner cart began its rounds.

He stifled a sneeze as he approached Tony.

His friend grimaced. "I know. Pretty overwhelming, isn't it?"

"I hate hospitals. I really do." Brian shook his head.

"You heard her, the feet felt like they had ridges. Good call, by the way."

"Thanks. So it's Hall."

Tony fidgeted. "I don't know for sure yet. My sources have all gone underground."

"Running scared."

"Yeah. Something big is happening." Tony stared down the hall, watching the dinner cart. Brian could almost see the wheels turning in his mind.

"Any ideas? The attack on Olivia couldn't be a coincidence."

"Nope. Stay close to our rescued angel. I'll be back when I learn something." He clapped Brian on the shoulder and turned to leave.

"I have a cell phone, you know."

Tony waved his hand by means of answer and disappeared around the corner.

Brian turned for Olivia's room again. The food cart caught his eye. It had progressed much farther in the brief time he'd been speaking to Tony. Farther than it should have, if it had stopped at every room. He used a supporting pillar at the nurse's desk to hide behind and watched the driver of the cart.

As men go, this man was unremarkable. Dressed in the traditional white uniform, he had sandy brown hair, was of medium height and stature. Unremarkable. He walked with a straight forward purpose, not hesitant, not careful he might miss something. He neither looked left nor right, nor did he glance at the list hanging on the

25

handle of the cart. Rather, he seemed to be focused on only one room: Olivia's.

Brian pressed his lips together. Trouble already. He considered his options. He could go around the corner through a connecting hall and come up behind the guy. The cart would be at Olivia's room by then. Or, and Brian nodded at this plan, he could step right up to the guy and take care of him, face-to-face.

He waited until the cart approached a maintenance closet. After a brief glance up and down the hall to discern there would be no witnesses, he moved out from behind the pillar, ducked his head, and walked toward the cart. As he closed the distance, he moved to the side of the hall as if he were trying to avoid a collision. As he passed, the sharp, acrid smell of the driver's breath breached the odors of the hospital. At the same time, he heard a low menacing growl and the man straightened to face him.

With no hesitation, Brian shot a quick punch in the driver's face. Stunned, the man staggered back and Brian moved in. He gripped the man's opposite shoulder and pushed him around until he was in a choke hold from behind. A cardboard cutout of Santa in his sleigh smiled at them from the opposite wall. The muffled noises of the skirmish seemed loud, so he coughed to cover the sound, hoping it wasn't enough to bring someone to investigate. As the cart driver clawed with his fingers at the choking arm, Brian dragged him into the closet and held him until he lost consciousness. Lowering him to the floor, he checked the man's clothes for identification. He found none. He flipped open his phone and called Tony.

"Hey."

"What?"

"I have someone for you to pick up."

26

"Are you kidding? Already? I haven't even made it to the car yet."

"Yeah, well, look at it this way: at least you don't have to look for another parking spot."

"Fine. I'm on my way back up. Where is he?"

"Maintenance closet, this floor." Brian hung up and stepped out of the tiny room. No one was in the hallway, so there truly had been no witnesses except on security camera and Santa. He was pretty sure Santa wouldn't tell, and Tony would take care of the video. He rolled the cart next to the wall and walked to Olivia's room.

Steeling himself, he entered and felt her gaze on him immediately. He wondered briefly if she'd heard something or could see far enough down the hallway to watch what had happened, but decided she couldn't. She said nothing to him even though he smiled at her.

Returning to his chair, he picked up his magazine, chose another random article, and began reading again. Still, he could feel her watching him the whole time.

Another attack, so quickly. He didn't feel comfortable trying to protect her here. The hospital was too open, too easily accessible. He wanted her some place he could control. He had to figure out how to get her on his turf.

Chapter 5

Why the hell were Tony and Brian so interested in
what shoes her attackers had worn? And what did the
smell of mud mean? Had the attackers been out
tromping around in a muddy field somewhere? Was that
what Tony was trying to discover? Was there another
attack before hers? Or had he and Brian been following
the costumed men from or across a field? Brian had also
had the smell of mud on him. Was this interview fact
finding or identity confirmation? The more Olivia
thought on it, the more she was convinced it was the
latter.

Worse, Tony had mentioned it would be Brian's
second overnight presence. It insinuated that they
expected a possible encore from the perpetrators. But
could he protect her, by himself, against those brutes of
men? She wasn't so sure, but they both apparently knew
what they were up against. Besides, with all the staff and
visitors around the hospital, how could the costumed
bear-men expect to prevail here? Still…

"Brian, what do you two know about these people who attacked me?"

He set down the magazine with a careful smile. His liquid brown gaze met hers. Even with the smile, frown lines creased his forehead. They'd been there since Tony left. She didn't like seeing them; they unnerved her. He said, "I can't tell you. Even if I did, which I can't, you wouldn't believe me."

She almost dropped her jaw. What the hell? "Try me. At this point, I'd believe anything. It's my life we're talking about here, and I need to know."

"I realize that. But I still can't tell you." He shrugged and picked up the magazine again. He held it higher to forestall any further questions. Olivia stared at the trashy cover. His answer sent her fuming. Damn him! And damn Silver! Of all the arrogant, secretive, self-serving, annoying posers who could have rescued her...!

Determined to not speak to Brian again ... ever ... she snatched the TV remote from the cabinet by the bed and jabbed the "on" button. The TV slowly warmed into life, and she clicked violently through the channels, one right after the other. She had no idea what she saw in the brief glimpses until she stumbled upon a shot of her apartment building. She stopped and listened to the anchor woman tell her story.

"—this peaceful picture last night. But it didn't stay calm. At approximately eleven p.m., an unknown group of assailants broke into the bottom floor of this apartment building and attacked the sole occupant, Olivia Bonaparte. Be warned, these images are graphic and not suitable for all audiences."

Brian lunged out of the chair and came to watch, standing beside her. For such a big man, he moved pretty damn fast. His musky cologne wafted past her in the breeze of his motion and the heady scent nearly distracted her from the news story. But then the camera scanned across the outside of the apartment dwelling and then showed an interior shot. The place was ruined, and her coat, which had somehow gotten ripped off her back during the fight, was crumpled on the floor near the end of the couch. Chunks of her wheat-colored hair littered the floor. She lifted her hand to her head to be greeted by scabs and thin patches. Damn! The news woman continued, "Ms. Bonaparte is in Boulder Community Hospital and is expected to make a full recovery. Police are conducting an investigation." Again, the camera swept the inside of the apartment. The place was devastated. It was obvious that a great deal of rage had caused most of the damage. And now, thanks to the media, the men who had done it knew she was still alive and where they could find her.

Olivia looked up at Brian, called a truce in her mind, and quietly said, "Your job is to keep me safe. Protect me from these thugs. Right?"

"Yes." His voice was just as soft, but he never took his eyes off the repeating scene on the TV.

"Do you feel you can do that here, in this place? Protect me from those vicious people? And protect yourself? Or any innocent people that might be in the immediate area?"

He looked down at her, his grim head shake mirroring his frown. "No. Not here."

She reached over and squeezed his forearm. "Then, let's get out of here. Go find my clothes in the closet, please."

There was no hesitation from him. He turned and did as asked. Olivia swung her legs off the bed and started removing the IV drip and pulse-ox monitor. He came back, shaking his head at her shoes. "I guess your clothes were ruined. This is all that you have."

She stared at the shoes and then up at his face. "I can't wander around in a hospital gown." He set the shoes on the foot of the bed, held up his index finger and then left the room.

Chapter 6

Brian walked down the hall toward the maintenance closet and Tony. Olivia's panic urged speed into his steps. Though he tried to walk quietly to keep from alerting anyone to his and Tony's activities, the heels of his running shoes squelched harshly on the white tile. Santa was where he'd left him, still guarding the closet and grinning like an oblivious fool.

A wheelchair draped with a blue hospital blanket blocked the door to the tiny room and Tony was inside, staring down on the cart driver. "Are you sure he's not dead?"

Brian shrugged and removed the blanket from the chair. "He wasn't when I left him." But, sometimes things happened. In truth, it had taken everything he had to not kill the man who'd wanted Olivia dead.

Tony leaned close and sniffed. "He reeks, but I think he's all right. Help me get him in the chair."

"You become a weakling lately?"

His friend chuckled. "Yeah, yeah. You're a regular Bob Hope. Just hold the chair." He sat up the unconscious man and then, with a heave, lifted and pivoted him. Then he dropped the driver into the seat.

The chair, though locked, pushed backward, shoving Brian into the hallway. He glanced at the nurses' desk and saw a physician staring at him. The doctor began walking toward him, white coat flapping with each step.

"Trouble coming."

"I'll take care of it," Tony said. One-by-one, he bent the cart driver's knees and placed his feet on the footplates. He straightened, stretched his back and motioned to the hall. "Go ahead and take him to the elevator. I'll join you there."

Brian nodded, threw the blanket over his passenger's body and pulled the chair back. Tony stepped out of the closet behind it.

"Hey." The doctor's voice came stridently down the hall, echoing smoothly off the flat tile. Two nurses poked their heads over the counter of the station desk to see the commotion.

Pretending he didn't hear the call-out, Brian wheeled the unconscious man toward the elevator. He pushed the button and turned to watch the show. Tony flipped open his wallet to a fake police ID, walked up to the doctor, flashed it and shut his wallet again before anything could be closely inspected. "I'm sorry we disturbed you. This man," he gestured toward the wheelchair, "escaped his guarded room on the floor below. We're just lucky we caught him so soon."

He leaned in conspiratorially. "He's a murderer, you know." He clapped his hand on the physician's shoulder. "Lucky for everyone, we caught him hiding in your maintenance closet."

Through it all, the doctor hadn't said anything. His mouth slowly opened more and more as the story continued. Now, he closed it with a snap and said,

"Well, thank you for handling it so quickly." He shook Tony's hand and returned to the nurses' desk.

The elevator arrived and Brian pushed his cargo onto it. He'd seen the bluff before. Still, it amazed him how willingly people believed it. Tony joined him and pushed the button for the basement floor. The elevator stunk of mold and sickness from the stained green rug. Brian breathed through his mouth, but he still could taste the stench. Trying not to think about what went into his lungs, he asked, "What excuse are you going to give for taking an unconscious man in white hospital uniform out of here?"

"We're not leaving the hospital. I'm sure we can find a nice quiet corner where I can question him. When I'm done with him, I'll take care of the video." Tony's voice, also, was tight, and Brian saw his friend was having the same problem with the smell as he.

Brian nodded at Tony's answer. It made sense to keep the man in the hospital. Why cause a problem when it could be avoided? "Maybe you two aren't leaving, but this is only the first attempt on Olivia's life after the attack. There will be more. I have to get her out of here."

"Does she know this yet?"

"Yep. She's waiting for a change of clothes."

"Locker rooms are in the basement too." Tony pointed his thumb to the right as the elevator doors opened. He pulled the wheelchair out into the narrow hall and turned to the left. Then he sucked in a deep breath and grinned. "Call me if you need me."

"Have fun," Brian called to his retreating back. For an answer, Tony began a colorful whistle rendition of the famous Seven Dwarfs' "Heigh-Ho" song that echoed off the walls. Brian smiled.

He turned to the right and walked toward the door of the women's locker room. The basement didn't smell as much as the elevator, but signs of age and lack of care showed on the cracked, dingy walls and the cement floor that needed more than one coat of paint. At the locker room he paused. Leaning his head against it, he listened for voices. Hearing no indication of anyone inside, he pushed open the door.

The locker room was modeled after most gyms, with rows of blue lockers and brown benches. Ancient beige tile with blue trim covered the walls. He found no clothes hanging loose anywhere, but he heard water running and headed that direction.

Turning left at the end of the last row of lockers, he came to the showers. Like the main locker room, they were built in a bygone day. Mildew crawled along the bottom and corners of the wall. The tile was cracked and even missing in a few places. The humidity climbed as he closed in on the curtained stalls. Sweat broke out on his skin. He still had on his jacket, and the heat was immense. The fake herbal scent of shampoo and soap assailed him. With relief, he noted only one shower stall was occupied. If there had been more, someone probably would have spotted him. The curtain covered the opening to the stall and an orange towel hung over the bar. Just outside stood a stool. And on that stool sat a set of folded and pressed medical scrubs.

Brian took slow steps, getting as close as he dared. The occupant of the stall seemed oblivious, splashing water and moving under the shower spray. He extended his arm and reached, leaning, for the green clothes. Snagging them with his fingers, he pulled back, bundled the scrubs into a ball, and then slid them under his jacket. Just as he was about to congratulate himself, the shower turned off and the towel disappeared inside.

He pivoted and strode out of the showers and the locker room as fast as he could. His running shoes squeaked on the damp floor, but there was nothing he could do about that. There now was a finite window of time before his activities would be brought to light. Bypassing the elevator, he ran to the stairs and vaulted up the steps three at a time to Olivia's floor.

At the first landing, he dug out his phone and called Tony. "You're on a time limit, buddy."

"How so?"

"Someone will be heading your way, looking for answers to missing clothes."

"What is it with you, today? Do you like creating problems for me?" Tony was silent a minute. In the background, Brian heard someone sobbing. Then his friend said, "Fine. I'll deal with it. Thanks for the heads up."

Chapter 7

Within two minutes, Brian was back, green surgical scrubs in his hands, a triumphant grin cresting his face.

Still, they were better than just a flapping hospital gown. Olivia struggled with them while Brian turned his back on her. She tugged the shirt over her head, but she couldn't pull it down. It kept getting hung up on the gauze on her back. The pants, even while sitting, were more than she could handle by herself, too.

"I need your help with this."

He turned around and blushed at her semi-nude condition. He didn't move, and he seemed to have trouble finding a place in the room to focus on. His gaze bounced from the TV to the door to her face to the TV again.

"Oh, please. This is no time for modesty." She held out one leg. "You're a full-grown man. I assume you've seen a naked woman before. It doesn't matter. Now help me so we can get out of here."

He said no more, but his face stayed red. At one point, while pulling up the pants with his face close to her belly, Olivia saw him puff out his cheeks and shake his head. He muttered to himself, but loud enough for her to hear, "It matters."

"Hurry." She snagged the tie strings at the belt from Brian while he placed her slippers. The more she rushed, the more her fingers fumbled over tying a knot. Finally, Brian pushed her hands away and tied it himself. Done, he navigated her toward the door as quickly as she could shuffle, given her injuries.

They weren't quite fast enough.

The chief nurse stopped in the doorway, staring at the two of them, openmouthed, holding a page open on her clipboard. It took her only a second to recover. She dropped the page, snapped the clipboard to her thigh and rushed into the room. Her tight baritone voice reminded Olivia of a drill sergeant she'd seen on some cheesy television show. Her name tag read Jackson. She had a smoker's gravelly voice. "What do you think you're doing?"

Brian said nothing, leaving Olivia to answer. She didn't have any witty or intimidating clichés, so she shrugged and simply answered, "I'm leaving."

"Oh no, you're not!" The drill sergeant nurse placed her hands on Olivia's shoulders and tried to steer her away from Brian and back to the abandoned hospital bed. An acapella version of "Jingle Bell Rock" played in the background, emphasizing the absurdity of the situation.

"No, you don't understand. I'm not safe here. No one is as long as I'm here." Olivia sounded delusional, even to herself. Maybe she was, but she knew for certain that Brian wouldn't be the type to worry unless he had reason. "Legally, you can't keep me."

The nurse tightened her grip. She pulled Olivia toward the bed, while Brian pulled toward the door. She kept saying, "Back to bed and we'll talk about it."

Olivia felt like the rope in a tug of war.

After a few more tugs in each direction, Brian let go and gripped Nurse Jackson by her upper arms, lifting her straight up, pivoting and placing her to the side. Disbelief crossed her face, but whether from his action or their continued defiance, Olivia couldn't tell. Brian said, "Excuse us, but we really need to be going."

"I'm calling security." With her mouth compressed into a thin line, she strode to the phone.

Brian jabbed his pointing finger toward her. "Do that, because there will be some very bad men coming here soon, looking for your patient. Make sure security apprehends them and the police are notified."

The nurse blanched and made her call.

Brian, throughout it all, had never stopped edging Olivia toward the door. While Nurse Jackson spoke with security, her back stiff and watching them, they finally made it out of the room. Spying a wheelchair parked by the nurses' desk, they headed that way. Olivia's hero's eyes were constantly moving, watching everything at once, it seemed. She was impressed. Really. For the first time, she felt quite safe.

A cardboard Rudolf chased Frosty around the base of the desk. More gaudy cutouts decorated the outsides of most doors. Red and green streamers crisscrossed the ceiling and a few strings of lights blinked competitively around bulletin boards and sitting area doors. Even the wheelchair was decorated with red and green tinsel. Brian balled it up and pitched it onto the floor as Olivia settled into her chariot. Then they were off.

They made it halfway down the hall when two guys with brown security uniforms stepped out of the elevator. One stayed in place and the other blocked the hallway in front of Brian and Olivia. Both stood with a wide stance and arms crossed. Neither was tall, but that was where the similarity ended. The man in front of the

39

elevator was blond and had brawny shoulders, like he'd played football in school. The other was dark-headed and skinny as a pin. Nurse Jackson closed in from behind.

Skinny seemed to be the boss. He held up his hands and spoke, "Why don't we go back to your room and talk about this?"

Brian sighed and let go of the wheelchair. Slowly, he pulled off his leather jacket. Then, with jerky exaggeration, he rolled his sleeves, all the while looking from one security guy to the other. Skinny stood firm, but Football's face went white and he stumbled back, reaching for his baton. Olivia didn't figure him to be the coward. Brian's actions failed to spook them both, so she made the next move.

Pivoting the wheelchair, she spoke to the angry nurse. "Look. We're leaving. You can't stop us. Legally, I have the right to go if I want. So, either my friend can make a mess of your guys, or you can help us do this right."

Nurse Jackson narrowed her eyes to slits that matched her still disapproving mouth. On the whole, she now looked like a pumpkin head political cartoon Olivia had seen once in the newspaper near Halloween. The artist had been poking fun at some senator who didn't like a reformation bill that had passed. Still, she had that stiff bearing. For a moment, Olivia thought she'd opt for the fight, but then Drill Sergeant Pumpkin Head Jackson gave a quick, tight nod and pivoted on her heel.

Brian winked at Football and Skinny. Then he piloted the wheelchair after the nurse.

Chapter 8

Brian left Olivia at the station desk and followed Nurse Jackson into the medicine room. Polished steel shelves and cabinets of bottles lined two pale green walls. A small sink flanked by more cabinets blanketed the third, as well as a cubbyhole for a small, lockable cart with medicine compartments. He assumed the nurse had gone in there to get something with which to sedate Olivia. When she saw him, she pushed him toward the door again, her lips grim, fury on her face. "Get out. You can't be back here."

He held his hands up to ward her off and said, "I need to talk to you privately. Listen to me a minute."

She dropped her hands to her hips and jerked her head in one quick nod. She said nothing, but couldn't quite stand still, shifting from foot to foot. Her reflection on the smooth cabinets swayed back and forth. He wouldn't have been surprised to see lasers shoot from her eyes or smoke billow from her ears.

"You know that guy that was found in the maintenance closet earlier? The one that escaped his guarded room and we found up here?"

Again, she gave a quick nod, but hesitancy had entered her gaze. Brian decided on a variation of the truth. "He came up here for one reason. To kill that poor girl out there." He pointed out the door in Olivia's general direction.

He continued, "We were lucky to catch him so quickly. The thing is, he's not alone. Like I told you a few minutes ago, there are more that will come looking for her. That's why I need to get her out of here. Not only to protect her, but everybody else up here." Now he waved his hand in an all-encompassing gesture. The nurse's gaze flicked to Olivia. When it returned to him, it was filled with worry and understanding. The anger still remained. This woman wasn't used to being thwarted, but she'd listen to reason.

"What do you need from me?"

"Stop stonewalling us. The longer it takes to get out of here, the closer those men come."

Nurse Jackson nodded and moved past him, empty-handed, her reflection elongating before it disappeared. It looked like he'd been right about her original intent to sedate Olivia. He turned, followed and stood with his hands jammed deep in his pockets while the nurse explained the forms. After a couple minutes, his phone vibrated. The picture ID showed Tony.

His friend's voice began without preamble. "This guy doesn't know much. He confirmed it was Hall who gave the order, but he doesn't know why."

"That doesn't help." Brian turned his back on Olivia and the nurse and walked down the hall. He reached his pal, Cardboard Santa, and stopped. So far today, the caricature on the wall had seen a lot of action, but he hadn't told a soul. He could be trusted with overhearing a phone conversation.

"No, it doesn't. But what's interesting is that it's not only Hall. There are quite a few families aligned on this."

"To kill Olivia?" He blinked hard. What could be big enough to make the families join together? There was a pause as both he and Tony thought on the ramifications. Nothing came to his mind. He stared at Santa, who also offered no insights.

"I have a description for Hall. He's a big man, not only heavily muscled, but also tall and broad. Has a heavy hand, especially when it comes to his son, Brett, who, by contrast, is built like a wire: tall, lean, and highly flexible. They both have sharp chins and heavy cheekbones. In the features, they're carbon copies of each other. But, in actions, they're as different as can be. Hall views his boy as a coward. He likes to bash him around, to toughen him up."

"Sounds like who we've been fighting."

"Yep." After a moment, Tony asked, "You still in the hospital?"

"Yeah. Got stopped by paperwork."

"That's the way of the world, my friend. I'm off to deal with the security video."

"You gonna leave the guy there?"

"What? He's in a hospital. I'm pretty sure he can find someone to give him medical attention." Tony hung up and Brian turned to stare at Olivia. What had she gotten herself into? This wasn't going to be any "babysitting" job. It was going to get bloody. More than it already had.

He watched the thumb on her left hand caress the paper while she signed. He wondered if she was even aware of her action. Watching, he felt a slow flush build

43

across his body. What would it be like for her to caress him like that?

He snapped that thought off, scolding himself. Olivia was injured and weak. People wanted her dead. She couldn't even begin to fight for herself. She needed him to keep her safe until they solved this problem. Everything he said to himself made him feel more protective of her. Which was good. But it backfired when he realized the defense instinct also made him more attracted to her. That was bad. As Tony had said, she'd leave him when she found out his true nature. He'd been down that road too many times not to know it. He was twenty times a fool.

With an exasperated growl at himself, he walked back to the desk and scooped the papers into Olivia's lap. Nurse Jackson opened her mouth for some sharp command or retort, but he cut her off, holding up his hand. "We'll mail these to you. There's no more time. We have to go, now."

He caught her furious gaze and added, "Call your security. Make sure they stay up here. Right now." Tipping Olivia's wheelchair onto its two hind tires, he pivoted it toward the elevator. He set off in a long, fast stride, settling the chair onto all four wheels while its passenger grappled with the papers and blanket.

Chapter 9

One of the papers Olivia had signed was the acknowledgement that she should contact the hospital if she had any trouble getting better on her own. She'd managed to slap that one onto the pile of signed documents before Brian dumped the rest of the papers into her lap and whisked her to the elevator like a madman behind the wheel of a formula race car. Olivia snatched the forms as they threatened to fly away. The blanket, too, seemed to want to misbehave and she worried it might tangle in the big wheels of the chair, so she fought with one hand to collect it into a lump on her lap. As they passed a cardboard Santa taped on the wall, Brian patted its head.

The elevator was still on their floor, and she couldn't help but look around for the two security guards. They were nowhere to be seen. Brian shoved the wheelchair into the lift, facing her toward the back. As the door closed, he punched the button for the ground floor at least half a dozen times. He was in a hurry, and that was fine by her. Still, his urgency unsettled her.

As they rode down, the small box intercom in the upper back right corner announced pages requesting that various hospital personnel report to the emergency room. It added to their tension. Brian had a hard time standing still, and his breathing came rapidly. He said nothing, but he punched the button two more times.

The ride was only four floors, but it seemed like forever they were stuck in that tiny box. The mustiness of the old green rug clogged Olivia's sinuses and, more than once, she stifled a sneeze. She stared at the plastic wood grain on the back of the elevator, not really seeing it. Who were these people who wanted her dead? Why was she their target? The foreboding she'd felt all along magnified and joined with the urgency. Something dark and sinister was going on here.

At last the elevator door opened. They entered the lobby and stopped short. The place was filled with distraught and injured people, as well as overflow from the nearby emergency room. Weaving through the traffic, Olivia picked up parts of the story and filled in the whole incident. A car had spun out of control on the ice, jumped the median and slammed into the first of two school buses filled with members, cheerleaders, and fans of a high school basketball team on the way home from a Christmas charity game. The second bus had rear-ended the first, and a minivan carrying more fans had plowed right into that. Everywhere she looked, she saw people crying. She wanted to stop and comfort them, but she knew the crowd would also be a good cover for someone who wanted to hurt her.

Brian was as nervous as a cat at a vet's office. He kept looking in every direction, like he expected someone to attack in the midst of all those people. His jumpiness affected her, and soon she was also scoping out the area. Still, he saw her would-be attacker long before she did.

Halting the painfully slow progress of her chair, he stepped beside her to meet a man with a syringe in his hand and a deep angry scowl on his face. Olivia's heart leapt into her throat, and she clutched the flimsy hospital blanket close to protect her. Brian, however, had a better idea.

He waited until the assailant was almost on top of them, then he stepped to the side, putting the man between the wheelchair and him, blocking the action from curious eyes. He exclaimed, "Hey, buddy! You look injured!"

Grabbing the wrist of the hand that held the syringe, he then plowed his opposite elbow right into the guy's sternum. As the man lost his air in a whoosh and bent double, Brian, still blocking the view with his hip, brought his knee right up into the attacker's face. The man dropped face-first onto the floor like an anchor. Brian yelled, "Hey! I need medical help here! This man passed out!"

Without waiting to see if anyone responded, he grabbed the handles on Olivia's chair and lurched toward the door and out to his car: a dark burgundy Fiat Spider. A fine powdering of dust covered the auto, and she noticed more than a few dings. It had definitely seen better days. She looked at the car and then back at the six-and-a-half-footedness of him. In an effort to lighten the tension, she asked, "Is there enough room for me in there, or should I ride on the roof?"

By way of answer, he narrowed his eyes and shook his head. Was that a glint of amusement? He actually had a sense of humor? She'd have to explore that further. Opening the passenger door, his voice showing mock exasperation, he said, "It's fine. Just get in."

Once she'd crawled from her hospital chariot to her seat in the car, he pushed the wheelchair to the side and climbed into the driver's seat of the car. Miraculously, he fit, though as he drove, she noticed he liked to hunch over the wheel and he clenched it tightly with both hands, as if driving was an unsafe necessity. The dings on his car gave testimony of that. She asked, quietly, "You're not a cop, are you?"

"Nope." He glanced at her anxiously.

"You're a private investigator?"

"We work with a lawyer and right now, I'm more like a bodyguard." He flashed a smile at her. "Trust me. You're safe."

She wondered why she was so willing to do exactly that. Trust him. True, she was in no shape to argue or escape, for that matter, but she could make life difficult for him, if she wanted. Still, he'd saved her life. Surely that counted as something.

The rocking of the car on Boulder's streets kept an easy rhythm, like a cradle with an infant. Olivia leaned her head back and let herself doze.

Somewhere in the night she woke, her eyesight fever-blurred. She couldn't get a grasp on her surroundings. Nothing looked right. It couldn't be her apartment. Then clarity seeped in and she remembered the attack, the hospital, and the escape. And Brian.

The low lights created dark ominous monsters from shadows of things she couldn't quite make out. She lay on a couch, behind a coffee table. Though there was no television, the place had a definite homey feel to it. Had he brought her to his house? Did his "special skills" work best here?

A tall, deathly-still figure stood to the side, not in front, of the living room window, staring out into the blackness. Brian? She certainly hoped so. She was too woozy to defend herself if it wasn't. Before she passed out again, she thought she felt someone smooth a lock of hair out of her face.

It was Brian who pulled her out of sleep the next time she woke, lifting her to a sitting position and then slipping in behind her to support her upper body. She supposed it was easier that way for him, but she still found it odd. But then, she was beginning to expect odd from him. His body felt warm and solid. Comforting. Safe.

A quick glance out the window confirmed it was still night. Table lamps had been turned on high, filling the room with light. There was no overhead light fixture. She identified the monsters of the dark as statuettes. The scariest shadows had been dragons and Chinese dogs. They stared at her now, mocking her earlier fear.

Brian held a stone mug in front of her. "Drink," he said in a gentle voice. "It'll make you feel better."

His warm breath bathed the nape of Olivia's neck and goose bumps sent shivers crawling across her skin. It added to her already spinning head. She couldn't even lean away from him if she wanted. But, she put her hand over his on the handle of the mug, holding it at bay. "Will it make me sleep again? I don't want to sleep anymore. It's too dangerous." At least that's what she tried to say. It sounded more like a mumbled bunch of gibberish to her.

Either he understood or he guessed at her objections because he said, "You need this for your fever, and you need to sleep. I'll watch over you." Stretching his arm, he neatly evaded her grasp. He pointed the mug at a full wineglass on the maple coffee table next to them. The round goblet held a dark red vintage. "See what you get for dessert?"

"Alcohol with medicine?" This time the words came out easier. And quieter. Did she really hear him say that? The wine did look good, though. Maybe she could have just it.

49

A smile entered his voice. "It's holistic. In this case, alcohol is part of the medicine."

Alcohol as part of the treatment. Olivia liked her new doctor-protector very much. She grabbed the mug and chugged it back, gagging with every swallow. Nasty stuff. It tasted like burnt garlic and skunk musk. It only reinforced her theory that holistic meant bad-tasting. Brian had the wineglass at the ready when she finished, and she took two huge swallows right away. Merlot. Probably a lot better quality than she could afford. It definitely shouldn't be gulped. Her protector behind her was comfortable to lean against, so she stayed put and sipped the complexities of the fruity wine. Besides, he kept the room from spinning around.

Eventually, though, she felt Brian shift beneath her, so she leaned forward with his help, letting him get to his feet. It wasn't until he was up and she looked over at him that she noticed a second half-empty glass of wine on the corner of the coffee table. It made her smile that he'd already foreseen that he'd be her pillow for a while. Or, maybe he hadn't planned it, but it worked out like that. Either way, it had been companionable and comfy.

Olivia sat twisted, halfway propped against the back of the couch, with one leg off the side. It occurred to her how little she knew of this man whom she'd come to trust with her life. He walked around her world, ordering it to suit his mission, even with a sense of humor. Yet he seemed to be almost a cardboard cutout of the perfect bodyguard: "Insert photo of mysterious hunky guy here." Guarded was the term she'd put on him, she thought. Very guarded.

She looked around the room, trying to get a grip on Brian's personality. Mellow blues played in the background, but she didn't know the musician. It seemed her bodyguard was an artist. A sketch pad and charcoal nub sat on the coffee table. With a start, she

50

recognized a mostly finished sketch of her sleeping. Other loose pieces of paper with charcoal drawings or landscape paintings were pinned on the walls between Chinese-type works mounted in heavy-looking gold frames. There wasn't an inch of bare upright surface. Dragons, horses, and cherry blossoms stared down at her from every angle. Even more loose sketches and paintings littered the tops of the furniture in the room, which appeared to be actual antiques, as heavy in design as the picture frames, with ornate carvings and inlay. Clocks, vases, dragons, gilded Chinese dogs and other weighted items covered the tops of almost everything. Even she could tell there was quite a lot of money tied up in that room. The only exception to all this was a tiny modern desk in the corner that looked distinctly out of place. Paper overflowed from its top and piled onto the floor.

Olivia's eyes lit on a dark chess board with what looked to be hand-carved pieces. She struggled into a fully upright position with both feet off the couch, sitting as people on couches should. He must have heard her because he turned from his sentry duty beside the still-dark window. She pointed at the chess board. "That's a gorgeous set."

He smiled and his deep brown eyes smiled too. His face became animated. And handsome. Very handsome. The dimples made an appearance and dug deep into his cheeks. Grin creases formed at the corners of his eyes. "You play?"

She shook her head and answered, "Not well." Truthfully, though, it was not at all. Miss Atwood had tried to teach her as a child, but finally wrote her off as hopeless at chess.

Brian didn't seem to notice her staring as he came to the coffee table and moved her wineglass to the side. "Would you like a game?"

51

Shrugging, Olivia said, "Sure, but, like I said, don't expect much of a challenge." Or any challenge, for that matter. But, at least he'd been warned. The fever could provide the excuse of a lousy player so he wouldn't know the extent of her inability.

If anything, Brian's grin deepened, and she discovered she liked his dimples very much. He fetched the board and brought the chair from his desk. His eyes sparkled and danced like they had swirls of glitter in them. The smile never left his face.

Chapter 10

After Brian set up the game, he walked into the kitchen for the rest of the bottle of wine. He felt as if his insides quivered like gelatin. Who was this woman in his home? Why did she move him so much? Why did he feel so protective of her? Was she a chance at his redemption? Or had he fallen prey to a rescuer syndrome? Somehow, he doubted either. And it wasn't just because of their situation. Protective, hell. He was plain out attracted to her. Had been ever since the first time he saw her fighting in the apartment.

Angry at himself, Brian shook his head to clear himself from the desire that had overcome him. He needed to focus on the task of keeping her safe, not romance her.

Yet, here she was. In his home, his private sanctuary. On his sofa.

He'd never met a woman as fierce and strong as her. Of course, the more he admired her, the more attracted to her he became and the more he fell for her.

He would do anything for her. Even kill. After all this time, he'd kill again to protect her.

Of course, he was living in a dream world. Love with her could never be. If she came too close and discovered the secrets he hid inside, she'd run the other way. If he had been Tony, he would seduce her anyway. Then dump her before she came too close.

But he couldn't treat any woman that way. Especially Olivia.

As he reached for the original bottle of merlot, he changed his mind on what he wanted to serve next. This wine had been strong and full-bodied; it helped to cover the flavor of the medicine. Now, he wanted something a little more subtle, a different merlot. He knew exactly which one he wanted. Opening the tall thin cabinet in the corner of his kitchen, he reached for one of the dark 2011s he'd cached to age. Though relatively new, it had buttloads of finesse. Perfect for a chess game.

His phone vibrated in his pocket, and he answered without looking at the identity of the caller. It would be Tony. "Yeah." He reached into the top drawer next to his stove and removed a flat-pronged cork puller. Glancing at the clock above the refrigerator, he saw it was almost two in the morning.

"It took me a while to get the security video from the hospital. I have to say, it's pretty damning. You walked right up to the guy and punched him in the face. Then you threw him in the maintenance closet. No hesitation, whatsoever."

"No way was he a hospital employee." Brian told him about the cart driver's behavior while he wedged the prongs of the puller on either side of the cork and then tugged. The bottle opened with a sigh and a deep thup. The cork was moist and clear of fungus. He sniffed the wine and compared what he smelled to the label. All good. Setting the bottle on a tray he pulled from a lower cabinet, he then found a small decanter and filled it with cooled water from the refrigerator. "He had a buddy too. We ran into him on our way out."

Now, his friend cursed. "They won't let up until she's dead. How is she?"

"You mean our angel? She's settled on the couch, drinking wine." Brian placed the filled decanter next to the merlot bottle on the tray and added a small towel. He reached into an upper cabinet for a box of almond wafer cookies.

"Dammit, Brian. Stop and think before you get involved with this woman. Remember the last two times?"

"I survived." His hand froze in mid-search. The last two relationships hadn't exactly ended stellar.

"Yeah, that's because I was there to pick up the pieces. I mean it, Brian. Stay the hell out of that corner. I'll come babysit her. You go to the other end of the house and leave her alone until I get there."

Brian had a fierce grip on his anger. It showed in his thin, tight voice. "Am I supposed to become like you? Seduce her and run? Never love anyone? Never be loved? I'd rather have my world shattered a million times than live like that. You need to mind your own damn business." The angry energy he held back came out in the flurry of his hand as he violently shoved boxes in the cabinet from side-to-side, searching for the misplaced cookies.

Tony said nothing for a minute. Then, in a voice as tight as Brian's had been, he said, "I'll go see Cujo, then."

At his friend's deflection, Brian felt his fury slowly leach away. He pursed his lips and blew out the final dregs of his anger before saying anything. "Good idea. He might know something about Hall. Check with Bellerophon, too."

55

"Why her?"

"To find out Olivia's part in all this." As Tony hung up, Brian's hand finally closed on the box of cookies and he brought them down to the tray. He stood, for a moment, facing the cabinets, leaning on hands balled into fists. Still, Tony was right. He was headed to a heartbreak. It was like watching a tidal wave approach a city. Olivia would hurt him; it would swamp him. She couldn't understand him. Would never, because she wasn't like him at all; she came from a different world. If she caught a glimpse of what raged within him, she'd be terrified. He needed to keep that in his mind at all times. His emotions were way too twisted up over her. Maybe, he should listen to his friend, this once. Leave her alone in the romance department and not pursue anything more. Friends only.

How the hell did he get back to that from what he felt now?

Chapter 11

As Brian returned from the kitchen with a tray, Olivia ran the basic rules of chess through her mind. Knight moves like an L. Queen could move any direction. Pawn could only move two squares on the initial jump. Bishop... Oh, god. What did a bishop do?

Brian set down the tray on the end of the coffee table. He settled in his chair and focused on the board in the same unwavering manner he stared out the window, sat in the chair at the hospital or forced her to drink that nasty brew. She took another deep swig of wine to fortify her courage. She had no doubt this man knew his chess. He'd be able to predict every pitiful move she made. She was in big trouble. She cleared her throat and asked, "Where did you get this set?"

"I won it." He was still focused on the board that hadn't had a single piece moved yet. Was he waiting for her to go first?

Dear God. She had the white army. She turned the board, placing the white army in front of him and forcing him to make the beginning move. As Olivia leaned back, she caught his startled glance. Didn't predict that, did he? She smiled and said, "Your turn."

He moved one of his center pawns. She supposed all the spaces had numbers and letters to designate them, but she'd never played the game enough to know. She moved one of her center pawns too. He moved another central pawn, but she moved one of her end ones.

She again wondered why she wasn't afraid of this man. She felt nothing other than comfort and safety with him. Yet, there was a closed feeling from him now. While he'd been in the kitchen, something had to have happened. She'd heard him talking. Had someone called him? The man who sat before her now was somber and too quiet. The twinkles in his eyes weren't there, neither was his smile. Trying to get him to open up, she asked, "You said you won the board. Was that in China?"

He nodded and moved his first white pawn one space.

She brought out a third black pawn. He immediately confiscated it. Damn! And he still hadn't said a word to help her understand him or why he'd suddenly grown so quiet. She thought to try a question that took an answer with actual words in it. Isn't that what was taught in marketing? Never ask anything that can be answered with "yes" or "no?" Get them talking. "Where were you in China?"

Glancing up at her, he said, "Everywhere."

She waited for more, but nothing came. So much for the great conversation opener.

Olivia tried again. "What was your favorite city?" She emptied her glass of merlot and eyed the bottle.

"I liked the Guilin Mountains." He pointed to some tall pointy heaps in a painting.

Now they were getting somewhere.

He reached for her empty glass and wiped it with the towel, and then filled it half way with water.

"Drink up." He did the same with his glass and waited until she downed the water and handed the glass back. Then he wiped her glass again, poured wine from the new bottle, and handed the glass back.

She tasted it and realized the reason for the towel and water. This wine tasted similar but softer than the other wine. She thought she liked it, but would reserve judgment until she'd had more. She realized it was her turn and moved her second pawn forward, onto a black square. Safe enough, she figured.

Brian leaned forward to move again and she realized her last play had left her first pawn unguarded. Instead of capturing it, he brought out another pawn and settled it into a position for her to take. Why would he leave hers and sacrifice his? Suspicion narrowed her eyes. Was he throwing the game? Before she accused him, she needed more evidence. Nor did she want it to be a big scene. She just wanted him to play right. And, she wanted him to keep talking.

"Those are real?" Olivia motioned to the mountain painting. She'd seen tons of those in paintings at restaurants, but she'd always thought they were misshapen artistic interpretations, like the Chinese horses with big hips and shoulders, but tiny heads.

Locking his gaze with hers, he said, "They're stunning. I could spend my whole life painting them."

Finally, a conversation! "Why didn't you?"

He slumped in his chair and sipped his wine. His gaze took a pained and far-off look. "It became too touristy."

"Surely there were some places there still unpopulated."

"Yes. But, my perceptions of them had changed by then."

Chapter 12

Carl Hall eased the black Chevy pickup along the curb and came to a stop in the fullness of the night. He opened the door and grabbed the top of it. He pulled himself out of the driver's seat, pushing on the steering wheel at the same time. He was a big man, not only heavily muscled, but also tall and broad.

His son, Brett, who slid from the passenger's seat, by contrast was built like a wire: tall, lean and highly flexible. Hall wondered if he'd ever been like that. Sometimes he even wondered if Brett really was his son. Then, one look at the boy's sharp chin and heavy cheekbones and he knew. In the features, they were carbon copies of each other. But, in actions, they were as different as could be. The boy was a coward. Something Hall was intent to remedy.

The five men who had been sitting in the bed of the truck clambered out, bumping and kicking the vehicle. Hall spun toward them with a glare. "You yahoos need to simmer down. It'll do no good to let them know we're here."

His men paused and then quietly began to undress. In the shapeshifter world, nakedness when moving from one form to another was just a fact of life. Buying new clothes all the time grew expensive.

He turned and grinned at the house. It was a hovel, really. Plain brown with white shutters. Nothing to get excited about. Nonetheless, it held something valuable. The girl was in there, somewhere.

He glanced at the bordering houses, both two story brick with manicured lawns. The neighbors were close, but it wouldn't stop him. That girl would pay for what her family had done. She would die tonight. And it would be painful.

Facing his men, he dealt out instructions. "This is a small place. If too many people come in, we'll be in 'each other's way. So, me, Trent, an' Clive will keep the guy busy while you," he gestured toward a tall, thin man, "take care of the girl. Got it? The rest of you keep lookout. We don't want the neighbors interferin'."

Chapter 13

Brian turned his mind again to the game. The trouble was, he had a problem concentrating because of her. He constantly had to fight looking up at her, ignore the loud tempo of his heart. It wanted to break out of his chest at her nearness. The cascade of tremors in his stomach seconded that sentiment. He forced himself still and focused on the board; answering her questions as simply as he could while the very scent of her drove his desire higher.

He studied the chess board and tried to map her next move. If he could understand that, he might understand her a bit better. He played whole game scenarios in his mind based on what he little he knew of her. She wasn't much of a player, though, barely a beginner.

Olivia would show her game, depending on what she did with the pawn he'd left unprotected. To his surprise, she didn't take it. Instead, she jumped to the other end of the board again and moved one of those from its home.

He studied her move and rebuilt the game strategy again in his mind, from first move to checkmate. The woman was easily the most unpredictable person he'd ever met. He caught himself smiling.

She asked, "How long were you in China?"

"Forever, I think. I visited and found the area very peaceful, so I decided to stay. Why didn't you take the pawn?"

"Why didn't you take mine? I can't imagine this game is very fun for you. Especially since you have to hamper yourself to not beat me so badly." Her tone sounded like an accusation to him. He held his breath, understanding that she felt betrayed by him. Even if she lost, she wanted to do it under her own power. He admired that.

Lifting his gaze, he gave a half smile and shrugged. "Any game is fun. I never get to play much anymore."

Comprehension dawned on her face and she smiled. "Okay. There seemed to be a hidden agenda, so I left it."

"No. No hidden agenda." Their gazes locked and an electric hunger filled the room between them. Of its own, his half smile bloomed into a full grin. His heart flip-flopped.

Her face flushed and the pheromones that were uniquely hers softly wafted to him. God, he wanted to go over to her and wrap her in his arms. But, he didn't. He couldn't get past the knowledge that she would eventually turn away from him. Still, their gaze continued, and he thought he should say something. But for the life of him, he couldn't think of what.

Then Brian heard them. Several intruders at the front of the house. Hall had found Olivia.

He lunged to his feet and stared out the window. A black Chevy pickup was parked in the street. Clear as day, he saw seven men unloading from the cab and the bed. He moved back from the window and turned his head from side to side, listening. Two of the men were circling around to the back. One stayed up front. That meant four were coming in. He presumed some were to keep him busy while another went after Olivia. Pointing to a second maple table butted up to the back of the couch, he said in a barely audible voice, "They're here. Some of them, anyway. Get under there, crumple into a ball and don't show yourself until I say."

Olivia scrambled over the back of the couch and across the table, trailing a deep scratch behind her. He wasn't going to worry about that. Chances were, there would be a lot more damage from the fight. It satisfied him, though, to see that she didn't seem afraid of him at all.

He turned to face the front window again and began to strategize the fight. They'd come in at the same time, but he'd want to handle them separately as much as possible. Moving to a stance closer to the front window than the back door, he kept as far from Olivia's hiding place as he could. He waited and cursed his cowardice at not wanting Olivia to see what he was inside. It wouldn't be easy, but he could handle the attackers in his human form, assuming they didn't all come in at once.

Glass shattered in the living room as one of the intruders broke through. At the same instant the back door ripped open and two came in through kitchen. Two had come fully as bear. Brian glanced from one to the other. Was one of them Hall? The third shapeshifter had chosen to remain in his transitory form: man and jackal combined. It made him able to use his arms. His skin was black as night, but human. His head was all jackal, like the head of Anubis.

Brian tensed and stepped toward the larger of the two bears, the one who'd come in the front. It tried to envelope him in a bone-breaking hug. He swung his fist in a jaw-breaking roundhouse and connected solidly on the side of the bear's face.

The attacking bear stumbled backward, landing hard against the sill. He came away with an angry growl, moving slowly, limping on the right side from glass cuts.

The man-jackal came at Brian, swinging and teeth snapping. The second bear flung its arms wide and lumbered toward him as well.

Brian blocked the blows with his arm and delivered several heavy punches to the man's thorax, driving him back and keeping ahead of the bear. He staggered and fell against one of the imported Foo dogs from the Han Dynasty. The statuette tottered and fell with a resounding crash.

Bending double, Brian drove into the bear's midsection, pushing him all the way back to the corner where the first bear still stood. The creature tried to wrap his front legs around him to crush him. But Brian's force landed them both on the antique nested tables and plant, splintering the wood and crushing the vegetation.

The jackal came from behind and pummeled Brian's kidneys with his man fists. While Brain turned and defended against the rain of blows, he also sought to circle around so the jackal was between him and the bear with the wide arms. He'd almost succeeded when the jackal apparently became wise to the strategy and began moving the other way again. This wasn't his first fight.

One bear struggled to his feet and lumbered toward them. The other stilled as a table leg pierced through his heart.

Brian lunged at the man-jackal, wrapped his arms around him, turning and ramming him against the remaining bear. The jackal bit down on his shoulder and tried to crush bone.

The push went all the way to the front wall again, shoving both intruders into each other and the plaster behind. The jackal loosed his hold and they both went down. The bear slumped heavily to the floor, but the jackal rebounded and Brian moved back to the center of the room as far away from the couch and Olivia as possible. This had to end, now. Unfortunately, it would finish in blood and death. He growled, not liking the thought, but seeing no other way around it.

The jackal gave a toothy grin. He launched at Brian.

Chapter 14

Olivia discovered she wasn't as small as she'd thought. She couldn't sit except with one foot under her, the other in front with her knee pressed against her cheek. The crown of her head pushed on the bottom of the table. If she moved, even a bit, she might bump the table and it might also move. Part of her would be exposed. She couldn't even turn her head for fear of her shoulder jutting out.

Without seeing it, she tried to choreograph the action in her head. Another heavy artifact shattered on the floor. The gilded dogs were the only things that looked that heavy. Now both were destroyed. A wooden crash came from the other side of the front window. She recalled a small bookcase that probably didn't exist anymore. No one spoke, except for the growls and grunts. It sounded as if animals fought, rather than men. Feet scuffled and fists repeatedly thudded against flesh.

One of the combatants was repeatedly knocked backward into the kitchen. Then she heard a heavy crunch, like a watermelon breaking open on cement.

Sharp-edged panic clawed through her. Was Brian the victor? Or victim? Her answer came in the vein of scrambling feet from the first waking attacker at the front of the house charging to the back. The breaking and crashing of objects picked up again. Relief pooled within her. Brian was still alive.

Two attackers down, one to go.

As the battle raged on, the table above Olivia lurched and tipped up on two feet. A giant bear paw reached down from over the top of the table. She held her breath. Her heart slammed against her ribs. She couldn't make herself any smaller. She pushed herself hard against the back of the couch.

The paw suddenly jerked away, accompanied by the sound of a deep claw scratching on wood. The table slammed back on all four feet, rocked and then settled. The fight changed tone to a heavy knocking that Olivia felt through the floor. It lasted only a few more seconds and then ended with another brilliant shattering of glass.

All was silent. Olivia shivered in her hiding spot, fairly certain Brian had won, but not entirely sure. And she was in no condition to fight anyone. Not that she did a good job of it the first time. She waited, breathless.

Feet shuffled toward her and Brian's hand stuck under the table. "You can come out." His voice was raw, like he'd been punched in the throat. She gripped his hand and, with his help, struggled to her feet. Her attention immediately flew to his face. Blood snaked out of a gash above his left brow, almost blinding him in that eye. More blood flowed from another cut on his lower lip. Dark red scrapes circled his neck as if he'd been choked.

"We've got to take care of those wounds. Where's your first-aid kit?"

He shook his head, swiping his blood-blinded eye and smearing a crimson arc across his temple. "There's no time. We need to get out of here. There will be more coming." He kept hold of her hand and snatched the blanket from the couch as they passed.

Olivia took the moment to survey the destroyed room. Broken antiques littered the floor. She'd been right, both dog statuettes had been destroyed. Torn canvases hung like drapes from fractured frames on the walls. Ornate furniture, in whole or part, sat at crazy, undefined angles. The loose pages of artwork had scattered under and over everything, like giant petals after a thunderstorm. A man in a bear costume lay propped in the corner where the desk had stood, table leg sticking out of his chest.

Brian didn't slow. He led her through to the kitchen. "If you're squeamish, don't look."

Those bastards had tried to kill her, twice now, that she knew of. For a reason she didn't know, either. She wanted to see their corpses. A body in the kitchen lay on its stomach, dressed in a full mask of something that reminded her of Egypt. What was it about the costumes? Another bearskin-covered body lay on the floor near the back door.

"Who are they? Do you know?" She pulled against Brian. "Let me look for some kind of identification."

"Later. We need to get out of here. Right now," he repeated and led her through the shattered kitchen door.

Outside, he wrapped the blanket around her, pulling it snug like an armor against more than just the cold. He gazed into her eyes, frowning. Worry lined his face. "Are you all right? Can you walk?"

"Yes, I can walk. Can you?"

He grinned and squeezed her hand. They cut across the backyard. Brian kept constant surveillance in all directions. His long strides meant Olivia had to scurry to keep up with him. Maybe he should have asked her if she could run. His homespun healing recipe seemed to still be working, even with the stress of fight and flight.

She looked behind them at the house. She didn't see anyone. "Why not drive?"

He glanced down at her. "They're waiting out front."

"And they're not back here?"

"Not yet. They've all gone to the front." He moved his hand to the small of her back, covering that part of the gauze, pushing and guiding her through a labyrinth of backyard fences, clothesline poles, and storage sheds. Their breath blew from their noses and open mouths like steam from train engines. Snow tumbled over the top of their shoes, chilling and soaking their feet.

Chapter 15

Brian felt the enemy, hiding in the night, blending their dark bodies with the even darker shadows. He could smell them now, counting the remaining shapeshifters determined to kill his Olivia. Their heavy steps couldn't be camouflaged. Two had returned to the street, including the one who had escaped through the window, who he thought was Hall. The last two from the back had moved forward and now hung out at the sides of the house. He could almost make out the gray profiles against black backgrounds. As he and Olivia moved away, he sensed the other two from the sides of the house moving with them. One from the front joined the pursuit. The remaining one, probably Hall, was undoubtedly calling in reinforcements.

He slid his hand in his pocket and closed on the smooth wafer of his cell phone. Pulling it out and flipping it open, he pressed the button for Tony. His friend's mumbled voice sounded thin and tinny. "What's up?"

Brian lowered the volume. He tried to keep his voice low and even. Olivia didn't need to know how bad the situation was becoming. He said, "I need you here, right now."

"Problems?"

"You could say that. Four broke into the house. There are more following us."

"Hall?"

"I think so." He guided Olivia around a neighbor's swing set.

"I can't leave you alone, can I?"

"Obviously not. Three are dead in the house. The one I think was Hall is in front, but he's injured."

"Where are you now?"

"We're headed to Marquis Park." The neighbor's chained dog walked stiff-legged toward them. Brain tensed, but didn't stop. Would it recognize him as alpha? A barking dog would wake up people and that would be bad. The last thing they needed would be to stop and explain the reason they were lurking through backyards in the dark. The hound hesitated, then tucked his tail and ducked into the doghouse without a peep.

"With some followers, no doubt." Tony's voice came out breathless as if he were running. Over the phone, a car door slammed and an engine roared to life.

"Three or four, I think."

"I'll meet you there." Tony's tires squealed in the background through the cell phone.

Brian disconnected and slid the phone back into his pocket. He glanced at Olivia, feeling his heart dive into its usual flip-flop. Dammit! Why did he flirt with her earlier, a big stupid grin on his face? How the hell could he forget his vow to be only friends so quickly? What was wrong with him? Did he really like to have his heart broken?

But he knew the answer: When he was in love, his past and all the mistakes in it disappeared. When he was in love, he felt whole. Alive.

And this woman beside him made him feel so very much alive.

He had killed for her. Would kill for her again, if need be.

He shook his head at himself, like he had so many times lately. Somehow, he had to crush his desire for her. But desire was the least of it. He wanted her body, mind, and soul. He was in love. And when she found out what he was, he'd have to deal with the repercussions. He wouldn't be able to hide within his human form forever. If Hall and his friends kept coming, he'd have to eventually let the beast inside him out to fight. And he was betting he'd have to do this sooner, rather than later.

For now, he'd have to stay sharp and ignore what he felt, before his distraction got them both killed.

Chapter 16

In the silence of their nighttime walk, Olivia became aware of other noises: the scuff of a foot on a snow-hidden rock, the creak of a fence being climbed, icicles falling, a low breath caught. She also noticed the barking of the backyard dogs had lulled into an eerie quiet. Alarmed, she looked up at her protector. "They're following us."

Brian nodded. His face was grim. "Yep." The pressure from his hand on the small of her back increased. Adrenaline spiked her pace. If he was worried, then she should be too. They reached the end of the housing. Across the street began a wall of frozen trees and thick icy undergrowth: Marquis Park. She knew the place. It was an untamed wilderness a couple miles in width and breadth, not really a park at all. It was only called a park because the city didn't want to do anything with the property at the moment.

They crossed the street and she slowed. Brian turned to her, questions in his eyes. She said, "It's dark with a million places they could hide and ambush us. I can't believe this is really the best option." Panic crawled through her, nesting in every pore, every cell of her body. Olivia had no doubt he could feel her trembling, but she hoped he put it down to cold shivers, not terror. She'd never told anyone about her unreasonable fear of the dark. Things hid so easily in the absence of light. Evil things. Harmful beings. Creatures she never wanted to meet in broad daylight even.

He smiled then, and she felt his thumb stroke her back where his hand rested. Shivers of a different kind rode up her arm to her spine and down to the backs of her knees. He said, "It's the best option for me to fight them. Trust me."

So far, her magic Chinese artist had rescued her from the first onslaught of bear-costumed men, helped her escape the hospital and defended her from the very same bear-men again at his home at the cost of all his antiques. She might still be terrified, but trust him she would, though she failed to see how moving out of the populace and into the wilderness would help them defend themselves. If it were up to her, she'd ring every doorbell until somebody answered, and then she'd hide inside. Then again, thinking of how the attackers had broken into Brian's place, maybe not. Given that, would any place be safe?

Olivia quit balking and they hurried into the park. The heady pine scent filled her nostrils and rolled deep into her chest with every inhale. This forest was like the frozen Colorado wilderness that surrounded Boulder. But, being centrally located, it had plenty of running water during the warm weather to support all manner of green life imported by birds or unsuspecting humans.

In the winter, skeletons of plants populated the park. Thick tangles of icy saplings tripped them. Ice coated vines twined high into tall, straight aspens, some stretching to nearby trees, creating a wall they had to work their way around. Stripped branches of icicle dripping pines hung low and at crooked angles, grabbing at them and scoring their flesh. They had to battle their way through. Once they breached this initial wall, it would be easier going because the tall trees, when in leaf, blocked the sun from the forest floor. Saplings starved out. The undergrowth was sparse.

As their large followers forged through the frozen brush behind them, they were easier to hear. Brian and Olivia knew exactly where they were. But it worked both ways, and the pursuers knew where their prey was also. It ratcheted up Olivia's fear level by at least 700%.

Brian didn't show any fear though. He acted as if he avoided miscreants every day by traipsing through the forest. As if it was something any normal person would expect to do. But then, maybe he did do this kind of thing every day. After all, he'd said he was a bodyguard. Maybe he was one of those survivalist nuts. She didn't think so, but how would she know from just one evening with him?

He shifted his guidance system from her back to her hand as he pulled her through tangles of vines, branches, and saplings. At times, he bodily picked her up and over some obstacle she couldn't quite make out. Icy logs became the bane of her existence. More than once, she found herself face down after bumping her foot on one while crossing. Her limited amount of energy drained quickly and the punch of adrenaline wasn't enough to replace it. She tried to keep up, but she moved slower and slower. It got to the point Brian carried her most of the time.

Every second, the great hulking shadows followed them.

Reaching a deep copse of aspen, Brian stopped dead. Here the aged trees spaced themselves far enough apart to allow the moonlight through. Saplings filled the forest floor. He looked back and forth, raising his chin. He reminded her of Miss Atwood's hound when he was trying to catch a scent. Then he turned to Olivia, both hands on her shoulders, face grim. "We're surrounded."

He narrowed his eyes at her. "Do you trust me?"

What? Was he kidding? Did he think she normally traipsed around injured in the woods on a winter night? Shouldn't he know the answer to that question by now? She'd intended a small amount of sarcasm to slip through, but exhaustion made her voice sharp. "I'm here with you, aren't I? Of course I do."

He frowned, let go of her, and stepped back. His body began to transform. The moonlight reflected off snow in the semi-open area and lit him in a muted glow. Olivia backed away even farther to give him room and to get a better view. But not too far, their followers were close. Thick gray hair sprouted from his skin and through his clothes, covering him. It moved in waves as his body changed and shifted. Dense ropes of muscle bulked on his arms and chest, straining his shirt until it ripped. His jeans split at the seams, exposing more bulk.

His face grew long in front of him, with a pointy nose and ears. Sharp teeth snicked into place, lining his mouth. Musk rolled off him. His hands grew long with scythe-shaped claws. The biggest change was his size. His rangy six-foot-six inches grew in stature and mass until he reached at least eight feet tall with the hulk of a football player. One massive paw swiped at the rags of his clothes and flung them to the ground. He stood in front of her on hind legs, a wild and untamed creature. One of legends and nightmares.

The man was a werewolf.

And impressive as hell.

The transformation took only seconds, and yet the world Olivia knew radically shifted in that time. The monsters that had always terrified her in the dark were real. Brian was one of them. Proof that they existed. It puzzled her that Brian didn't frighten her though. If anything, she felt even safer. He looked more like a wolf, even on two legs, than the fabled werewolf.

Through it all, he kept his gaze on her as if to get confirmation of something. She took another step back, just to get a good view into his eyes. What did he want? Approval? No. Acceptance. She gave one quick nod, and it seemed to satisfy him. Not only did she accept him, she absolutely approved. His musk surrounded her, sparking something primal within. She forgot about her pursuers, the dead man in Brian's house and the dark forest surrounding them. Her hands itched to run through his dusky fur and trace the firm muscles on his chest. She hoped he wasn't some kind of hallucination and she was really lying on his couch, dreaming.

She stopped dead at the sudden realization of what she felt and had been thinking. It wasn't the attraction that bothered her. She happily admitted she had interest in the man. What bugged her was the smoldering burn she now felt deep in her belly. Dear God! She had the hots for a werewolf!

Chapter 17

Brian had kept his transformation as slow as he could, given the circumstances. There wasn't much time though: Hall's three men had joined with some reinforcements and were circling for the attack. He didn't want to alarm Olivia any more than necessary, halting at the halfway point. She needed to see he was still a man, but wolf also. He watched her, waiting for signs of horror, fear, and revulsion. His heart would break. He would suffer. Someday he'd move on.

He braced himself.

Then, something magical happened. Instead of panic, her gaze turned into one of acceptance and approval. He held his breath. Could this be real? True, it was a long way from the lightning bolt of attraction they'd shared in the house, and it might move into the "just friends" realm, but he'd take it. Anything was better than seeing terror on her face.

A sweet blush of pheromones hit him. Olivia was attracted to the wolf as well as the man. She could be a freak, turned on by animal sex. Though, he couldn't really see her following the whole animal erotica scene. Most probably she was just a devotee of the romanticized Hollywood werewolves. Still, his heart dictated that he'd take what he could get. At least for now.

Her face reddened and her eyes widened. More pheromones bloomed into the air between them. The scent of her filled his nostrils. She was his. Her desire urged the animal side of him to growl his longing to her. He almost did, too, but there was no time. He just hoped she still wanted him when this was all over. She could have a change of heart. Or come to her senses.

Dark shadows menaced from beyond the grove. Thick rolls of bear musk curled over him. Regretting the circumstances that brought them together and now might separate them again, he broke the spell and pointed to the top of a tall, thin Aspen. It would be easy for her to climb, not so for the bears. They'd have to change to human. That would make them more vulnerable.

Olivia shook her head. "I can't reach."

The tree had lost its bottom boughs; she would need a boost. Brian scooped her up as if she were a squirming caterpillar. Though he longed to hold her close, he launched her at the lowermost limb. He held his breath until she landed neatly on top, scrambling for a hold on the icy trunk. Her blanket, which had miraculously traveled with her in the vertical flight, got snagged and ripped away to flutter to the ground. She began a slow climb, stretching from one icy branch to another, no doubt losing skin on the way.

Olivia didn't look good. Exhaustion showed in the deep wells of her eyes and the haggard, but determined set of her jaw. She slipped and slid, losing her grasp more than a few times. It worried him. It would do no good to save her life here if she couldn't heal. She needed rest.

While she climbed, he continued his transformation, putting more energy into it. He was out of time. The familiar ache bit at his bones, added to a sharp agonizing lance of pain that happened only when he rushed the change. He gritted his teeth and dropped onto all fours. He was strongest in his between form—the werewolf. But speed would be what won this fight, and he was quickest as a true wolf. He could wear down his adversary until the real muscle, Tony, arrived.

Some of Hall's reinforcements had arrived, and his men were nearly in place now, crashing through the woods toward them. Brian smelled mostly bears, but their scent was strong and overpowered the odor of the others. He had no idea what they were, but they hung back and didn't approach. He neither smelled nor saw Hall himself. Apparently, the fight at the house had injured him too much and was as much as the bear had wanted in person.

Fully wolf now, he backed against the base of Olivia's tree where he would make his stand. Either he would win this fight or he would die protecting the woman perched in the tree above.

Chapter 18

Below Olivia, growls and guttural noises echoed from tree to tree as the enemy pushed into view. They showed no hesitation, as if the giant wolf hadn't been standing there. Three of them came close, leaving more hidden amid the murky shadows. These three were all dressed as bears. Her mind jumped unbidden to the night in her apartment: the deep bruising kicks, the panic and the assurance of her death. Red-brown fur. Had that been only last night? Were these the same men?

Even in the dark, she saw the cinnamon fur that fluffed their size to larger than a normal man, though one towered over the others. To her, they all looked impossibly huge. At that moment, she finally understood. These men weren't in costume; they were like Brian. They could change from human to bear and back again. Hence the reason for Tony's questions about shoes. He had to be sure who, or what, had attacked her.

She also understood why Brian had chosen this place to make his stand. These bear people were desperate to kill her. No house could stop these fiends.

Nor would anyone, innocent bystander or no, be safe. He had to get them away from the populace of Boulder. Fear for him tightened Olivia's throat, almost choking her.

Brian was fully wolf now, on all fours, snarling at the attackers from the base of the tree. The bears lunged and tried to circle him to get at her. The wolf dodged and danced back and forth. He first snapped at one hairy beast and then at another. She tried to remember what she'd learned about wolves from Miss Atwood, but she'd been a poor student. The only thing she remembered was that their jaws were some of the most powerful in the world. The large ones could crush a man's skull.

Brian was large. He was very large.

The wiry saplings sprang back as they were knocked into or trampled, tangling and slowing the bears' swats. Though spaced wide enough to allow the saplings to grow, the bigger trees, like the one where Olivia perched, grew close enough to make movement difficult for the bigger bears. One of the bears, in trying to club Brian, crashed his furry fist into her tree and the vibration ricocheted through the trunk into her bones. Bark and ice flew. She clutched harder to her branch.

The bears could take down her tree. They could also climb. As men, they could climb faster. No matter which way she looked at it, she was doomed if Brian failed. The magnificent wolf darted in, snapping and biting like a rabid creature, avoiding the clubbing fists and the crushing arms of the bears. Clumps of red fur flew. More creatures—mostly bears, but also a stag and two giant lizards—joined the fight from the shadows of the forest. As he defended her and the fight moved in an arc from her tree, the largest bear changed to man and, naked, began the climb to where she huddled.

Olivia called to her wolf. "Brian!"

83

In a blur of motion, the wolf launched onto the back of the man and killed him. Protector, indeed. She approved of Brian's "other skills."

The body fell. One of the two remaining bears hooked his claws under her wolf's rib cage and threw him against the next large tree amidst a shower of ice and snow. With a soft whine and a solid thump, Brian dropped to the ground and lay still. Her heart thudded loudly as she looked for any signs of life. From her perch, she saw none. The other creatures milled about on the ground, watching her. A small bear began to climb her tree, growling. With a start, she realized he was small enough that the aspen could support him as an animal. Her branch shook with every step he took.

She scrambled higher, slipping on the ice-covered branches, and shouted, "Tell me! Tell me why you want to kill me! What have I done?"

The beast didn't answer. Each branch he climbed, she also retreated another. The tree swayed with the weight of the bear. Twice, her foot slid out from under her, leaving her flailing over open air. The stag below shook its antlers at her.

A loud shot rang out. Bark exploded an inch above the bear's head. Tony's voice filled the forest. "If you make one more move to hurt that woman, I'll drill a silver bullet right into your brain. Then I'll change, and I know that you know exactly what I am. I guarantee none of you want to tangle with me."

The bear looked over his shoulder, as if considering his options, and then dropped to the ground. He lumbered off with his friends, but not far. She heard them waiting in the woods. In her panic to get to the ground and check on Brian, Olivia slipped more times than not, adding yet more skinned places and bruises to her collection. When she finally reached the ground, he was waking naked in human form. She snatched up her blanket and wrapped it around him, falling to her knees. Worry crowded fear and everything else from her mind. "Are you all right? What can I do?"

He seemed surprised, but a smile came. "Yeah. I'm okay." He slowly eased himself into a sitting position, leaning against the tree. As he moved, the earlier fight's gash opened again. He swiped at the blood seeping from his brow with his hand and then held the heel of his palm against the wound.

"Of course he's okay. That wolf can take a beating. Isn't that right?" Tony's voice came from where he crouched over a decapitated body.

She rounded on him. Fear made her voice sharp and high pitched. Tears scalded the rims of her eyes, and she blinked hard to keep them back. "Where were you? If you had been here, no one would have gotten hurt or killed. For that matter, how come you let them go? Why didn't you question one of them?" To Olivia, her voice sounded frantic. She glanced at Brian, hoping he hadn't noticed. He had an amused smile directed at his friend, waiting, she supposed, for the answer.

Tony stood and turned to face her. He carried a backpack, walking closer, placing his feet precisely in front of each other with no effort. He didn't smile, but his eyes glittered like blue fire. Everything about him spoke of danger. She assumed from what he'd said that he also had an animal form and wondered at it. She made a mental note to be more careful with him. His voice was smooth as the ice that filled the forest, but it had a steely quality underneath. He said, "A, I was on the way here. It takes something called 'time' to navigate the streets. And B, I have already questioned one of them. These men aren't who we want." He stopped speaking and held her gaze, as if daring her to say another word.

She kept her mouth shut.

85

He dropped the bag beside Brian and kicked his foot. "Get up, you lazy cuss. You may have convinced her you're mortally injured, but not me. You still have work to do. They aren't giving up, and she's still in danger. This is Hall's show and he's thrown mostly his own clan of bears at you, but I'm willing to bet more from other families of shifters are on the way. I'll hold them off as long as I can, then join you at the truck. You know where it is."

With that, his body stretched. Soft white and black fur sprouted through his skin and clothes. Like Brian, sharp fangs lined his mouth. He dropped to all fours. Claws and a long tail grew from his body. His clothes fell to the ground in shreds. Brilliant blue eyes glittered against the fur on his face. A feral cat odor billowed from him. Before Olivia stood a huge white Bengal tiger. Where Brian had been all power and muscle, this creature was lithe and sleek. He was the most beautiful cat she'd ever seen. Also one of the most dangerous.

She became conscious of her slack jaw and open mouth. She closed it with a snap. Now his name, Silvani … Silver, made sense to her. It also made sense why the bear had left when faced with a lone gunman: he knew of Tony's alternate body and didn't want to tangle with him unless he had reinforcements.

She rocked back on her heels and stood as Brian slowly raised himself from the ground. The backpack contained a complete change of clothing, more than one set. It looked like these two had been down this road before. She pivoted to look the other direction while Brian dressed, though she was sure it amused him to have the tables turned. She thought she caught a glimpse of moving shadows among the trees, but it was so dark she couldn't tell for sure. How many bears still wanted her dead?

Questions flooded her head. First and foremost, who were these people? And, was she really awake? She felt like Dorothy in the Land of Oz. Tigers and wolves and bears, oh my!

The blood from Brian's brow gash had slowed to a bare trickle when he handed her the blanket. She happily wrapped it around her shivering body, soaking in the warmth he'd left in it. The wool still held the remnants of his wolf musk interlaced with his natural human scent, and she inhaled deeply. What that did to her insides could be written in a pornographic romance novel. Longing filled her, like a sharp sweet pain, but was it for the wolf or the man?

Brian reached for her hand, leading her deeper into the woods. The tiger followed, softly growling, with his mouth open. She remembered cats often "tasted" the air for their prey. A fair distance behind him, she heard the rumble and stomp of bears. At a spot where the brush and trees narrowed and choked the ground, Tony halted and turned to face the oncoming beasts. He looked over his shoulder at Brian and Olivia, and she thought he might be laughing, but really, how could she tell if a tiger was laughing? Still, he looked happy as he crouched low, tail whipping, facing his adversaries.

Chapter 19

Brian's heart soared. Olivia had made it clear that she cared for him. She'd even defended him from Tony. Even if it had been a reaction to his fight for her, a rescuing syndrome thing, she still cared for him. At least for now. He absolutely would take it.

The dark blanketed them in softness, and the snow muffled their footsteps. On nights like this, Brian normally liked to walk these woods. They gave him a peace, unlike any meditation or exercise. Here, he could vent until all his angst left. He could, and often did, walk until any sorrow or heartbreak flowed out of him, leaving nothing but calm. Sometimes those walks took all night; he'd never been a saint.

She spoke, keeping her voice low. "Does it hurt?"

He hesitated. He'd been caught up in his own little world and was unsure of what she was talking about. He guessed. "The faster I change, the more it hurts. But a person gets used to it."

"So, was that a fast or slow change?"

He almost smiled at his cleverness. He'd been right about what she wanted to know. "Fast with a stop in between."

"Can you heal yourself by moving to the other … you?"

"Pure fiction, created by Hollywood. I'm as mortal as everyone else."

She was silent a moment, concentrating on climbing over an icy, felled tree. Then, "How many of you are there?"

He hesitated. Talking like this was difficult for him. Not because he didn't want her to know, but he didn't want to worry or frighten her. Still, if there was any chance they could be together as a couple, he needed to be honest. "Of all of us? There are quite a few. Obviously, there's no census taken. But there are several large families in the Boulder area. A little over 300 of us, I think."

"Families. That's what you call each … breed? Species?" She slipped on a patch of icy leaves and her grip tightened on his hand. He held her up, wrapping his arm around her waist.

A grimace of pain shot across her face. "I think your magic medicine is wearing off."

"The adrenaline makes you run through it quicker. I'll make some more as soon as we settle somewhere."

"I hope that's soon." She said nothing but one look at the deep furrows on her cheeks and the black hollows under her eyes and his heart crashed. She was in a bad way. The herbal remedy he'd learned in China could only do so much. He needed to find someplace she could rest, fast. He'd like to go for the truck, but it was too far. She'd never make it. They needed to stop and rest. Let her regain some energy. He kept his arm supporting her and scanned the trees and fallen logs, looking for a place to hide.

Behind them, distant muted sounds of Tony's throaty snarls blended with crashing trees. The noise echoed in near silent tones from the wall of frozen bark around them. Brian glanced again at Olivia. She gave no indication she heard. In truth, he wasn't surprised. Most humans couldn't hear what he and his brothers could.

"Can you identify other … shapeshifters when they're in human form?"

"I wish I could. It would make our lives so much easier." He helped her across a jumble of rocks and small boulders. The always present scents of the forest's natural spice and musty leaves seemed to close around him. For the first time, they failed to comfort him. This was a conversation he didn't want to have with Olivia.

"What do you mean?"

He sighed. He might as well confess. "We'd heard rumors about this guy gathering his family for something—we didn't know what. We weren't entirely sure the guys we saw were shapeshifters. But, we decided to follow them to find out, instead of confront them to find out. We saw them stalking you and stayed close, to stop anything they started. But, they didn't stop you or say anything that would give us a clue as to what was happening. Instead, they were smart and followed you all the way to your apartment. That's when they changed to bear and attacked you. We came in right away."

"So, you could have stopped it before it happened." The accusation was clear in her eyes when she looked at him.

He jerked his gaze away. His culpability in her near death dug deep into him. He tried again, and failed, to meet her glare. Again he sighed. "We thought you could be one of us. A shapeshifter could protect herself from these guys better than the average human. An attack on a non-shifter isn't done. It's too brutal with no way for the human to defend against it, except by gun. That's why we hung back and followed. We thought we had time, in case we had to intervene."

Olivia's movements were slow and disjointed. Noise came from every step she made. They'd be easy to track if Hall's men got past Tony. Brian glanced back that direction, but neither saw nor heard any sign of pursuit.

For a very long time she didn't say anything. "So, who are these ... people?"

He squeezed her hand, glad the focus moved to something else and not to his failure to stop the attack. Still, he was pretty sure she would return to it. She had every right to hate him. He hoped she didn't. He hoped she could understand their reasoning. But he wouldn't blame her if she held him responsible for what happened to her. If she didn't want him anymore. He wasn't too fond of what he'd done, himself. "The man's name is Carl Hall. He runs a construction company in Boulder. He and his buddies unofficially consider themselves the police for our kind. We don't know why they want to hurt you."

"Hurt's an understatement."

He had no answer to that.

"I haven't done anything wrong!"

"That's why we need to speak to him." Before this war, or whatever it was, got even further out of hand.

Chapter 20

Brian and Olivia forged deeper into the park, threading through frozen vines, saplings, underbrush, and dense copses of aged trees. The latest punch of adrenaline had long since abandoned her. She stumbled over everything and nothing. Her vision, never good in the dark, narrowed to a few inches beyond her eyelashes. She felt crappy and her back and kidneys burned deep within her. Each jarring step churned her stomach. Bile scored her throat, and she swallowed hard to keep from vomiting. Throughout it all, Brian never let go of her hand and, though he had been injured in both fights, he let her lean heavily on him, even lifting her over difficult footing.

His confession of how he could have stopped the attack kept her silent. She would have to think more on this, but not now. It would have to wait until later. She only had enough strength to concentrate on getting through the forest.

They reached a large open area with a wide rushing stream, frozen only on the edges. The gurgle of the icy water sounded unnaturally loud in the silence of the winter night. Four to five feet off the bank, moonlight outlined lumps of snow in the shapes of a ring of stones and logs. Someone had camped there during the fall. Looking around, Olivia had no doubt it was a beautiful spot when warm. It was beautiful now. Snow graced everything on the ground, softening harsh lines into gentle swells. Trees stood tall, reaching for the stars, coated with ice. They reflected the purity of the moon with a peaceful ethereal quality, not unlike how crystals reflected the warmth of the sun in colors.

Brian apparently didn't notice. He led her all over the clearing, packing the snow, then into, and back out of, the woods more times than she wanted to count. She followed in a zombified state. She wanted a warm place to sit. After that, he took her to stand by the stream while he brought a handful of charcoal and ash from the fire pit. "Rub this on the bottoms and tops of your shoes and up your ankles. We'll head upstream in the water until we can find a hiding place." He busied himself, showing her the way to do it.

Olivia barked a short laugh. The whole thing was beyond surreal. She was soon to be covered in ashes and protected from killer bears by a werewolf. All this at Christmas time. Truly, she could have read this in a fictional book. At his deep frown, she sobered. It would never do to let him think she wasn't taking his rescue efforts seriously. She took the ash and stared at him. Was the man crazy? "Won't the ash wash off?"

He grinned and her mouth, on its own, smiled back. She couldn't stop it if she tried. Something had changed between them since he'd become wolf. He seemed more open, as if hiding the secret of his alternate self had been holding him back. Now that it was out in the light, he acted more relaxed. She heartily approved of the change. He said, "Yeah, but it'll add to the confusion of smells."

"You think they've gotten past Tony then." Bending over wasn't good for the dizziness in her head. She stopped and stood upright a moment to let her vision calm before bending again to work on her legs.

"If they haven't yet, they will soon. He's fierce and strong, but there are too many of them. He'll eventually have to give way."

"Have you ever fought him?"

Finished with his task, he shook his head and reached over to help her put the final touches on her legs. "Tony? No. I'd prefer to stay out of that corner."

Done, they straightened. Olivia rinsed her hands in the stream and wiped them on the blanket. They still smelled like rotting ash: acrid and sour. She shrugged and said to Brian, "Just so you know, you were pretty impressive."

With a small grin, he dipped his head in thanks and took her hand. She looked around the clearing and the ice trees in the moonlight one last time, and then they were on their way again. The stream decidedly cooled her already chilled feet, flooding over the tops of her snow-soaked shoes. She couldn't feel the sharp stones or whether she was lifting or placing her feet. She stumbled time and time again. Brian often glanced back at her, concern on his face. He seemed to be measuring how much more she could take.

Twice, Olivia would have landed face-first in the stream if it hadn't been for his hand balancing her. She had an earthquake going on inside of her, and she kept her teeth clenched to keep them from chattering. Icy dampness crawled up her legs as her surgical pants absorbed water into them. The blanket dipped again and again into the stream and weighed heavily on her. At last, he pointed ahead to a large fallen tree with a dislodged root ball that camouflaged a small opening. "You need rest. We'll hide there for a bit."

The minute she opened her mouth to speak, the chatter broke out. "W-won't they s-s-smell us?"

"I'm hoping the trick in the clearing will convince them they can't trust their noses. It should keep them frustrated and following the stream."

Brian and Olivia stayed in the frigid water until they were directly in front of the tree. Brian pushed her ahead of him as they cut straight across the land toward it. He held his hand on her shoulder as if he could keep her from falling that way. Though, remembering the size of the in-between stage of his, the werewolf, she suspected he might actually be able to do it. At the opening, she balked, pretty sure her temperature had spiked to well over a hundred by now, even though the ice bath probably cooled it. But she didn't want to be first into their hiding place. She had a thing about putting any part of her body into someplace she hadn't checked. Feet didn't go into boots without inspections. Whole bodies didn't go into underground caves without checking everything out first. Besides, it was dark in there. "I'm n-not going i-i-in there s-sight unseen. There m-might be s-s-snakes or s-something."

He narrowed his eyes at her. "Snakes. In winter?"

Admittedly, it had sounded lame, but she felt crappy. Stubbornness abounded when she suffered. Even though she was warming, now that they were out of the water, and the shiver began to lift, she didn't want to go into that dark hole. Olivia shrugged. The motion dislodged the blanket yet again and Brian caught it before it fell to the ground. He came close and bundled it around her, tucking it tight against her arms. Worry etched his handsome face. "You may not know what's in there, but you definitely know what's out here. Take your choice."

That was true, but she still hesitated. It wasn't a girly thing. She preferred to think of it as a careful thing.

95

With an exasperated snort, he pushed past her and disappeared into the hole. She heard him exclaim and suddenly he came out, pretending to wrestle with a root as if it were a python.

In spite of how miserable Olivia felt, she laughed. She wondered if he'd learned one of her "special skills" or if sarcasm came naturally to him also. After working so hard earlier in the night to make him open up, she began to think she'd made a mistake. She'd never dealt with a wolf-man before. Maybe she'd bitten off more than she could chew. She said, "S-sarcasm will get you n-nowhere."

Her amusement ended as quickly as it came when she remembered his earlier confession. True, she was now safe because of him, but she'd also been injured because of his reluctance to stop Hall. Thinking on it, she felt like she was swimming in a deep well. It hurt her head.

Brian's face showed that he'd guessed where her thoughts had gone. Concern, grief, and guilt battled in the way his downturned mouth and brows set. Deep lines cut into his face. He opened his mouth to say something, then hesitated and finally closed it slowly. He looked away, staring at the skeletal tree branches around them. After another moment, he sighed deeply and brought his attention back to her. "We need to get inside."

Still she hesitated. Not because she didn't want to go, but because she couldn't quite get her thoughts marshaled again. The only thing she could focus on was what felt like a betrayal. She wanted to push it aside to think on later, but it didn't want to go.

He growled in a low and throaty voice, breaking through and forcing her full attention on him. Her bad feelings receded. The sound of his voice thrilled and also terrified Olivia. It was a do-not-test-me command. "Into that hallow. Now move." He pointed.

She went.

The little cave was just that: little. And it smelled like wet earth. Not surprisingly. It was going to be a tight fit for both of them, but on the upside, it would build warmth quickly. Perhaps too much. Oxygen might become a problem. She broke off a piece of root and pushed experimentally in a few places where light glimmered through. She found a promising gap toward the back, made it bigger and huddled under it hoping there were no winter spiders. Her breath echoed harshly back at her. Brian, in the meantime, was busy outside, brushing fresh snow across their tracks. He also built a curved wall of snow about a foot away from the front of their entrance. Anyone looking from the stream, except at an extreme angle, wouldn't see the opening. Or so they hoped.

The opening dimmed as Brian wedged his shoulders through. He glanced at the space Olivia had left him and then met her gaze. She had no need to guess at his meaning. Six-foot-plus of man needed more space. She retreated to the farthest wall to give him room, mourning the loss of her tiny beam of moonlight. She tightened her blanket around her, trying not to think of creepy-crawlies that might not hibernate through the winter.

It took a lot of shifting, bumping, and squeezing her against the dirt wall, but eventually, Brian settled beside her in their cozy earth abode. Any nasty little bugs that had been in there with them were probably squashed in the process.

Beside Olivia, Brian sat hunched over in the small space, and her memory flashed back to him behind the wheel of his Fiat. She decided to offer a temporary truce in the matter of his wrong-doing. At least until she had brain power to do some serious thinking on it. She nodded to his snow sculpture outside their front door. "Nice wall."

"Thanks, Nice window." He glanced at the air hole she'd made and grinned in the dusky light. She caught a glimpse of dimples making deep wells on his cheeks. Despite her recent confusion about him, she still liked what she saw. The werewolf was sexy.

Chapter 21

Brian pressed his finger to his lips. Olivia nodded to show she understood to keep quiet. He relaxed a little. She seemed to be making an effort to overlook his devastating mistake. At least for now. Still, sooner or later there'd be a reckoning. He was no longer afraid of her not accepting him. She'd accepted his greatest secret. Somehow, they'd work through this problem.

She needed to regain her energy. Though her voice had been soft, he hadn't missed the slur in her words when she complemented the wall he'd built. She'd reached the end of her reserves. He glanced at her in the tiny space. The moonlight coming in through the air hole she'd created shone down on her. Her eyes were brown pebbles in darkly pooled rings that stood out even more on her pale and drawn face. He tucked the blanket tighter around her, and she smiled weakly at him.

Their earthen hiding place barely had room for the both of them. The curved dirt walls and jutting roots pressed them hard against each other, their faces inches apart. The closeness of their quarters held Olivia's natural woman scent near him. As if that didn't drive Brian's pulse higher already, when he returned her smile with a grin of his own, her scent bloomed around them. It mixed with the deep base smell of damp earth and made for a heady intoxicant.

He breathed long and slow through his nose, trying to calm his racing blood. In her condition, she didn't need any romancing. Without a doubt he knew that, but all he wanted to do was to wrap his arms around her and hold her close.

Damn him and Tony for waiting to stop Hall and his men! And damn Hall! By now, the police were probably arriving at his house, called by some concerned neighbor, no doubt. They'd find the place a wreck, blood everywhere. Hall would have had the body removed from the kitchen. A man with a jackal's head would cause too many questions.

Brian could never go back to that house. Even years from now, if he bought it from the city, where it would default to, one of his neighbors would be sure to recognize him. No. He could never go back. He wouldn't miss any of his things. They could all be replaced. But that kitchen. He'd surely miss it.

Chapter 22

Olivia huddled in the moonlight peeking through the entrance to their miniscule hiding place. The pinpoint of light she'd made from above shone between her and Brian. The dark was anathema to her. She was sure furniture moved in the lack of light. Miss Atwood had often comforted her as a child when she'd woken in the night, screaming about monsters in the closet or under the bed. The head of the orphanage had slept beside her until she drifted off to dreamland again. She'd told Olivia there were good things in the darkness, too, so she learned to tolerate it. But when she'd left the orphanage, Miss Atwood had never warned her that she might someday find herself in a black hole in the ground. Come to think of it, she'd never said a word about men who changed into animals either.

She and Brian sat in silence. More questions burned inside her, but fear of discovery kept her tongue mute. Though warming from their body heat, their cave was still frozen. It also held a measure of moisture. After some time, her fever, which had seemed to lower due to

101

the ice bath provided by the stream, began to climb again. A spasm of shivers overtook her. The harder she tried to control the quakes, the worse they became.

"Take off your shoes and tuck your feet in your blanket," Brian whispered in her ear. He again rearranged her blanket across her shoulders. Her shivers continued and deepened, setting her teeth into a continual chatter. He wrapped his arms around her and pulled her against his chest, grunting in pain as she settled against his ribs. She tried to pull away, to keep from hurting him, but he held her firm, placing her head against his shoulder. Bundled close, she even tucked her feet under his thigh. She breathed in the nimbus cloud of his natural scent and relaxed against him. She listened to the strength of his heart and his deep, full breaths. She fit perfectly against his chest, and she wondered what he thought of that. If he even thought of it at all. She felt like a teenage girl with her first crush, waiting in anticipation of their next interaction. She wanted to know if he thought of her as that teenager, or if there was a possibility of more. Despite his part in her injuries, she still wanted him.

They waited in silence, listening for any bear scuffs, growls, or anything that spoke of imminent danger. Olivia warmed bit by bit. Because of the wolf part of him, she suspected he had hyperthermia, which was something she deeply appreciated at that moment.

Brian lifted his hand and, when he brought it back around her, it was smeared with blood. She sat up and looked at him. His eyes were closed and he had leaned his head against the back of their hiding hole. The gash on his brow was oozing and once again, his eye was completely covered in blood. His heightened metabolism would probably mend him quickly. This cut, though, looked deep. She dabbed the corner of her blanket against the injury until the blood abated and whispered, "This cut won't stay closed. You're going to need stitches."

"Most likely." He didn't whisper, but his voice was soft and low. He raised his head from the dirt wall and watched her from inches away with his deep brown eyes while she cleaned the drying blood from his brow. Olivia felt a slow flush creep up her spine to her neck and cheeks. Their whispers were so low she doubted anyone more than two feet away would have heard them. He asked, "Did I scare you?"

"What? The wolf?" She shook her head and looked directly into his big dark eyes. For some reason, she felt it was important he knew this. "No, I wasn't frightened."

"I'm glad." His smile was as gentle as his voice, and it sent shivers of a different kind through her body. He lifted his hand and ran his thumb down the side of her face. Olivia blushed even deeper, even though she was pretty sure he couldn't see it. But then, he wasn't only a man, and maybe he could. Maybe her attraction to him was a rescuer type thing. Or maybe it was the wolf. Or maybe she didn't care. She liked the way it felt, the way she felt next to him, and the way her body reacted to his.

"Kiss me." Brian's soft husky voice sent thrills through her. He lifted her chin with his thumb. His lips found hers and held them. His tongue traced the inside of her lips and pushed against her teeth. She opened to him. As his tongue entered and stroked hers, he crushed her against him. She couldn't get enough of him and sent her tongue twisting against his. This wasn't a simple attraction. Oh no. This man turned her on and on and on. Her body heated from the inside out and an ache began deep in her belly, headed south. And, judging by the way his nostrils flared, he knew it. A moan escaped her throat, and his breathing deepened and quickened.

With one swift move, he turned her so that she leaned across the front of his body, laying in his arms. He kissed her again, slower this time. His tongue made explorations into the depths of her mouth, around the inside of her cheeks to the smooth ceiling and the backs of her teeth, always returning to tangle with the wetness of her tongue. While he held her in one arm, his hand stroked her back, her neck, her hair, and her face. Suddenly, she was burning hot, and all feelings of illness dissipated. She struggled to escape the heat of the blanket, but it had twisted with their movements and held her like a cocoon.

Brian stopped then and pulled away, his breath as ragged as hers. His gaze roamed across her face for what seemed like a long time. His eyes were dilated large with passion, yet his tender smile moved Olivia more than even his kiss had and she caught her breath. This was no high school crush. He traced her lips again with his thumb and gave her a warm, sweet kiss. Then he cocked his head toward the entrance of their hideaway. "Tony's here."

"How do you..." And then it hit her. He'd heard Tony like he'd heard the bears at his house. It was going to be rough being with a wolf. There would be no secrets between them.

Brian frowned at her unfinished question, but then Tony poked his dark head into the cave, and that ended all possibility for a conversation. He hesitated, frowning, but then smiled at them both and said, "I'm sorry to interrupt your moment of burgeoning intimacy, but those bears aren't going to stay gone forever. We need to get out of here."

"Damn," Olivia said softly and reached for Tony's extended hand. If she could have, she would have growled, herself. Talk about poor timing. And thanks to the creatures within the men, not only did Brian know

104

how she felt, but she was sure Tony had picked up on it also. Curse Mother Nature and her pheromones! She let the tiger-man pull her out of the opening of the hiding place.

"Yep," came Brian's voice from behind her.

Outside, the air was crisp and clear, and dawn's lemonade pink, purple, and orange streaked across the few clouds that darkened the deep blue sky above. It was going to be a beautiful day.

Chapter 23

Brian crawled out of hiding and straightened, still watching Olivia. She stood with her back to him in a patch of early morning sun, arms overhead, stretching as high as she could. The sun shone on and through her hair, making it look electric and otherworldly. Her scrubs shirt had lifted with her movement, raising high above her slim waist. At the same time, her pants had shifted lower, exposing the top of the cleft between her buttocks. He couldn't drag his gaze away. What it would feel like, running his hands over that smooth skin?

She turned, lowering her arms, and their gazes snagged. She smiled, and he couldn't help himself: he grinned back.

Beside him, Tony fidgeted, breaking the spell, and Brian glanced at his best friend, noting the crimson blush and how his attention now traveled through the tops of the trees. Tony had never before been embarrassed by affectionate displays. Or was it something more? Was he attracted to Olivia too? She wasn't exactly his type.

Brian handed Olivia her shoes and returned his attention to his friend. He narrowed his eyes and asked in a tight voice, "What's up?"

Tony glanced sideways at him and gave a tiny shake to his head. "I got a snoot full of pheromones when I shoved my head into your honey house." He gestured to the hiding place. "Any woman would look good to me right now. Even one I'm not interested in." As he turned toward the truck, he tapped Brian on the chest. "And you need to uninterest yourself too."

Brian cursed and snatched his friend's arm. "I don't care if you approve. As if I need your permission to spend time with her. To do anything, for that matter. You need to back off. Right now. Or you and I are going to have trouble. Get me?"

Tony glanced at the hand cuffed around his arm. He jerked his eyes up to look at Brian. "You want to do this? Now? Here? Over a woman?"

Brian let go. "Not particularly, but you need to stop trying to run my life."

Tony looked away, into the trees. He pressed his lips together tightly and gave one quick nod. Then he pushed into the wintery brush and headed for the stream.

Brian reached for Olivia's hand to follow, but found her with only one shoe on. She held the other at arm's length, staring at the icy water that dripped from the tip and shoelaces. Her bare toes were curled tightly as if in anticipation of the torture to come.

He laughed, a happy, healthy laugh. How long had it been since he'd done that? Tony had been wrong. This woman was good for him. "Do you need help?"

She sighed and shook her head. "No, I got it. Just working up my courage." She dropped the shoe on the ground. It landed upside down, with the toe pointing back at her. Using her shod foot, she uprighted and straightened the offending shoe. With a sudden jerk, she

107

jammed her toes in the sodden canvas and reached down to tuck the heel in place. Done, she straightened.

"You're a rip-your-bandaid-off-fast kinda gal, huh?"

"Yeah. Let's go." She reached for his hand. Her voice sounded strong, but he was sure that strength was only a punch from the erotic energy they'd shared earlier. It would only be a matter of time before she went downhill again.

Together, they scrambled to catch up to Tony, but found him waiting on the other side of the stream, a few hundred feet into the forest. He was busy inspecting the cuts, scrapes and myriad of bruises along his arms. When he saw them, he grinned ruefully. He caught and held Brian's gaze. "No dates for me for a while."

Brian relaxed. His friend was letting him know that their skirmish was water under the bridge. He'd been worried. Tony could hold a grudge. Though, in truth, it was his own grudge to hold against Tony for his interference. Not that he would. Or could. He smiled in return.

The trees and bushes were denser on this side of the stream, as if wanting to keep intruders at bay. Thorned shrubs snagged at their clothes. Branches reached low, pulling at their hair. Ice and snow still managed to find their way through the bare web of tree limbs to coat the ground and rotting leaves. Formidable. Brian seldom came through here during his night forays.

They'd struggled for close to fifteen minutes while Tony, in the lead, regaled them of the skirmish with Hall's men. Occasionally he glanced back at Brian and Olivia's clasped hands.

During a pause in his monologue, Olivia asked, "Where are we going?"

Tony spoke. "Well, the cops are, no doubt, at Brian's place. So I thought we should try for my cabin.

108

It's perfect. It's secluded and deep in the woods. We can always take to the lake."

Brian looked at Olivia dubiously. "Can you swim?" He could, though he didn't like the water any deeper than he could see through.

"Better than a fish."

A pleased smile on his face, Brian said to Tony, "Sounds perfect." Of course she could. She was one tough cookie. Though he hadn't missed the fact that her voice was softening. Her surge of amorous energy was rapidly wearing off and the fever showed on her face again. "We need to stop for supplies."

Tony nodded at Olivia. "Medicine."

"Clothes." Olivia had worked hard to keep her condition hidden, but with all the efforts of earlier in the night, it was obvious to Brian that she'd reached the end. She moved as if drunken and near-blind.

Finally, she fell.

Brian scooped her into his arms like a small, soggy child, grunting when he felt a sharp lance of pain in his side. He carried her the rest of the way to the Escalade while Tony broke trail for them. Once trundled into the front seat of the vehicle between the two men, Olivia drifted off to sleep.

They stopped at a Chinese grocery. Brian carefully lifted Olivia's head off his shoulder, reached into the dash of the truck, and removed a wad of cash. He ran into the tiny shop. The stench of burned grease assailed him. There wasn't much in the way of groceries, just a few bulk bins of rice, noodles, and root vegetables. A single table sat beside a kitchen the size of a closet. The one redeeming value was the wall full of herbs and holistic potions. It didn't take long for him to find what he needed. He added a box of cookies at the counter and paid, then dashed back out to the Escalade. While Tony drove, Brian mixed the medicine. Olivia's fever was high. Too high. It worried him.

He held her close and poured the drink into her mouth in small doses. She refused any cookies. Her heart pressed to his, she drifted off to sleep again.

"While you were inside, I made a call to an old friend of mine," Tony said softly. He turned onto Baseline Road and searched the store fronts they passed. At last, he drove behind a small boutique that had male and female mannequins in the window. They pulled behind a robin's-egg blue Nissan. A red-headed woman with pert features and an oversized beige coat climbed out of the car and walked to Tony's driver side window. Her lips were a bitter line.

"I should be angry with you, Tony, for the way you dumped me. Yet, out of the blue, you call with an emergency. And here I am, doing your bidding like a little mutt at your heels."

Brian watched Tony turn on the charm. "Thanks, Theresa. You don't know how much I … we … appreciate this."

"Zip it. I don't want to hear a word from you." She scrutinized Brian and Olivia. "She's a size six. But you're a giant. I'm not even sure I have anything that will fit you."

With that, she pivoted on her heel, walked to the back door of a shop with the name "Miss Tique" and twisted her keys in the lock. Then she disappeared within.

Tony fidgeted with the knob on the keychain, and Brian couldn't help but ask, "She saw through you? Is that why you broke it off?"

"A little bit, yeah."

Brian grinned and cracked down the window. Olivia didn't budge from her deep sleep.

After just a few minutes, Theresa returned and dropped a pile of clothes on Tony's lap. "These might be a bit short for you," she said to Brian. Turning to Tony, she said, "Don't call me again." Without waiting for Tony to answer, she returned to the store.

This time, Brian laughed. "I like her."

Tony stared at him with feigned indignation. "That hurts. It's deserved, but it hurts." Then he grinned and started the SUV. Pulling back onto Baseline, he turned toward the Flatirons. The road became Flagstaff Road and they climbed steadily, passing the flat wedges of rock that protruded from the steep sides of the mountains, giving that particular range its name. Twice during the trip, Olivia woke and each time, Brian gave her more medicine to drink.

Chapter 24

Olivia didn't fully wake until the following day in the cabin. She opened her eyes from a dream about wolves, Bengal tigers, and bears. Rolling her head to the side, she found Brian sleeping beside her. He lay facing her on a bed, curled under a sheet and using his hands as a pillow.

His eyes snapped open.

This startled her so that she took a moment before she spoke. "I suppose you heard my breathing change." No, there would be absolutely no chance for any secrets with a wolf.

"Yep." His voice was sleep-soft and raspy. Claw and bite marks crisscrossed his chest and a deep red and purple bruise bloomed across the left side of his rib cage. His brow cut was clean and had scabbed. She noticed a couple small stitches there. Another colorful bruise covered his right cheek. The scrapes around his neck from the fight in his house were fading to brown already.

It pleased her that he assumed they would share a bed. "How long have we been here?"

"A day already."

"How long have you been asleep?"

"A couple hours." He lifted his arm, draped it across Olivia and pulled her close. He closed his eyes again and murmured, "Sleep."

She'd done nothing but sleep, and she seriously thought she couldn't, but the deep easy breathing of the man beside her lulled her, and soon she drifted off with him.

The second time she woke, her bladder had an urgency that could not be ignored. Moving carefully, she slid off the bed and padded to the door. On a chair, she found a couple changes of clothes, one close to her size. Thank goodness. The scrubs she wore were covered in mud and they stank enough to wake the dead.

One of the two men had a good judge of female measurements. Olivia's bet was Tony. Though, she still didn't know Brian that well, and it could have been him just as easily. The other set of clothes looked big enough for Brian.

"Tony's on guard. Don't let him startle you," Brian called from the bed as he stretched and rolled over to face the window. She noted that he'd pushed the sheet off his upper body and was naked down to his waist. She wondered about the rest of him. Was he naked all the way down? His long lean torso invited her to run her hands across it, and she regretted the circumstances that kept them physically exhausted and apart, though they were what had introduced the two of them.

She'd have to rectify the apart thing though.

Her bladder made a second bid for her attention, and she turned and ran, bundle of clothes in hand. She wanted a shower before she dressed. Two doors sat side-by-side on the wall next to their room. She chose the

113

closest one, reasoning the spaces between all three doors dictated this smaller room was either the bathroom or a closet. Luck granted her wish, and she found a cramped, rustic pine bathroom containing a pedestal sink, stall shower, and energy-saver toilet.

After she relieved herself and showered, she dressed in the clothes chosen for her. The jeans were an off brand, but the blue, brushed cotton shirt was tailored. The underwear, bra, and socks were no frills, but fit well. She tossed the stained and smelly scrubs in the trash and wandered into the great room looking for Tony. Despite the size of the bathroom, the cabin wasn't all that small. The great room was about forty to forty-five feet in each direction. Adjacent to the bedroom wall was an open kitchen area. Beside it stood a ladder that leaned against a small loft crammed with boxes, blankets, snowshoes, and the like. A wineglass and a hanging pan rack swung above a long island that separated the kitchen from the rest of the room. One step down from that was a roughly furnished pine dining table. Two steps below that was the living area, which contained a brown leather couch, matching chairs, and an Oriental rug.

The wall directly across from the kitchen area was nothing but a floor-to-ceiling window with sliding glass door. In the corner of it and the bedroom wall burned a homey fire in an antique woodstove. The final wall, on the other side of the kitchen, contained a door to the outside, a small window and an even smaller desk. Blond pine logs rolled up the three walls and across the chandeliered ceiling. The floor was solid pine planking.

Not seeing Tony, Olivia went to the picture window and stared out. Their cabin overlooked a secluded cove of a frozen blue-green lake. No other houses could be seen amidst the snowy forest, but she saw a power boat tied to the dock. Still no Tony. Because of the fire, she knew he hadn't gone far.

Frowning, she wandered toward the kitchen. Her head felt tight, which meant she had a migraine coming within the next ten or twelve hours. Not that this surprised her, given all she'd been through. Caffeine will help. Besides her head, she felt pretty decent. She did some tentative stretches to test the extent of her healing and was pleased to note, besides a hitch where the stitches tugged on her skin and a deep-seated ache in her kidney, she once again had almost a full range of mobility. Her ribs felt good, still a little sore though. She inspected the myriad of scrapes and bruises. They'd mostly faded to brown. It seemed Brian's magic healing potion was exactly that. Though, she cautioned herself, she had just woken up and might go downhill again. She rustled through the cabinets and found decaffeinated instant coffee. That wouldn't do much for her head.

Hearing a soft sound behind her, she turned around and came nose-to-nose with the white Bengal. His fangs were only inches away. To her credit, Olivia didn't shriek, but she sucked in an amazing amount of air while her stomach felt as if it jumped through the roof of her mouth. She closed her eyes and slowly blew out her breath through pursed lips. When she looked again, Tony had gone back to human form and was pulling on a pair of dress pants, his back to her. He turned around, shrugging on a white oxford shirt, and sat at the dining table in the great room. Any body builder would be jealous of the six-pack on his abs.

Though Brian, with his sensitive ears, might have heard them already, Olivia kept her voice soft. "Asshole. I think I lost three years off my life."

"Just three? I may be an asshole, but, it's your ass I'm guarding." An arrogant grin creased his face, but then he frowned as she continued her search. "What are you looking for?"

"Real coffee. You know, the kind with caffeine. I have a headache coming." Now in a whole lot less than ten-to-twelve hours, thanks to Tony. She sighed.

"The maker is in the first cabinet at the bottom. Coffee's in the freezer."

In the freezer. Why didn't she think of that? It made perfect sense because everyone kept their coffee in there, right? She stopped and took a deep breath. There was no reason to be churlish just because of a prank. The migraine was definitely coming soon.

Once the coffee was brewing, she sat at the table across from Tony. "So, tell me about you. All of you."

"Okay. Education time." He leaned his chair back onto two legs. "Our kind are called by many names ... shapeshifters, changelings, animal people. Individually, we've also been known through time under other names and titles. Most ancient cultures have some kind of mythology about us. We've been called gods, and we've been demonized." He pointed toward the bedroom where Brian slept. "He and those of his family have been known as 'werewolves.' We've been worshipped and petitioned. The Druids, American Indians, and many other cultures believe that animal spirits guide them. We're not inherently evil, nor can we convert humans by bite or blood sucking. Not even Brian's kind can do that."

"You've been around a long time then."

"Pretty much since forever. We live a long time too. That man you want so badly in the other room is over four hundred years old. We can produce offspring with others of our own kind or sometimes with humans. We cannot crossbreed with those of other families, however."

116

Olivia blushed at the mention of her desire for Brian. She really wished Tony's nose hadn't been so keen. She didn't mind most people finding out who interested her, but somehow Tony's knowing bugged her. Then she focused on the over four hundred years old part. Wow. To his credit, Brian didn't look a day over thirty-five. "How old do shapeshifters get to be?"

Tony chuckled. "He's still a pup, if you want to know about his stamina. He could live to well over two thousand."

She felt her blush burn even more brilliant. Her temper was beginning to rise. Of all the arrogant, self-aggrandizing comments! Tony seemed to think he knew so much about her when he hadn't the foggiest idea. She opened her mouth to cut him down to size, but then bit back her words. He'd saved her life twice now. Anger was not the way to respond. She took a grip on their conversation and turned it to a safer direction. "The world must be full of shapeshifters."

"Not so much. We have a high mortality rate, due to our dual lifestyles."

Olivia would have to think on that awhile. They could live to two thousand years, but usually died much earlier. She didn't like the sound of that in regards to Brian. She asked, "What's your part in all this?"

He shrugged. "Someone has to help those of us who break the peace, who don't know how to control the animal within. No one else will give them a fair shake. They can't even show their true nature. Most of the time, they get in trouble because of a conflict between their other self and the laws of society. Sometimes, though, we have to deal with someone that has become truly evil."

Someone who had become truly evil. Another thing for her to think on. "Is that how you met Brian? Because he was in trouble?"

"He'll probably tell you himself, but he was in trouble. Not quite evil, but very close. He couldn't reconcile with the wolf. When it would break loose on him, which happened often, he killed."

China. Guilin Mountains. Now she understood the pain in his eyes when he spoke of that place and the tourists.

Tony continued. "He came over here to make a new start. But you can't run from who you are, and that wolf just wouldn't let him be. After a fortnight, he broke loose and mauled some loser who'd gone down the wrong alley. That was in New York City. Brian went to a local police station and turned himself in; he'd had enough and just wanted to die. But as luck would have it, a lawyer friend told me about him. She got him released on insufficient evidence, and he and I have been working together ever since."

Insufficient evidence. Since the wolf killed the guy, they'd had no evidence tying Brian to the crime. Probably made them mad. Olivia went to the kitchen and brought back two cups of coffee. "Like AA for changelings?"

"Something similar." She thought she saw his chest puff out with that statement.

"And you, have you ever gotten loose?" She sipped her coffee and burned her tongue, wishing she'd waited.

There he paused, looking at his hands as if seeing the scars and violence hidden there. "I think we all do, in the beginning."

She tried her coffee again. The burn earlier had numbed the center portion of her tongue, but the rest of her taste buds worked fine. The coffee had a nutty, toasted flavor and tasted great, though she'd never heard of the brand before. Being from Boulder, she assumed it was some kind of an organic variety. The smooth roast comforted her. She understood her need for that. She'd feel better if she had a grip on the whole wolf-tiger-bear-shifter thing. "Why do these bears want to kill me?"

Tony shook his head, his face grim. "I don't know, but I'll find out. Though, I have to tell you that bears are notorious for withstanding interrogation." He smiled and drank from his cup, watching Olivia through the steam.

Chapter 25

Brian dozed, waking occasionally to listen to Tony's and Olivia's murmurs. At last, he dropped into a deep sleep. His dream began in a simple, quiet forest, much like the one they'd just left, Marquis Park. It was in the full throes of summer. Trees were in heavy leaf. Shrubs carried long branches of berries. The stream bubbled and tumbled in its bed while fish and tadpoles cavorted in the shallows.

He pressed through the high growth of spike-covered bushes. The deeper into the undergrowth he went, the more confused he became. Olivia appeared beside him. At least, it should have been her, but he couldn't quite see her face. Together they walked through the forest, hand in hand.

Then, as always, his dream stumbled into the hellish. Menacing shadows stretched to the ground from the treetops. They enveloped the forest. The darkness became absolute. He couldn't even see Olivia's hand in his own.

Brian struggled to turn the dream around, to return to Olivia. The forest lightened, and he was beside her. The brush parted way for them, long vines draped from the trees like banners. She turned and stared into his eyes, but he still couldn't make out her features.

The shadows reappeared. They had scythe shaped claws and sharp canine fangs. They snapped and growled at him. Again, Brian fought to regain the happiness of the earlier dream. He called to Olivia, and she came to him. Her face was hazy, shifting with distortion. Still, he knew it was her. She leaned in to kiss him. He was happy. It was a happy dream. They talked about being together forever.

Again, the sky darkened until he couldn't see anything. Out of the dark, images of sharp, jutted mountains formed. His guilt screeched at him. It crowded everything out of the forest. He looked for Olivia, but she was nowhere. He found himself in the Guilin Mountains, near the Li River in China. Babbling voices reached him. Chinese was a second language to him; he should have been able to understand them, he'd spent enough time there, but he couldn't.

Sun-tanned farmers' hands grasped at him, clawed his skin, pulled out his hair. He ran and they followed. A giant mango tree stood in front of him, filled with ripe, fragrant fruit. As he reached for a mango to slake his thirst, the tree burned red. The fruit in his hand became rotten. He dropped to all fours and ran, now a wolf. Still, the enraged people followed.

Seeking refuge, Brian bolted into the back of a shallow cave. A ring of people brandishing knives, clubs, and torches crowded around the cave mouth. They threw burning twists of hay in after him. Some blazed on his coat, searing through to his skin. Branding him. More and more flaming hay twists flew into the cave. He couldn't stay or he'd die. Yet, they'd kill him if he tried to flee the cave. With no good choices, snarling, he leapt into the crowd.

Brian jerked awake. He lay on his stomach, his hands curled beneath him; his right one pulsed with pain from the lack of circulation. What a nightmare that had been. His insides still shook with the trauma of it. He tried to roll to his side, but the sheets had wound tightly around his torso and legs, trapping him. Slowly, he wriggled his arms free through the small space available near his head and stretched them out to the sides, uncramping and working his wrists.

He was drenched in sweat, and it rolled into his eyes, stinging them with salt. Remnants of the dream still haunted him. As it had most of his life. As it always would.

When feeling finally returned to Brian's fingers, he began extricating himself from his soaked sheet. Patiently, he tugged the opening at his neck until it was large enough. He pushed the cocoon down to his hips. Then he pulled himself out. Freed, he sat on the edge of the bed and opened the window. The frigid winter air blew across his damp body, cooling it. The last traces of his nightmare dissolved. From the front room came the sounds of Tony's and Olivia's voices.

He sat like that for a long time and waited for his insides to stop quivering. This had been one of the worst nightmares he'd had in the last few decades. Something was different this time, though.

"Why Olivia?" His whispered voice sounded harsh in the silence of the room. He found no answers. With a yawn, he shut the window. He rolled flat onto the bed and let himself drift off again.

Chapter 26

Tony set down his coffee and continued watching Olivia. Steam curled from his cup toward the ceiling. She took another sip from hers, using it to hide behind. Those blue eyes could pin anyone to the wall.

She got fidgety. "What?"

He tapped his fingers on the table. "Brian and I have been friends for a long time. Be careful with him."

She shook her head. "He won't hurt me."

"I'm worried about you hurting him. The wolf is very sensitive. So is Brian. He takes things seriously."

Ah. In other words, don't break his heart. "Got it."

"Good. As I said, he's a good friend." He now stabbed his finger at her.

Was that a threat? Really? Usually, it was her friends threatening her boyfriends. She'd never been on this side of it before. Offended, she said, "Relationships go the way they want. They can't be predicted. I can't guarantee either of us won't get hurt. But I'm not after anything. And, though the wolf is certainly nothing I've encountered before, that's not why I'm interested in him." Or was it?

He stood and turned his back on her, starting toward the loft ladder beside the kitchen. "As long as we understand each other."

That was the final straw. Fury burned through Olivia at this man's arrogance. Before she knew it, she was on her feet, leaning across the table. "Look, Tony the Tiger, you really are an asshole. You don't know me. You don't know my past. Yet, you feel you can threaten me. If you honestly were Brian's good friend, you'd be happy he found someone, even if it only lasted a short time, even if it caused pain in the end."

He turned, surprise on his face.

Her words dripped with sarcasm. A small voice in the back of her mind said Caution! but she bulled ahead. "I saw how much luck you have with relationships, chatting up the nurses, trying your charm on every woman you can find, even one barely alive in the hospital. Buddy, you're the last one who should be giving advice or thinking you had any answers regarding relationships. Your longest relationship is probably with a magazine."

His eyes glittered. With feline speed and precision he stepped close to her. She realized how foolhardy her words had been, but it was too late now. Anyway, she'd never been one for hiding her feelings. He leaned across the table until she could feel his breath on her face. He spoke in a low voice. "Round one and two went to me. Round three goes to you. But don't think you can sit in the winner's chair yet. The war is still to be decided. Be careful, little sister." With that, he pivoted on his heel, jerked off his shirt, and vaulted up the loft stairs.

Olivia picked up her coffee cup and went into the kitchen for a topper. "Asshole."

124

From the loft above she heard a chuckle. She looked up in time to see Tony's face watching her from over the edge of the loft as it changed into the pale softness of the Bengal. He winked a brilliant blue eye at her and then whisked away to his hiding spot.

She closed her eyes. This whole shapeshifter thing had a high learning curve to it, and her head wanted to explode. She felt like she was always on the losing end of any conversation, much less an argument. She needed to talk to a plain old human, but that wouldn't be happening for a while. Taking her coffee to the couch by the window, she settled down and watched the lake. Waves of snow scrolled across its frozen surface, pushed by the wind. Bare tree branches shook at the sky as if daring nature to do its worst.

It amazed her how many people thought they owned a person because they did a favor. She could see this man, Tony, a savior to shapeshifters, was no different though. Friend to Brian he might be, but she resolved to get out from under his thumb as soon as possible. Once they were on even footing, then perhaps he would be tolerable to be around, for as long as Brian and she were together.

For that matter, who was to say Brian wasn't trying for a little action on the side as long as he had a captive play toy? Which was fine with her, actually. The thought of sex with Brian invoked the memory of his long lean body lying near naked next to her and she heated deep inside. She glanced toward the loft, where she'd last seen Tony, but caught no sight of his white fur. She hoped he didn't smell the rise of her desire. Damn pheromones.

Crossing her legs, she concentrated on her coffee.

Within a couple hours, she felt the first stirrings of cabin crazy. Pacing in front of the window didn't help. She tried taking a nap on the couch, but she'd slept so much lately that her eyes flew open the minute she closed them. The coffee didn't help.

Her stomach growled. Olivia decided to focus on food and rooted through the kitchen, checking out the larder. Apparently the boys had stopped for food somewhere during the trip. Boxes and cans filled their cabinets and fridge to jam-packed full. She decided on a bowl of cold cereal. It became a two-handed operation, holding the two neighboring boxes in the cabinet with one hand while she tugged out the brand she wanted. In the end, she had to pull out two extra boxes to sandwich with hers so she could put them back on the shelf together. She added milk from the fridge, noting the fresh cream sitting in the door shelf. Someone had put some money into stocking the place, as if they were going to be there awhile.

She ate at the table, staring out the window. Her headache hadn't left, but it hadn't progressed either. It hung in the back of her skull, threatening and making her scowl. It wouldn't take much to push it over the edge, and Tony was still lurking on the premises somewhere. Olivia finished her cereal and washed her bowl, spoon and cup in the sink. Then she went to search the bathroom. There had to be some drugs of some kind there. She pulled open the mirror front of the medicine cabinet and stared at the bare shelves. No help. The only other place that could have held any medication was the shelf above the toilet. Though she shoved aside the stacks of towels, washcloths and toilet paper, she found nothing to prevent or dull her impending migraine. Sputtering her frustration, she returned to the front room.

Tony couldn't be seen and she walked to the sliding glass door that led to the deck. Cool air might help her head. The moment she put her hand on the handle, the white Bengal jumped in front of her, growling softly.

126

She had no idea where he'd been hiding. One minute, she was alone, the next, he was there. He bodily pushed her back, as if saying, "You're not going out there."

"I'm going cabin crazy. I'm not used to sitting around. Exercise is what I need." She felt foolish speaking to a jungle cat, so she reached again for the door handle. Tony snarled and gripped her wrist in his mouth. His bite was gentle, but firm, leading her to realize he brooked no argument in his decision.

"Fine," she said and settled on the couch again. He stared at her a moment. She raised her hands in defeat and repeated, "Fine."

Perhaps he took pity on her, but shortly after he left, he returned as a man, dressed and with a bottle of aspirin, a glass of water, and a deck of cards. "Poker?"

Olivia nodded and snatched up the bottle. "Anything at all." Drugs and relief from boredom. She could almost forgive him. She downed three pills.

He dealt the cards and they played in silence except for the occasional words they needed for the game. The hours passed slowly, but they did pass. Periodically, Tony paused the game to listen or pace from window to window. Once, he bolted from his chair and ran to the loft. She waited, barely breathing, ready to race to the bedroom to wake Brian. But Tony came back, re-buttoning his shirt. They'd been playing a little under five hours when the bedroom door behind her opened and a fully dressed Brian wandered to the bathroom. When he came out, she halfway expected him to return to bed, but he came to where they sat and settled on the back of the couch behind her, watching the game.

"Who's winning?" His voice had a sleepy slur to it that added a western accent to his words. His dark hair was rumpled, and he rubbed his eyes, yawning.

Tony pointed at her. "Olivia's kicking my ass." He dealt the final round of cards.

127

She nodded. "A little humility is good for you." A lot of humility would be better. She laid down a royal flush and leaned back against Brian, watching Tony's face contort from disbelief to exasperation to the thin lips of negation.

He tossed two pair onto the table and stood. "Well, Brian, if you're up, then I'm gonna head back and see what I can see."

Brian also stood and nodded, wiping sleep from his eyes. "I'm up."

"Then I'm out of here. See you when I know something." He lifted his hand in a farewell at her and practically ran out the door. She should have been offended at this offhanded treatment, as if he'd had too much of her and couldn't wait to get away. But truthfully, she was happy to see him go. She wanted some time alone with her magic, skilled, Chinese artist.

Brian waved his hand in a circle. "I'm going to take a look around outside. You stay here." He opened the door and slipped out into the snow, tossing his clothes and changing to the wolf.

If he had been Tony, Olivia would have saluted and given her best "Yes, sir!" But it wasn't, and she was happy to wait. She walked to the window and watched Brian fade into the trees on the far side of the house, weaving between the trunks. His dark fur blended with the tree bark and dark pine boughs. As he moved farther away, she soon lost sight of him. She waited at the window. He would return. And when he did, she wanted him to know she kept an eye out for his safety, too.

She was still at the window and watching when he, in naked human form, came out of the trees on the near side of the house. As far as muscle, Tony had nothing on her Brian. The man had an amazing physique. He moved with a lithe grace, huge bulks of muscles bunching and rolling with each step. And he was well endowed in the

128

sexual department, she noticed. She watched him until he got too far around the corner of the house for her to see him anymore. When he opened the door, in his jeans and pulling on his denim shirt, she turned around and crossed the floor, stopping just a foot away. "All clear out there?"

He nodded, never once taking his gaze off hers.

She smiled at him. Tony was gone. They were finally alone. Heated desire singed through every cell of her body.

An answering fire lit in his eyes and he murmured, "Come here." He reached for her hand and pulled her into his embrace. Crushing her to him, his lips came down on hers, devouring them. Her heart swelled and her breath was swept away. She finally understood when heroines in historical novels swooned; she felt she would pass out just from sheer desire to have this man's body tangled with hers. He traced her lips with his tongue, and then dove it into her mouth, filling it, ravishing it, while he stroked her back and hips.

Olivia' flattened her hands on his chest muscles, and she let them wander across their smooth lines and span the breadth of his abs. She couldn't get enough. Her fingers, like carnivorous creatures, feasted on every contour of his abdomen, every line, tracing them again and again. Then they rose to the smooth stone of his chest, rubbing across his nipples.

Kneading the base of her spine, and then squeezing her buttocks, Brian pulled her hips tight against his captive erection. He lifted his mouth away from hers and grazed his lips across her face in tiny kisses. She couldn't catch her breath. Zings of fire sparked from where his lips touched her throughout her whole body and a ragged moan broke free. She slowed her hands, and reached down to unbutton the top of his jeans.

He smiled at her then and, with a low growl, scooped her into his arms and carried her to their bed. The wolf was so visible in his eyes, she shivered.

Chapter 27

Brian carried Olivia in his arms, hoping she didn't hear the heavy drum of his heart. It felt as if it would lunge right out of his chest. He wanted her like he hadn't wanted anyone in a long time. No, it was more than that. He needed her. In every way. Her smile calmed the raging torrent of emotions inside him. He wanted to wrap himself around her, completely envelope her.

She looked at him like he was the answer to all her dreams and desires. Like he was a hero. It made him feel foolish, vulnerable and indestructible all at the same time. He was no hero, but for her, he'd try to be one.

He lay Olivia on the bed, following to lie beside her. His blood burned to be with her, but he didn't want to just have her in passion and fire, he wanted to love her. He wanted this to mean something. It already did to him; he wanted it to for her as well.

Already she scrambled with the zipper of his jeans. Her face was flushed and it made the pupils of her eyes seem larger. Tiny green flecks speckled her eyes, lending them more to hazel than brown. Brian wondered if passion had brought them out, or if they had always been there and made a mental note to check later. He wanted to know everything about her, to love her, but not hurt her.

Shaking her fingers loose, he took her hands and kissed each knuckle.

She stilled at the sudden change of pace. She asked, "What's wrong?"

"How do you feel?"

Her eyebrows knit together. "Fine. I feel fine."

Still, he hesitated. He wanted Olivia so badly his whole body hurt. Every time she touched him his skin tingled and a quiver settled deep inside him. Yet, she'd been so grievously injured, and so recently too. Could he really be so selfish as to jeopardize her health for the sake of making love to her now?

Olivia took the decision from him. She reached up with both hands and placed them on either side of his face. She pulled him close. "I promise to tell you if anything, and I mean anything, feels uncomfortable."

Slowly he nodded, agreeing. There were, after all, more ways than one to make love to a woman.

He propped on his elbow and cupped the back of her neck with one hand. Lowering his mouth to her throat, he kissed and nipped her gently. With his free hand, he unbuttoned her shirt and cupped her bare breast, rubbing his thumb across her nipple. His desire for her focused and became sharp in his blood, like a thin wire. Her hands floated like birds across his muscles inside his shirt and down his back, becoming more insistent as her breathing quickened.

His hand moved lower, undoing her jeans and sliding beneath her waistband, around to her back, lifting her abdomen and pelvis against his. His bites and kisses trailed after his hand, stopping at her breasts. He rolled his tongue around and around each nipple and softly nipped them. The already pronounced tips hardened, and Olivia moaned, breathy and low. He loved her breasts. They were neither too large, nor too small, but seemed to fit perfectly in his hands. In his mouth. He flicked his tongue back and forth across one, then the other nipple, drawing more breathy moans. The sound of her passion moved him. Made his heart tighten with emotion. Staring into her face, he thought he'd never seen a woman more beautiful. Her eyes were closed and she was biting her lower lip.

He let his free hand roam across her body, stroking, massaging and squeezing every curve down to her buttocks and around front, grazing across her soft mound. She opened her legs to him. That simple act, that trust, nearly drove him to break his vow of making love slow and easy. The ache throughout his body showed him just how badly he wanted her. He didn't think he could get any harder, and he wanted to plunge himself deep inside her with every ounce of strength he had.

Abruptly, he stood and pulled off her jeans and her lace panties. While he peeled out of his clothes, she watched his erection spring forward in freedom. He stood a moment, letting her see what belonged to her now. He wasn't small by any measure. She smiled, crooked a finger, and beckoned him. Need for her infected him like a plague, and he growled, pouncing on the bed, covering her with his body, making her his prisoner. The heat of her sex burned against him. He kissed her deeply, filling her mouth, stroking her tongue with his own.

His free hand rode her curves down to the wetness between her legs, where he slid his fingers into the heat hidden there. She caught her breath and shuddered. It spurred him as if he was a racehorse, and he wondered if he would make it to the end of the ride. He'd never lost control before, never let himself become lost in a woman completely. But this woman, Olivia, brought him to the brink.

He raised his head and backed down her body, tracing a long line with his tongue until he reached her cleft and found the sensitive nub buried above it. First he traced the edges of it, then he lapped it, matching the rhythm with his fingers inside.

Her breath came ragged, and she spread her legs wider. One hand tangled in his hair while the other twisted the blankets beside her head. Her hips pulsed with the rhythm of his tongue. The crest of an orgasm came on her and her body bucked and clenched around his fingers, seeking of its own to pull him in deeper. It almost undid him. He raised himself and moved over her, pushing her thighs farther apart with his own.

His need for her had control of him. The only thing he wanted was to be buried deep inside her, moving as one with her. No other thought entered his mind. Holding himself off her body, he rubbed the head of his shaft against her cleft, wetting it with her own juices.

"Yes, inside me," she whispered.

In one smooth motion, he entered her and slowly pushed in all the way. She gave no sign of discomfort and, to his pleasure, she took him all. It was as if they were meant to join together. He slid almost all the way out and then shoved his full length in again and again, quicker each time. Looking down into her flushed face, he still saw no signs of unease or pain. Another climax was close upon her. He lowered himself on top of her, capturing her breast with his hand and her neck with his mouth. He flicked his thumb over her nipple, bit her neck, and settled into a driving rhythm. Within three strokes, she reared her hips up under him as her second orgasm washed across her. It gave him deeper access, and he buried himself as deep as he could get. Her

134

contractions against his erection brought him to his own climax.

Everything stilled and centered on the explosion within him. It started at the base of his shaft and spread throughout his body like a long jolt of electricity, over and over. Sweet agony. He slid his arms beneath her and held her against him, pulling her into his moment, Olivia's whimpers hot in his ear.

They lay coupled together for what seemed a long time. Then, as his erection relaxed, he moved out of her and rolled onto his back, pulling her to lie against his chest. "You still feel all right?"

She laughed. "Beyond all right."

He smiled and kissed her. Stroking her hair, he thought about how to tell her what he felt for her. That his attraction was more than just sexual. Despite any efforts to the contrary, he was in love. But, had he really fought that hard? What would she say? Would she reject his love? He didn't think so, but the possibility existed.

"Do you feel different as a wolf than as a man?"

Surprised, he turned to look at her, trying to fathom her reference. It took him a moment to realize she'd been talking about changing to the wolf. "I used to think so, but as I learned to control the wolf, I stopped seeing us as two individuals. We're just different forms of the same man."

"So, you're as bad-ass as a man too?"

He couldn't help but laugh at that. He'd never thought of himself like that before. She really did think of him as a hero, of sorts. That worried him. It also made him vow to cross hell barefoot, if necessary, to keep her safe. "I suppose."

"You and Tony have done this before? Gotten into situations where you've both had to change to the animals? There were two sets of clothes in that

135

backpack." She ran the back of her finger along his jawline, sending tingles through his spine.

He nodded, not looking at her, taking hold of her hand. His heart flooded with love for her. He wanted to tell her, needed to tell her that he wanted her in his life forever. That this wasn't just a fling. "It's sometimes necessary."

Oblivious to his rising emotions, she said, "Tony used a silver bullet. I always thought of that as myth, written for the movies."

He rolled his eyes. "It is. Tony uses that bullet because it's his signature. Tony Silver." He pressed her against him. Talking about Tony was the last thing he wanted to do at that moment.

Chapter 28

Brian stood in front of the window and the darkening whiteness outside, dressed in nothing but jeans that slung low enough to show the points on his narrow hips. The glow from the fire highlighted the muscles in his back and thick shoulders. They seemed to ripple as he moved. He seemed more animal than man in that moment. He had the remnants of a sandwich in his hand and, while Olivia watched, he jammed the last quarter of it into his mouth as one bite, wiping his fingers on his jeans. His head swiveled from side to side as he scoped the oncoming twilight, the lake, and the surrounding terrain, keeping an eye out for movement and listening for anything amiss.

She knew he heard her coming out of the bedroom, but he didn't turn away from his sentry duty. She also knew he wouldn't until he made sure they were safe. She came up behind him, dressed in the other half of his clothes, his denim shirt, and slid her arms around his waist, leaning her cheek against his smooth, hard back.

She breathed in the maleness of his scent and a tiny thrill burned through her body.

It had been two days since Tony had left. In those two days, she and Brian had talked, laughed, and loved. They had cooked too, finding delight in making their favorite meals for each other. Nobody made spaghetti like she did. Nobody. And Brian loved it. She found that he was a better cook than she, which was saying a lot, actually. He made an unbelievable mushroom tomato soufflé that melted in her mouth. She prided herself on her gourmet skills, but he was a maestro. But then, he'd had over 400 years to practice.

With his hyper-metabolism and the magic herbal medicine he continued to concoct, his bruises had faded to pale brown already. His cuts were well on their way to healing too. As for her injuries, her bruises, cuts, and scrapes were still dark, but mending. The only problem areas remained her kidney and her ribs.

He lifted his arm now, letting her slide around the side of him, still with her one arm wrapped around his waist. They both watched the sun make its final bows, sending cascades of tangerine, burgundy, and hot pink across the sky, snow, and ice crusted lake.

She said, "It's beautiful. We should stay here."

"They'll find us."

"Not if we find them first."

His body shifted as he turned to look at her. He didn't answer, so she continued. "Then, after we take care of business, we can come back here and live." For as long as their relationship might last.

"You mean it? You'd want us to live here?" His voice was soft, hesitant.

She looked up in his eyes. "Absolutely."

A kind of wonder crossed his face, and he cupped her chin in his hands. She was pretty sure he would have kissed her then, but he straightened, turning toward the door. She could tell his keen ears picked up something and, after a few seconds of listening, he said, "Tony."

"Damn that man." He was forever ruining a good thing. She scurried to the bedroom to dress.

Within ten minutes, a tired Tony walked in their door. The circles below his bloodshot eyes were as dark as bruises, and the lines in his face were deep-set. Though, his hair, per his usual, didn't have a lock out of place and his clothes looked pressed. He withdrew a gun, a silver .357 Ruger, from the back of his belt and sat at the table, throwing a folder down in front of him. Olivia stood at the bedroom door, just finished dressing, having decided on a speed shower first. Brian was still dressed as he had been: jeans, no shirt, no shoes. Tony leaned his chair back onto two legs and crossed his feet on the table. Though she was sure both men knew she was there, Tony spoke to Brian without acknowledging her presence. "I beat the hell out of him, and he still wouldn't talk. The rest of my sources dried up too. Everybody just disappeared."

She frowned. Beat who? One of the bears? Obviously, someone they'd spoken privately about, probably during the trip here, after she'd fallen asleep.

Brian said, "Something scared them."

Tony nodded, clearly enjoying the melodrama. "Finally, I cornered that little rat down near the veterans' hospital. He rambled and said a lot of stuff, but one word caught my attention: Griffin."

Brian tucked his chin as if in surprise. "Griffin?"

"Yep. Fierce and brutal. Blindingly loyal. High moral compass. Often stereotyped as evil by those unfortunate enough to cross them."

"Extinct." Brian glanced up at her, presumably to make sure she followed the conversation. She nodded and came farther into the room, sitting at the table opposite Tony, who now leaned forward, picked up his

139

folder, flipped it open, and rocked his chair back on two legs again.

"Bellerophon came through. Good idea, Brian." His attention focused on the folder, Tony began. "Olivia, who are your parents?"

She shook her head, unsure of where Tony was going with this. But, wherever it was, it scared her. "I don't know who they are—I'm an orphan. Is that about me?" She stood and reached across the table for the folder he held, but before her fingers could close on it, Tony jerked it out of her reach.

"Tony, she can't be a griffin. The last two, a mated pair, were killed over two hundred years ago." Brian paced the length of the table, rubbing his mouth and chin with his hand, his frown as deep as hers.

She couldn't believe what she was hearing. "I'm only twenty-three. It's physically impossible for me to have parents who died over two hundred years ago. Tony, what are you saying?" The uncomfortable feeling grew inside her. She stepped back from the table.

"You were raised at Miss Atwood's orphanage, right? It has long been known as a safe haven for shifter orphans."

Brian stopped and glanced from his friend to Olivia and back, his eyes wide and alarmed. He slowly turned to fully face her. She could almost see the possibilities clicking through his mind. Behind him, the last of the sunset colors disappeared outside and dusk took over.

Her voice rose, and now it was her turn to look from one person present to the other. "I don't know anything about shapeshifters hiding at the orphanage. I'm not one of them, and I'm no damn griffin! I would know. I would have changed by now. Doesn't it usually happen at puberty?" Brian's panic unnerved her, and that bad feeling just grew and grew. This couldn't be happening. She stared at him, silently begging him to find a way out

140

of this predicament for her, to find a reason it wasn't true.

Instead, he slowly said, "Well, not necessarily. It usually happens at puberty, but not always. Sometimes it takes a long time. There have been documented cases of onset at four and five centuries, even." He looked at her now as if she were a complete stranger.

His sudden acceptance of Tony's stupid idea cut through her like a lance, and tears stung her eyes. "For God's sake, I'm only twenty-three!" Her voice thickened with distress, and she sounded like a petulant child.

Tony asked, "Did Miss Atwood ever take you on a field trip? Did you ever leave her compound while you were there?"

Now that just confused her. "No, I... Why?" What would field trips have to do with anything? Unless he meant to find out if she'd had contact with anyone else in the outside world in Miss Atwood's orphanage. Why couldn't he just ask a question straight on?

"So you had no way of knowing the true passing of time while you were there."

Again, she looked from one man to the other. They were both staring at her like she was some kind of monster. "This is preposterous! I think I would have noticed 200 years going past. I'm not evil! I'm only twenty-three! I'm not a griffin!"

Chapter 29

Olivia turned her back on Brian and Tony. She ran, half-blind from her tears, for the sanctuary of the bedroom, reasoning that if she tried to leave the cabin, they'd stop or track her. Fear did one of two things to her: it either really pissed her off, or, as in this case, when it was coupled with betrayal, it sent her into tears. And she'd be damned if she'd break down in front of either of them. She reached to close the door, but Brian was right on her heels, already closing them both in and turning on the light. She said, "Go away. I don't want to talk to anyone."

He didn't budge. He just looked down on her with those brown eyes of his filled with concern. She went around to the far side of the bed and sat, sniffing and choking back sobs. What a nightmare. How could either Brian or Tony consider this to be true? There was no way she could be a griffin. Her backlit reflection in the window stared back at her while she worked to get her emotions under control again. Brian followed and settled in beside her, waiting.

After what seemed like forever, he said in his always gentle voice, "Tell me about Miss Atwood. Was she kind?"

Olivia nodded, sniffing and wiping the final dregs of tears from her face. She had no tissues, so she wiped her nose with her hand, hoping this wasn't too unmannerly for him. "She was the best. Always patient with us and ready to tell stories. When someone adopted one of the kids, she made a cake and we all celebrated. We also had a party for any outstanding event or sometimes because we hadn't had fun like that in a while." She smiled in spite of her tears, but sobered quickly.

"How long were you with her?"

"All my childhood. I never found a home with anyone else. Truthfully, I don't think she tried to find me one too hard. She said I was her special favorite. One day, she told me to leave. She said I'd turned eighteen and couldn't stay. It can't be true. How could I not notice 200 years going past? The length of the year I know now doesn't seem any shorter."

He nodded and picked up her hand, her unsnotted one, rubbing it back and forth with his thumb. "There are herbs, like Belladonna and Dong quai, that can help people not notice the passage of time. I want you to think really hard. Did it seem like you were there longer than most of the others?"

She didn't like this at all. Each word, each sentence seemed to point to Tony's conclusion. "I guess. Not as long as some, though. But longer than most. You don't think too clearly about things like that when you're young. It never bothered me because I had Miss Atwood."

They sat silent for a long time, Brian patiently beside her. Whether he was waiting or trying to figure out something to say, she couldn't tell. For her part, she

143

couldn't wrap her head around this new twist in her life. It couldn't be true. Could it? Was she really a griffin? And over 200 years old? She turned to him. "Tony's good at what he does, isn't he? Is he ever wrong about these things?"

Brian shrugged, his dark gaze locked with hers. "He's wrong, but not very often."

"But, how can I be this evil thing? I'm not that way."

He pulled her against him and said, "No one says you have to be evil." She heard his voice echo in his chest. It sounded safe. Comforting. Honest.

Olivia spoke to the echo, "But, if Tony's right, then I am this griffin. Won't evil be in my nature? Isn't that what he said?"

"Not necessarily. True evil is very rare. Usually, people are branded with that stigma because of ignorance and fear. Take me for example. Because I didn't know how to live with the wolf, I did some bad things. I'm not evil, though I've been called that. In fact, most of my clan are considered evil, but rarely are."

She turned her head and stared at her reflection in the window. She had nothing left to say. All her arguments had an answer. Could it be true? That sinking feeling inside her certainly seemed to think so. She felt betrayed. A bit by Brian, though she had no trouble forgiving him. He'd seen the possibilities and had been trying to help her accept them. And she could forgive Tony too, even if that ground against her because she was still looking for a way to get out from under his enormous ego.

Brian pulled away and stood, reaching for the denim shirt she'd discarded earlier. He didn't take his gaze off her, and she squirmed under the scrutiny. What must he think of her now? She was supposed to be an evil monster. How could he want someone like that?

It occurred to her that Miss Atwood was also a shifter. No matter what creature she was, Olivia couldn't forgive her for her transgressions. She had loved the older woman as a mother. And Miss Atwood had loved her too. She was sure of it. Yet, she'd betrayed her. Anger blossomed within her. She wondered what manner of animal the other woman was inside. Something sneaky. Rat? Snake? The trickster crow? Even if all this was wrong, and Olivia fervently prayed it was, she wanted to talk to that woman. With extreme prejudice.

"Why now? Why didn't they come to kill me when I was young?"

"They most probably didn't know." He buttoned the shirt and slid his feet into socks and sneakers.

She let him see her skepticism. "You think anyone could keep that a secret … for two hundred years?"

"I don't know. If anyone could, Miss Atwood would be at the top of the list. She's been around longer than anyone can remember. She would know all the tricks. We'll find out for sure. I think Tony has plans to visit the orphanage."

She certainly wanted to be along for that ride. She said, not asked, "So, you think it's true, then."

Brian wrapped his arm around her shoulders, pulling her against him again. He lifted her chin so he could look in her eyes. "I don't know. Time will tell, but we'll deal with it together. Now, let's go see what Tony wants to do."

Together sounded good, but who knew how his emotions would change if she became this evil thing.

They walked out of the bedroom, hand in hand, Brian in the lead. She was trying to clean her snotty hand on her jeans and didn't notice he had stopped until she actually bumped into him. Peering around him to spot what had caused the traffic jam, she saw that Tony,

145

too, was standing at stiff attention, staring toward the front of the cabin, his weariness no longer visible. Then, as one, they both snapped their heads to the right, their attention on something she couldn't hear.

"Eight," her Brian said.

"Yep," was Tony's response.

The bears must have found them. She stood behind Brian at the bedroom door, thinking about how that might have happened. She whispered to Tony standing beside the dining table, knowing that a normal man wouldn't hear it, but he would. "They followed you."

He glanced at her with a wry smile, his bright blue eyes wincing. Score the big one for her. She was out from under Tony Silver's huge ego, finally. And, judging by the wince, he knew it. Olivia could have danced a jig right there, except Brian was busy pulling her to hide with him behind the pine kitchen island.

Tony joined them. "What do you want to do?" This he asked of Brian. Not her. This time it didn't really bother her. She was still basking in the glow of her victory.

Brian tipped his head. "Fight until we can make a hole big enough to get her out?"

Tony acknowledged her presence with tight lips and a glance. He nodded. They both edged toward the end of the island.

"Wait," she said. "If you two are going to the party in costume, then leave me the .357."

They both stared at her.

"Do you two really think I have no skills whatsoever? You already know I can swim. I can shoot too. Miss Atwood taught all of us orphans. I was grand champion every year." She held out her hand. Tony hesitated, so she snapped her fingers. "C'mon. We don't have much time."

He was slow about it, but he forked over his pistol and three speed loaders. She thought she saw a glimmer of satisfaction in Brian's eyes. Or was it amusement? And with that, they rounded the corner. She rose enough above the counter to watch them leave, but they were too quick, changing as they moved, and all she saw were tatters of clothing on the floor. She glanced at the door and saw Tony's white, striped tail whisk out of the cabin.

Chapter 30

Brian stepped out of the cabin and into the fading light, Tony at his heels. He chose to stay in the half-wolf, half-human form, the man-beast. He was stronger there, and he had a feeling strength would win this fight. He was the legend now, the monster. He was werewolf.

Tony, on the other hand, was always best as full tiger and never stopped at the halfway point, the Paladin.

Unnatural silence surrounded the clearing. The air was crisp and heavily scented with pine and the wood smoke from the cabin's chimney. It carried another scent too. He smelled shifted bears; their odor was different than natural bears. Specifically, he scented Carl Hall and at least two others from his family. Humans carried varied scents, so it was hard to identify shifters in that form. But now, in animal form, he could smell the human all over them.

There was another jackal and a couple of wolves. Somewhere, there was a solitary stag. Of all the shifters, the one that worried him most was that big buck deer.

They were quick and deadly with both their antlers and their hooves.

Tony peeled off to the right, circling the house. He had his mouth open, tasting the scent of his prey, his long tail twitching with excitement.

Brian forged straight ahead into the darkness beneath the surrounding trees. The musk of his enemy was strong here, caught by the heavy boughs of the towering Ponderosas. Snow crunched under a heavy foot on his left, and a lupus shadow on his right lunged at him. Brian knew this one. He was part of Cujo's pack. Brian had been invited to join them when he'd first moved into the Boulder area, but he'd declined, wanting his solitude. The offer had remained open. This one had been one of the pups at the time. A reactionary, if he remembered right. No surprise he'd shown up here. His inexperience showed in that he chose to fight a werewolf with a full wolf. He was destined to lose.

Brian met him head on. Behind him, the other shadow materialized into a black bear. It didn't join the attack, however. Instead, it loped into the clearing, headed toward the cabin.

The young wolf wouldn't let go. Twisting, Brian swung his foe against the nearest Ponderosa with a solid thump. The wolf grunted, but hung on.

Again, Brian wheeled his adversary against the tree, putting every bit of strength he had into the move. This time, the stunned wolf loosed its hold and dropped to the snow and pine floor of the forest, unconscious. He wasn't dead, but certainly out of the fight; Brian grunted with satisfaction.

His sharp ears picked up the sounds of more breaking branches, hisses, and snarls from the other side of the cabin. Tony was hard at work too.

The clearing was a slight incline toward the center building, and the black bear was only gaining speed, its

149

shorter forearms better suited to that incline. Brian would never catch him as he was. He shifted fully into the wolf and sprinted after the bear, catching it twenty feet from the giant picture window that covered the front of the cabin. No way would he let anyone hurt Olivia.

He launched into the air and landed on the animal's wide back and rolling shoulders. He couldn't get a purchase through the thick, coarse hair. The bear stopped and slung its hind end, pivoting on its front, with surprising speed. With no grip, Brian tumbled off, mouth full of fur. The black bear reared up to its hind legs, mouth agape, mawing loudly.

Brian jumped to his feet and darted around the beast. He growled and worried the other shifter's hindquarters. Without turning, the bear swung his nearest arm straight back, clocking Brian on the head.

He yelped and fell back, dazed. Shaking his head didn't seem to help dispel his dizziness or the ringing in his ears.

The bear fell forward to all four feet and lumbered toward the cabin. Brian charged after him.

Chapter 31

Olivia was almost relieved to hear animal growling, snarling, and crying. Silence had filled the cabin and surrounding area. It had stayed way too long. She had to admit that it had unnerved her. A mighty crash sent a black bear through the big front window. He got up groggy and stood in uncertainty for a moment. That's all she needed. She took careful aim and squeezed off a bullet. He dropped like a stone. Brian's elongated wolf face peered around the corner of the broken window and then disappeared. She thought he was just checking on her until he drove another bear, a grizzly this time, through the window and into the front room. This one rose to his feet still swinging. She'd shot moving targets, but they were somewhat predictable, not wildly erratic like this animal. The one thing she did know was to not rush the shot, so she waited until she got the hang of the action.

Brian kept the bear occupied from the front. She knew he'd be listening for her, so she said in a soft voice, but loud enough for him to hear, "Drop." He did exactly that, throwing himself to the floor amid the glass shards. She fired. She misjudged the bear's turn a little and didn't hit him. Brian was up and at him again. She came out from behind the kitchen counter and walked right down to the bear, aiming. She wondered if he'd been one of the men in the apartment or the woods. Anger flooded her. This man was trying to kill her. A step out of paw range, she fired. This time, she hit her mark.

Lowering the gun, she said to the wolf Brian, "Sorry. Moving target. Got the hang of it now." Her anger hadn't left with the bullet, but instead solidified in her heart. These bear people may have started this war, but she intended to finish it. She wanted to kill every one of those men who attacked her based on only rumor. Yet, somewhere inside, she knew she'd become as blind as them if she did.

Her wolf bowed his head and leapt out the window. Within minutes, he was back, lowering his front end. It took her a moment to realize he wanted her to climb aboard. She didn't really want to leave. She wanted to put an end to this war tonight. But, she also trusted Brian and Tony. If they thought it better to leave, then so did she. After all, they'd been around this shapeshifter world a lot longer than her.

She frowned. "I can ride a horse. Wolf remains to be seen." She climbed aboard.

It was an odd sensation and very unhorse-like. Whereas a horse's barrel-like body was broad and somewhat rounded, suitable for a rider to grip with his legs, the wolf's chest was narrow and deep with a finely tapered waist behind it. It took a few strides to situate herself, but by the time they reached a full run, she pretty much had her seat.

A large wolf, not as big or as dark as Brian, loomed to her right and she took aim. "Firing."

152

She let go with the bullet and Brian stumbled to the side with a loud, "Oof." The other wolf dropped even as she grappled to stay seated, fisting huge chunks of her wolf's neck fur. Searing pain from her wounded ribs shot through her body and, for a moment, she honestly thought she'd be sick. Brian had been right; she was still plenty injured.

"Sorry," she said with a grimace. "No more shots to the side. Straight on or straight behind." Glancing back, she saw the smaller wolf flailing to rise. Then she saw a streak of white attack it. Give him hell, Tony.

Olivia had two shots left in the revolver, and she contemplated changing them now. Just as she decided she would, a big albino buck deer appeared only ten feet in front of them, head lowered and antlers ready. Brian reared back and rocked to the right, almost unseating her. She wrapped her legs tighter. They kept turning around the buck until he was directly behind. He pivoted with them, pawing grooves in the deep loam and keeping them always facing the points of his antlers. He charged, digging his feet deep into the frosted forest floor. She let him have it. This time went much better; no stumbling steps and one dead deer.

Tony joined them, and they raced through the woods. She reloaded and tucked the .357 into the front of her waistband and settled low over Brian's shoulders like a jockey. It seemed that they were running in that forest forever, but when they met up with a highway, they turned to run beside it, taking to the trees again when traffic approached. Both Tony and Brian seemed tireless, but she worried. Though mostly healed, Brian had those recent injuries, and carrying her added weight had to be wearing him down.

Tony led the way, like a white ghost, racing toward their destination, which Olivia suspected terminated at Miss Atwood's orphanage. They veered away from the highway and paused at a secluded spring for a quick drink. Warm water bubbled from underground, heating the clearing enough so that no snow covered the dry glade. The trees also showed bare bark and needles on the half that faced the spring.

Her suspicions about Brian were confirmed. Whereas Tony looked tired, Brian fell back on the moonlit brown grass, huffing hoarsely. His wolf face was haggard and he kept his eyes closed. She turned her gaze on the tiger, who seemed to know her concern. Nothing needed to be said. He got to his feet and loped away into the forest. She watched over Brian, smoothing his soft fur as he slowly drifted off into exhausted sleep. She didn't think he'd hear a whole army of bears, or whatever, from three feet away. Even though without a coat and cold, she caught herself nodding off, so she marched around until her head cleared. Then she stood at the edge of the clearing, leaning against an aspen, rubbing her arms and watching her wolf.

She wondered when he'd become her wolf. It had to have been in the woods, when she watched him defend her. Or, had it been in his house, before he'd ever shown his other self to her? Or had it been in the hospital, when she woke and he'd been watching over her. Yes, she decided. That had been it. Was she falling in love? She felt no silly giggles bubbling inside, no heartache clinging to the edges of her dreams. She felt no overwhelming desire to blind him to all women but her. Watching others who claimed to be "in love" had taught her these were the signs. She had none. Yet, they somehow fit together. And she couldn't see her life without him. Was that love?

About forty-five minutes after he left, Tony reappeared in man form, dressed in cowboy duds. He swung a bulging fast food sack in one hand and clothing in another. She hadn't even heard him walk through the

154

woods. Disgusted with herself, she flopped down on the ground near Brian.

Tony tossed a coat at her. He chuckled. As if knowing her thoughts, he asked, "Do you expect to be able to hear like we do?"

"I expect to at least be a decent lookout, but apparently, I can't even do that. Anyway, if I'm supposed to be this mythical griffin, shouldn't I hear better than I do?" She gently pulled on the parka, favoring her ribs, reinjured from the sideways shot that sent Brian stumbling. Maybe she'd even re-broken the mending seams. Her kidney still felt bruised, but no worse.

Reaching into the bag, Olivia snagged the first burger she found. She was naturally carnivorous, but when tired or in need of comfort, beef was the meat of choice. And this burger, though subpar, tasted fantastic right then. She closed her eyes and let the heavy grease and burnt leather flavor roll around her tongue. Heaven.

"Your abilities will most likely change when you do," Tony said.

She opened her eyes. She knew he meant to be reassuring with his words, but they only drove deeper the assertion of her nightmare other self. She thought he sensed her despair and they were silent a few moments, listening to Brian's heavy breathing. Well, at least she was listening to Brian, because she apparently couldn't hear anything much farther away.

Eventually, Tony said, "You handled that gun really well."

Catching what she thought was a hint, she pulled the .357 out of her waistband and held it out to him. He waved it off. "Keep it for a while; you may need it again."

That brought up a topic that had been bothering her. "Why don't the men after us use guns?"

155

"Tradition. Arrogance. As a shifter, you feel immortal."

"But, you aren't. Injuries carry over to the other form. Dead as animal is dead as man, right?"

He nodded, locking his gaze with hers. "Just don't get dead. Either way."

She didn't like the sound of that, but she still re-tucked the pistol and finished her burger, eyeing the bag again. She reached for it to snag another charred beef delight. Spasms of pain shot from her side, snatching her breath away. She slowly retreated from her intended quarry.

Tony, who no doubt had heard the catch in her breath, reached over and plunked the burger bag into her lap. "Bones heal slower than soft tissue for our kind. We need both you and Brian to return to healing, but first we have an errand. Then we need to move farther away." He looked off into the distance. "Shifters usually remove their dead. It causes too many questions in the autopsy room. Hopefully the police won't find out about the skirmish at my cabin. I hope I can go back there someday."

"Me, too." She loved that place. She shoved the food bag out of her lap; the pain had removed the last bit of her hunger. She needed more of Brian's magic drink, but they'd left the last of it at the cabin. "I don't suppose you have any aspirin in your pocket, do you?"

He shook his head and stood. Picking up the bag, he dropped it on Brian's wolf flank. "Rise and shine, sleepyhead. Here's breakfast."

Brian lifted his long, lupus head and shoved it into the bag. He snuffled and rooted a moment and then emerged with a sandwich, chewed it and swallowed it, paper and all. As he ate, he slowly changed back into man. He sat and reached for the clothes Tony brought for him and worked his legs into the jeans. Then he

156

reached into the bag for a second burger which he unwrapped this time. Cramming half of it into his mouth in one bite, he stood and finished pulling on his jeans. He grinned at Olivia, his cheeks gopher full. She gave him the best smile she could muster. Adrenaline is a wonderful thing. It can make a person feel invincible, even when badly or mortally injured. When it wore off, however, the reality of injuries sucked.

Brian was helping her to her feet in an instant, concern brimming in his eyes, despite the caked blood from his new injuries, including a really nasty one on his neck. He helped her back to the highway and into their acquired vehicle, a pearl white 1968 Chevy pickup that Tony had swiped earlier. The owner had strangely dropped the keys when faced with a snarling and spitting 600 pound albino Bengal tiger. The inside had been done fully in cherry red leather. She felt bad stealing it, but not bad enough that she wanted to begin their cross-country journey on foot again.

They turned around and barreled down the highway, the old Chevy rocking and heaving at its top speed of 110, Tony at the wheel, heading toward the camp again. They didn't discuss their final destination, but they all knew. Miss Atwood would be surprised to get a visit from Olivia. Especially with the company she now kept. It seemed odd to her that this world she'd entered was more real to her now than the one she'd lived in just a week ago. Shapeshifters had become part of the norm for her, and no matter what happened with her griffinness, or not, she'd never be the same again.

Chapter 32

Brian held Olivia close to him as the old Chevy sped down the highway. The owner had taken good care of the antique truck. Its engine purred evenly and matched the whine of the tires below them. The heater worked well. Too well. Despite several adjustments to the controls, the heat continued to pour through the floor vents. Both windows were rolled half-way down by the time they came to the long road leading to Tony's cabin.

Tony switched off the headlights and slowed to first gear.

Brian craned his neck and scanned the area. Nothing moved under the towering Ponderosas. No vehicle lights shone through the woods, nor did any appear behind them as they cruised past. It appeared they'd eluded their pursuers by doubling back.

"I don't see anything. You're good to go." He spoke softly, and then laughed at his low voice, as if their enemies could hear him inside the truck.

The Chevy picked up speed again, but Tony waited to turn on the headlights until the road curved around an abutment in the mountain.

In the silence, Brian's thoughts returned to their conversation just before the bears and crew arrived. Olivia was a griffin. Well, maybe. No, scratch that. Probably. Miss Atwood was known as being a tough old gal that was as crafty as they came. If there was a rumor about a griffin, it could have only come from one source. And it was probably true.

His heart surged within him. Olivia was a shapeshifter! She was a natural part of his world. If she rejected him, it wouldn't be because he was a wolf. Unless she just plain didn't want him. But, one look in her eyes and he knew that was untrue. It was as if the weight of a thousand boulders lifted. Relief flooded through him. He hadn't realized how heavy that burden had been. How much he'd held back because he'd, deep inside, expected her to come to hate the creature within him. It was possible that the griffin may not tolerate his wolf well, but that could be taught.

Another thought hit him. There were no others of her kind. She was alone. Even more than he. He squeezed her close to him, looking down when her face turned up to his. He needed to find a way to tell her she'd never be alone. That, no matter what happened between them, she would always have him in her corner.

Before he could speak, she said, "You said the griffins were extinct. How?"

His gaze involuntarily shifted to Tony. His friend's face turned hard. He kept his focus on the road.

Brian answered. "There was a war."

"A war? Between who? The griffins?"

He hesitated. Trees flipped past in the headlights of the truck, counting the seconds before he spoke. Finally, he said, "Between the griffins and just about everyone."

159

Olivia was equally silent for a moment. Then she quietly said, "Tell me."

"It was in the day of the dragons—"

"Wait! There's dragons?" She jerked upright, her gaze like a child's, brightly searching his.

"Extinct," came Tony's voice.

She twisted to look at him. "It was thought griffins were extinct, yet, here I am. Assuming I am one. Couldn't dragons still be alive too?"

He shook his head, not taking his eyes off the road. "Not a chance. Dragons have been gone since the war, just over a thousand years ago. Compared to that, the extinction of the griffins is a recent occurrence."

"But still."

"That long ago, one would have popped up. Like you did." He glanced at her. Then, the corners of his mouth twitched. "Assuming you're a griffin."

She scowled at him and turned back to Brian, effectively dismissing Tony from the conversation. Behind her, Tony's face lit into a full grin.

Brian would have to speak to him again. The dynamics between those two would have to change if he hoped to live peacefully. That would have to wait until later.

"The Great Griffin Wars," he began. "It all started with two men and one woman." He glared at Tony over Olivia's head.

Tony glanced at him, eyebrows raised. "Different situation."

Slowly he nodded. Again, it would have to wait until later. He continued the story. "Thousands of years ago, dragons and griffins ruled as supreme shifters jointly. Dragons were known as strong and wise. Griffins as loyal and fierce. They were evenly matched and neither bothered the other. Dragons demanded sacrifice from humans. Griffins just took what they

160

wanted. It had always been that way, would be today except for a woman."

"It's a love story, isn't it? I can tell. I love romances."

Of course she did. Brian loved that about her. Even though she was terrified of what she might become, she still grasped at fairy tales. He smiled at her. "It is the worst kind of love story. A human woman, who, strangely, no one remembers her name, was pledged as a sacrifice to one of the dragons—"

"They ate people?" She caught her breath.

"No. They stole the women away for their pleasure."

She blushed. "Well, that's better, I guess."

"This woman was one of the most beautiful women anywhere. The dragon was named Bartheleme. And he wanted her more than anything. When time came for the sacrifice, the woman was tied to the sea cliffs near her village. As Bartheleme approached to claim what was rightfully his, a griffin by the name of Efar snatched her from the rocks and flew away. The dragon, being heavier, was slower and never caught Efar."

"This sounds like a fairy tale."

Tony said, "Where do you think they come from? Folk tales are based on truth."

Olivia flicked her gaze toward him, but returned her attention to Brian immediately. "What happened next?"

He grinned, enjoying her attention. He'd tell her stories all day long, every day, if it kept her staring at him like that. "War happened. Between dragons and griffins. Eventually, other shifters joined in. Most took the side of the dragons. Griffins were protective and loyal, but they scared everyone too much with their fierceness. Once they got started, they couldn't be stopped. One day, there weren't any more dragons. But the shifters that had fought alongside them continued on until there were no griffins either."

"Or so they thought."

He hugged her gently. "Yeah."

"Could this by why Hall wants me dead?"

"Hall doesn't strike me as the type of person who would reignite a war because of an ancient vendetta. I think there's something personal in it."

She sputtered her lips together. "Great. Just great."

Chapter 33

It had now been six days since the first attack in Olivia's apartment. Yet, it seemed a lifetime to her. Everything had changed. Yet, nothing had. The world was still the same, she just saw it with opened eyes.

As she, Brian, and Tony pulled into the driveway of the orphanage, dawn lit blandly across gray clouds. The place hadn't altered a bit in the few years she'd been gone. Maybe the old chimneys on the main house missed a few more bricks and the ridge of the barn swayed a bit more, but it essentially looked the same as the day she'd left. A few children dressed in thick, well-worn coats were already up and at their chores: milking the two cows she remembered as Jess and Bess, feeding the thirty or so hens and collecting eggs. Several roosters paced the sides of their pen closest to the hens, pausing to crow. Judging from their size, they'd be dinner one day soon. Memories of her doing those very same chores flooded her, and she pulled in a deep breath until a shot of pain from her ribs grabbed and stilled her for a moment.

Melita, an orphan herself and Miss Atwood's assistant, came out to meet them. Forever the flirt, she beamed directly onto Tony's presence. She gently shook her head, settling her blonde curls to frame her face. By the time Brian and Olivia came around the front of the truck, the other young woman looked like she was ready to bear Tony's baby. If only she knew his other form…but then, maybe she did.

"Melita, we need to speak to Miss Atwood," Olivia said.

"Olivia! I'm so happy to see you." The blonde woman squealed. That alone made Olivia take a step away from her. They'd never been friends. When Melita moved in for a hug, Olivia extended her hand quickly for shaking. She was having trouble standing and breathing, she would collapse under the pressure of a hug. Anyway, the whole friend thing had to be a show for Tony.

She asked, "Where's Miss Atwood?"

Melita put on a sad face, one Olivia remembered from her acting classes. "Oh, honey. I'm afraid she's passed on. Someone broke into her office and killed her. It was just terrible."

She stepped closer to Tony, who obliged by putting his arm around her. He looked as if he was eating it up. He murmured, "What did they take?"

She shook her head, still with the sad face. "Nothing at all. What was there to take?" When she glanced at Olivia, there was a glint of something hard and dangerous in her eyes. And a spark of triumph.

Fury blazed in Olivia. Injuries be damned. She strode over and jerked Melita away from Tony, biting back the nausea that rode the lance of pain she felt from her wounded ribs. "Enough with the acting, little missy. You're going to tell us what you know." As Olivia finished the statement, Melita's body slimmed and elongated. Olivia found herself with a writhing mass of snake coils in her hands. The other woman's golden hair had changed into a wide cobra hood with eye markings inside. The rest of her body followed suit, changing into golden-striped sleekness. Her clothes slid down the length of her to the ground. Her face, however, remained human. Olivia dropped her and jumped back, wiping her hands on her jeans. She'd never been one for any kind of snake. In her way of thinking, they were sneaky things, always trying to surprise her.

Brian and Tony circled Melita. Brian stepped on her tail. She reared up at him, her golden hood flaring wider behind her head, but Tony anchored his fingers around her throat. Never a fool, she closed her hood and lowered to the ground. Tony moved away from her and focused his bright blues on Olivia. She realized it was her show now. She was kinda liking this not-being-under-his-ego thing.

She was now sure Melita had been the one to give up the goods on her griffinness. She almost asked how Melita found out about her, but she lost nerve. Instead, she asked, "What did you find out?" She wrapped her arms around her ribs, choking back tears from the pain; the effort of grabbing the snake had a cost.

"I hated you ever since we were children. You always got the best of everything. Everybody had to be nice to you, or we'd be harshly punished. I discovered that Miss Atwood talked in her sleep. And since she'd always favored you, it stood to reason that she was speaking about you in her dreams." Melita stopped, a poisonous glare on her face. Clearly, she thought she had finished speaking, especially to Olivia.

Tony cleared his throat. His warning caused her to jump. It was apparent to everyone that his amorous actions with her earlier had been a calculated effort to extract information.

Olivia approved. She said to Melita, "So you told someone. What exactly did you say?"

"I told them what Miss Atwood had said in her sleep. That's it. I swear. Then they broke into the office and killed her." Melita started to cry. The vision was surreal: a golden cobra with human head shedding tears. It unnerved Olivia. She also didn't believe the little actress. She'd seen it too many times. She didn't think the boys believed it either.

She said, "I rather think that's all a lie. You're the one who broke into the office looking for my folder. Miss Atwood stumbled upon you, so you killed her. Then someone came looking, and you told them what you'd learned."

An ugly eruption of anger flashed across Melita's pretty face at the words. "There was no folder about you. Whatever that old witch knew about you, she took to the grave." In a snap, she shifted the rest of her to snake and slithered across the yard to an open shed. None of the three tried to stop her. Olivia, for one, didn't want to face a deadly cobra, though she felt sure they could defeat her. Melita had answered every question they'd had, but they still didn't have the answer they wanted: was Olivia a griffin?

Brian said, "I need to get supplies." She suppose he meant for his brew. She hoped he did. Tony helped her back into the cab of the still warm truck.

She asked him, "What now?"

His face was grim. "We find a place to lie low and get you both healed."

"And then?"

He shrugged. "Wait and see what's in the wind."

They were silent until Brian returned a good twenty minutes later. He climbed into the truck beside her. His face, hands, and shirt collar were wet, and she saw that he'd cleaned off the dried blood. A patch covered the

wound on his neck. Probably better that way, so he
didn't scare people. He also had a thermos that he
uncapped and handed to her. She didn't even hesitate. In
truth, the flavor of his holistic medicine was beginning
to grow on her. Or maybe it was a different brew. He
had to use what he could find, right?

"What's in this?"

"You really want to know?"

"I do." She didn't, but then again, it was something
to talk about.

"Eucalyptus, burdock, nettle, ginger, raspberry leaf
and a touch of hops." He smiled. "She didn't have any
catnip."

"Catnip?"

"For the animals within." He pounded his chest
with a closed fist. Him, Tarzan. Her, Jane? Or Her, Evil
Bird With Mega Killing Abilities?

Brian took the thermos, drank, and recapped it. He
reached into his pocket and produced wraps and
bandages of all types and sizes. Picking a particularly
wide roll, he began tightly wrapping her ribs right over
her most recent bandage and her clothes. The pain was
blinding and almost beyond bearable. By the time he
finished, the tears she'd worked so hard to choke back
flowed down her cheeks. He pulled her close and held
her against him as the whine of the tires on the pavement
took them into the mountains.

Chapter 34

Brian sat in the moving truck, staring out at the wooded road. The midday sun shone through pine interspersed with occasional bare-branched aspens and cottonwood. It glinted off the snow that layered the ground like a field of picked cotton. The occasional deer on the side of the road startled at the truck's approach and dashed off into the undergrowth of the forest. The wolf in him sat up to take notice, but he was just too tired to do more than watch the deer run. It seemed as if he, Olivia, and Tony had been in the truck forever.

The day had started decently enough, albeit with a pale gray overcast sky. Now, however, the clouds had taken on a deep charcoal color to them. A storm wasn't far away.

Olivia had kept the pickup's old radio on one station or another. The music faded in and out with every turn of the winding mountain roads. Leaning against him in the crook of his arm, she softly hummed the songs and alternated between looking out the front windshield or his window. Tony had settled into an easy driving rhythm befitting a man who was used to traveling by auto for great distances.

They were in the mountains, currently on Route 72, driving roughly parallel to the front of the range.

The radio station faded out and disappeared altogether. Olivia turned to Brian and asked, "Where are we going?"

He glanced down at her, turned on by the gentle curves of her lips. Memories flooded him of the hunger she'd shared when pressed against him. He lifted his other hand and ran his thumb across her soft mouth. "North."

She blushed and her greenish-brown eyes grew smoky and large. After a second, she asked, "That's it? Just north? Why?"

"There are fewer people. The ground is tough and dry. It's less conducive to growing lawns and building homes."

She settled against him again, facing the front. Turning her attention to Tony, she said, "You've been driving awhile. Why don't you let Brian take over?"

Tony glanced at her, his eyebrows raised. "Have you seen him behind the wheel? Not a chance I'm letting him in the driver's seat."

"Then let me."

Brian grinned. That would never happen. His friend liked to think he was in control. The master of his own destiny. Nobody drove for him. True to his prediction, Tony didn't answer, nor did he slow the truck. After almost a minute of waiting, Olivia returned to staring out the windows, a storm cloud of her own on her face.

Leaning close to her, Brian whispered, "I actually engineered it this way. See, he has to do some of the work. This is the most he can manage, poor fellow. He's tough in a fight, but driving is about all the higher thinking he can handle."

"I heard that." Tony glared at Brian in mock indignation.

Olivia laughed. Immediately, she wrapped her arms around her injured ribs. "Oh! Ow! Stop. Laughing makes me hurt." Still, she didn't stop giggling.

Brian grinned and watched the trees flip by. After Olivia's laughter subsided, he quietly said, "It's back to the basics."

Olivia frowned. "What's that mean?"

"It means we have to start over: food, water, and clothes."

Tony nodded on the other side of the pickup. "Lodging. Someplace secluded." He pointedly looked at Olivia.

As if she didn't hear him, she said, "We also need money and a map. Something that will show where there might be cabins of some kind. We left everything behind in the cabin, even our phones. We can't just steal the provisions like we did the truck. Nor can we break into a cabin."

Brian wasn't quite sure what Olivia was thinking. She hadn't said a word about taking the truck. If she had a problem with them helping themselves to what they found, then they all had a problem. "We can get some cash wired to us."

As if reading his mind, she said, "The owner will eventually get his truck back, right? We're just borrowing it for a while."

"We are. Don't worry." He'd have to make sure they left it somewhere it could be found. He almost laughed at himself. Olivia was certainly good for him. He was becoming an honest thief.

Tony lifted his hand and checked the gas gauge. His friend said, "Speaking of the truck, we're low on gas."

"Time for some new wheels anyway. This one stands out too much," Brian said. "We passed a turnoff to Estes Park about a few minutes back. Let's double back to that."

"Yep." Tony slowed the truck and stopped. He jockeyed it back and forth across the road until they were facing the way they'd come. Then they were off again.

Chapter 35

They didn't make it to Estes Park. The gas gauge on the old truck was faulty. Twelve minutes from the time they turned around, and just on the far side of Allenspark, the truck lurched and sputtered. Within another minute, it quit running altogether. Tony dropped it in neutral and let it coast as far as it would go, but the road had tiny rolling hills. When it reached a speed slower than they could walk, he pulled to the side and parked.

Tony dismounted. Brian patted Olivia on the leg and hopped out of the truck. When she started to scooch to Brian's side to exit, he held up his hand. Motioning to the radio and center dash, he said, "You need to try to wipe any fingerprints off there." He tugged the sleeve of his shirt over his fist and rubbed his passenger's side door.

She glanced at Tony and found him polishing the steering wheel. Following his lead, she buffed the radio with her shirt tail.

Once finished, she slid out and stood at the side of the road a moment. Their options were to go back to Allenspark or to continue on. None of them said anything, but by mutual agreement, they all turned toward Estes Park. The storm clouds above continued to build into a platinum and charcoal threat of rain. The temperature rose and humidity bore down on them. Though it was January, sweat slicked their skin as they walked. The reflected heat from the asphalt had melted the snow, so they at least had that going for them. Olivia's biggest worry was that one of their beloved followers would now find them. One look at Brian's face, and she saw it worried him too. Tony, on the other hand, kept his expression bland, as if it was an everyday occurrence to be attacked and then run out of gas during the escape.

She liked that Brian walked close enough to her that they often nudged each other. It warmed her and made her smile.

Them. She'd used that word a lot lately. What would she do if she wasn't a shapeshifter? She tried to picture her life as usual: picking out makeup, fighting off patrons at the bar, home by ten or eleven at night if she had no date with a non-sleaze. Did she want that now? Normal? What about Brian? She tried, but she really couldn't picture her future without him. That, in itself, frightened her. Would a normal life have room for a werewolf?

She decided she definitely didn't want normal anymore. Too many things had changed. She'd changed. She didn't know where she fit in the grand scheme of this dual world of shifters yet, but she wanted to stay here. And yes, she was falling in love. She could no longer pretend her attraction to Brian was a lust-borne infatuation or curiosity for the wolf. She was in love with him, no matter where they ended, no matter what

173

form he, or she, took. The thought thrilled and terrified her. Did he feel the same?

They trudged along the right shoulder of the thin road. Traffic was light, so there was little chance of hitchhiking. That meant they would have to walk until they found a suitable replacement in the vehicle department. She had napped in the truck, but the boys had been awake since well before the fight at the cabin. She worried about them. Brian had deep circles etched beneath his dark brown eyes. His mouth had settled into a grim line. She tried to remember the last time either one of them had a full night's sleep. Their two nights at the cabin hadn't exactly been restful. They'd taken full advantage of Tony's absence.

As for Tony, he didn't look much better, and Olivia wondered if he'd had his own midnight liaison during his sojourn.

Either side of the road rose to sharp mountain tops, thick with various types of trees. The smell of pine and wood smoke permeated the frosty air. Someone had a campfire nearby. Twin Sisters Peak as well as the famous Longs Peak were somewhere close, but she couldn't see them yet. They were hidden behind the peaks that surrounded them. Tributary roads tied in with theirs, and she supposed they were populated with private cabins.

As they rounded a turn in the road, a sign about a quarter mile away came into view: Gaines Lodge. That's when the heavens decided to open. Ice-cold rain pelted down on them, stinging their skin. They picked up their pace, almost to a jog, though they all felt near collapse from exhaustion. As they neared, she saw that the sign at the front door boasted a gift shop as well as a café. Her stomach growled at the possibilities. Oh, to have some money! The parking lot was packed, with every slot filled. In the last row of spaces, the vehicles nosed up to a fence that bordered the far end of the lot.

Brian said, "I see a 2010 Equinox. Silver. At the fence."

"Perfect. I'll call Bellerophon," Tony said.

As they entered the lot, they separated for their respective jobs. Olivia was to be Brian's lookout while he broke into the Equinox.

"Who's Bellerophon?" she asked, once they reached the fence. It was the second time she'd heard that name. The SUV was near the back of the lot, probably an employee's. She stood hunched in the rain and shading her eyes so she could watch the café windows and front door, her back to him.

"Our lawyer." Then, as if to forestall her next question, he added, "She's a shifter too."

"How's she going to help us?" A fellow at the table in the second window of the café glanced outside at her. She tensed, ready to sound the alarm. But his gaze didn't settle; she was just someone waiting in the rain, probably for a person inside. Brian stayed hidden.

"She'll get us money, ID, phones, and a car that isn't stolen."

His words sparked something deep inside to clutch at her heart. They were not only in trouble with Hall and the pursuing shifters, but they were now fugitives of the law. That thought froze her. She had to clear her throat before she could speak. "How often does this happen? You seem pretty comfortable stealing cars." Tony exited the lodge and slogged through the rain toward them, head bent.

The sounds behind her stopped dead. Brian turned her toward him and met her gaze. "Do you trust me?"

"You know I do."

"There's a difference between trusting someone because you have no other choice and trusting them because you desire it."

"I do trust you."

He expelled his breath. "Good. I promise I'll answer all your questions. But we don't have a lot of time right now. We'll talk about this later. I know it's important to you, so I promise I won't forget."

She hesitated, but then nodded. Still, she could feel a small frown crest her face as she turned back to the door. What had she gotten herself into?

The Equinox started as soon as Tony reached them. They jumped into the SUV and took off.

Chapter 36

The rain stopped as suddenly as it had begun. The heat in the truck was on high as Brian drove into Estes Park. It didn't take long, but he'd kept checking his rearview mirror. No one had followed them from Gaines Lodge. Nor did it appear that Hall and his henchmen had found them. That was a fair piece of good luck. And encouraging.

"I'll let you two off at the meet and join you after I ditch the Equinox."

Tony nodded, but Olivia chose otherwise. "I'm going with you."

Brian had to wonder if her choice was because she wanted to be with him or wanted not to be stuck with Tony. "Go with him. I won't be long."

"I can help you clean off the fingerprints."

He glanced at her and got snagged in her mesmerizing brown-green gaze. His heart frolicked in his chest like it did every time she looked at him. He couldn't argue with her. Grinning, he said, "Good enough."

He let Tony off at the restaurant where they were to meet Bellerophon: Ginger Pie. Then he drove three blocks deeper into the city and turned right twice. While he drove, Olivia busied herself wiping the radio. By the time he parked behind a tiny strip mall, she'd moved on to the passenger's side door. Together they finished cleaning fingerprints from the vehicle. They walked quickly to the restaurant, Olivia's hand in his.

Arriving at Ginger Pie, he held the door open for her. Tony was seated at a table dead center on the left wall of the restaurant. Most of the other patrons sat spaced throughout the room, but mostly on the other side near an ancient jukebox. No one sat close to their table. A small stack of dish towels sat on the corner of the table near Tony. He gave one each to Brian and Olivia and said, "I ordered the special for us." He pointed at the chalkboard near the kitchen. TODAY'S SPECIAL: COLOSSUS ANGUS BURGERS WITH BUFFALO SAUCE.

As he dried his hair, Brian turned to Olivia. He leaned into her and spoke just above a whisper. They didn't need anyone overhearing them. Not that he thought anyone could anyway. "While we wait for our food, I'll answer the question you asked earlier." He glanced at Tony, making sure he'd keep an eye on the door. He needn't have worried; his friend's gaze was constantly roving the room.

Turning his attention to Olivia, he said, "Yes, we steal vehicles, and other things, occasionally. It's one of the drawbacks to what Tony and I do. When a shifter gets in trouble with the law, it's not like a normal human. Often, the shifter, when trapped in prison, will change and kill. That exposes us all. It can't be allowed. Understand?"

"So far."

"Our job, mine and Tony's, is to step between the law and the shifter long enough to get other options in place. By the time the shifter turns himself in, Bellerophon is able to barter for a better situation. Most shifters in the legal system are experiencing their animals for the first time. They just don't know how to deal."

"Have you ever gotten in trouble for helping someone?"

He shrugged. "Not so much."

She nodded and tucked a loose strand of her beautiful honey blonde hair behind her ear, brows knit together. Brian could imagine the gears grinding in her brain. He almost smiled, but thought better of it. She probably wouldn't appreciate his levity at that precise moment.

After a brief pause, Olivia asked, "If you know you have these situations, why steal cars? Why not just have a fleet of them ready?"

He grinned. He'd used a similar argument with Tony when he'd first joined the cause. "We don't want anyone to know we're helping these people. It's easier to catch us if we keep cars. Then it's all over. No more shifters will be helped."

"Are there any shifter criminals? I mean, habitual? Or really bad ones? Other than Hall, I mean."

"Sometimes," he answered softly, thinking of his past. He'd been damn lucky to have been found by people who believed in him, to have their help. "But the same holds true. If a shifter gets found out, it'll expose us all. We can't have that. And despite all evidence, I don't think Hall is a criminal in the classic sense."

He thought that would end the conversation, but she persisted. "No. Hall just wants to kill me. So, if he does kill me, for example, what do you do? According to what you tell me, he can't go to jail."

179

"Oh, he'll go to jail all right. There are jails run by our kind, those who understand the animal side. We try to place our people there. But he'll never find you."

It seemed to satisfy her, and he was grateful. He really didn't want to go much further into this discussion. He wasn't quite ready for her to learn about his past. She should know it, but he would tell her in his own time.

The end of the conversation coincided with the arrival of the burgers. They were, indeed, colossal. And very juicy. He leaned over his plate to catch the drips as he bit. Off the top of his head, Brian couldn't recall a better tasting slab of ground beef. Angus, for sure. The fries were beer battered, which he normally didn't like, but even they tasted good. Through a mouthful, he asked, "What's that saying? Hunger is the best spice?"

Tony and Olivia both nodded, their mouths crammed just as full. It was then, of course, that someone walked in. Tony swallowed an unchewed mouthful of burger and stood, hurriedly wiping his lips with a wadded napkin. There was only one woman who made Tony toe the line. Brian could tell by the fire in his friend's eyes that it was probably the lawyer. He also stood and turned around.

To say that C. Angelique Bellerophon was beautiful was an understatement. Her pale blonde hair cascaded in waves around a perfectly oval face. When she pulled off her shades, crisp blue eyes pierced through each and every occupant of the room. Her lips were full and formed a perfect cupid's bow. She was slim, but curved nicely in her cream-colored suit. She wasn't tall, only five-seven, but her always present three-inch heels brought her close in height to most men. And judging by the faces of those males in the room, she'd be spending the night with every one of them while they dreamed.

180

She looked good, no doubt about it. He'd been interested in her, in the beginning, but he'd gotten over that. She was just too … something … for him. Controlled, maybe was the word. Or hidden. Yeah, that was it: hidden. He'd trade a thousand of her for one Olivia.

Tony met Bellerophon halfway across the floor and kissed her square on the lips, branding her as his. "Lana."

"I've told you, Tony. Don't call me that." Annoyance filled her voice, and she frowned at him. Then her gaze lit on Brian and slid past him to Olivia, who was still seated at the table, watching with narrowed eyes. Was that jealousy? He could almost see the griffin rising within her. If it was true, and she actually became a griffin, she would be a moving force in the world. It pleased him that she considered him to be her property. Again, he had to fight to not smile. He didn't quite make it though.

"Brian." Bellerophon reached her hand to him. "You look happier than I've ever seen you."

"Angelique." They shook hands. Brian turned toward Olivia, laying his hand on her shoulder, showing his connection to her. She looked very relieved that he'd only shaken hands with the lady lawyer. "This is Olivia."

"Ms. Bonaparte." Bellerophon glanced between the two of them as she shook hands with Olivia. A light of understanding crossed her face. "Now I see why Brian is grinning like a schoolboy."

Tony pulled out the empty chair for her. She sat and said, "I could have sent one of my boys, but I couldn't pass up this opportunity to meet you."

"You made good time," Brian said as he settled back in his chair.

"Well, the community is abuzz with news of our new friend. I knew it would be a matter of time before you phoned me, so I had my boys do some shopping in preparation. When you called, I came as fast as I could."

"Councilor, did you break the law?" Tony asked, his eyes full of mirth.

"Yes, Your Honor. I'm afraid I exceeded the speed limit." This she said with a deadpan face. Then she grinned and reached into her clutch bag. "Luckily, there were no cops."

Pulling out three cell phones, she slid one in front of each of them. The next trip into her bag, she returned with three thick stacks of cash, which she also dropped one in front of each of them. One final trip brought out a set of keys. She handed them to Tony.

Olivia picked up her bundle of cash and flipped the end of it. "I'm not sure how long it will take to pay you back."

Bellerophon smiled and gently said, "Honey, do you honestly believe that any one of us, who can live to 2000 years, isn't stinking rich? Think about it. It would be near impossible. And, if you are who we think, then you have the wealth of a whole race dumped into your account."

Olivia blushed. "Brian said you're a shifter. May I ask, what?"

"I'm a Firehorse."

"Firehorse. What is that?"

"Exactly what it sounds. I'm a horse." Bellerophon tugged her hair. "But, this all goes to flames if I want."

"I bet it's beautiful."

"So I've been told." She glanced pointedly at Tony. Rising from the table, she said, "You need to get going, and so do I. Call me if you need me or when you know something. Whichever comes first."

182

She gave a soft laugh, kissed Tony on the cheek and strode out the door, every male eye in the place following her.

Brian leaned into Olivia. "She's a good lawyer, but she's not the kind I would consider a friend." Tony raised his eyebrows at that, but Olivia rewarded him with a deep sigh and bright smile.

Chapter 37

The vehicle Bellerophon brought them was a faded blue Chevy pickup. Nothing fancy. Olivia guessed it was probably purchased privately instead of from a dealership. An effort to stay hidden. Tony drove them farther north, but moved deeper into the mountains. It had now been seven days since the initial attack at her apartment. Yet, it seemed like years had passed.

Through a series of twists and turns over paved and rock roads, they discovered an abandoned cabin hidden in the foothills above the city of Walden and a few miles from the Arapahoe Wildlife Refuge. The hut had no view, other than trees, trees, and more trees. Though the situation seemed to fit the mission of the AWR, she didn't think the officials who had built the nearby park had their kind of wildlife in mind while planning the location.

The cozy cabin had only the main room and a bathroom. She and Brian got the solitary bed in the corner, while Tony took the couch after giving them a stern warning to please refrain from bedroom Olympics.

She thought he might have been jealous because he didn't have a partner. He didn't have to worry, though; with the way she felt, she just wanted to cocoon under the heavy quilts until she died. And that's pretty much all she did for the next twenty-four hours. She had no idea what Brian and Tony were doing during that time, but mice would have made more noise than them. Except for the dosing of Brian's brew, she rarely woke.

Late on the following day, when she stayed awake for more than an hour or two, she sat on the bed and faced Tony. He was stretched across the length of the couch, frowning and reading a brown and torn novel about combat pilots in the Congo. She asked, "What's the plan?"

He looked her up and down. "We're not ready." Then he returned to his book. He'd started growing a slick black beard and mustache. She wondered if it was just from lack of razor or for camouflage. Dark half-circles hung below his eyes and his hair, though combed, didn't have his usual primping. Was that from worry, tension, or the couch?

She asked again, "What's our plan?" She knew he had one, and she had a right to know it.

Through the window, Olivia caught a glimpse of Brian outside, picking through a stack of firewood. He still had telltale signs of exhaustion, cuts, bruises, and other injuries on him. He'd healed well for the most part, though, and seemed to be his usual laid-back self. He'd also started a beard and mustache, but curly brown. He wore the coat Tony had given her in the clearing. Behind him, sat the ancient blue Chevy truck. She still missed the pearl white 1968 Chevy. It saddened her, though she knew the necessity of getting rid of such a recognizable vehicle.

With an exaggerated sigh, Tony marked his place and set down the novel. "No plan, yet. We're waiting on you."

At her perplexed look, he added, "To finish healing. And changing."

If anything, he confused her more. And scared her. What did he mean? "Finish changing?"

"Do you really think a normal human could deal as well with everything you've been through, as badly injured as you've been? Have you noticed how much you sleep? How much you eat? Do you think that's normal?" His brilliant blue eyes held her gaze.

She felt breathless, but not from excitement. Was this real? Could she be changing? "M-maybe," she stammered. "Maybe the doctors misdiagnosed. I couldn't have been injured as badly as we thought. And I'm just tired from everything we've been through." She had to admit, it sounded hollow and very implausible. But the alternative scared her. Terrified her, actually. It kept her rooted, completely immobile. She was actually becoming this evil thing. This griffin.

Brian walked in, whistling, and saw what must have been panic on her face. He shut the door and carefully placed the wood in its home next to the fire. Glancing from Tony to her, he came around the couch and took her hands. "Together," he said, as if he knew exactly what the conversation had been.

Olivia almost said, "What together? You're not going through this. You're not becoming evil incarnate." But then, she remembered his past and what Tony had told her and she nodded. Together. At least until she showed her true evilness, and then there would be no more togetherness. Brian wouldn't want her. He would leave, and she would be alone.

She took a deep breath and asked the two of them, "What other symptoms can I expect?"

186

Brian said, "It's different for every shifter, but one thing is an increase in metabolism, which means you'll be hungry all the time and you'll heal fast. An eagle can see over a mile away, so you should too. You'll be able to hear better also. The lion has a keen sense of smell, but he's your back half, so I don't know." He shrugged.

Tony added, "If I remember my griffin mythology right, you'll be stronger in human form."

Great. No help there. That stuff she'd already figured out on her own. She could add one more to the list. She was certainly becoming testier.

Two nights later, she woke in a heavy sweat, her side of the bed soaked. Brian rolled over and looked at her. In a flash, he lunged out of bed, pulling her to her feet and to the door. "Outside with you."

"Outside? Are you kidding? It's freezing out there!"

"Trust me on this."

She tried the trust thing, she really did. It lasted for about half a second. Then she pulled back. Brian, never easy to sway, almost lost his balance. He hollered over his shoulder, "Tony! A little help here, please."

In an instant, Tony was beside him, jerking open the window. It annoyed her that they'd apparently known about this overheating thing and hadn't included it in the increased metabolism conversation. He and Brian grabbed her by her shoulders and bodily shoved her toward the window. She rapidly progressed from annoyed to pissed, and she started swinging her fists. It didn't do any good. Even though her punches connected with flesh a couple times, the boys kept up the steady drive forward. She no longer could think clearly. Instinct took over and she locked her stance, leaned into her two bodyguards, and pushed. The forward movement stopped.

Tony abruptly let go, stepped back, and then swung his fist into her temple.

187

Chapter 38

To Brian's horror, Olivia dropped to the floor of the cabin. Without a single second's hesitation, he whirled and threw a punch that landed squarely on Tony's jaw. His friend's head whipped to the side and he staggered several steps back before falling on the coffee table. The small table wasn't built to take that kind of punishment and it collapsed; one leg splintered in half while another broke off the table completely and skittered across the floor to stop near the front door. He pulled himself to his feet. Even with only the moonlight shining into the room, the fury on his face was clear.

Brian was too angry to speak, so he just stood there, waiting, his fists balled and ready. Suddenly the tiny cabin seemed way too small for the two of them. For a moment, they only glared at each other. He knew Tony didn't want a fight any more than he did, but fight he would, if need be. Tony's cell phone rang, but he made no move to answer it. After the third ring, the caller either hung up or left a message.

Tony broke the silence. He worked his jaw back and forth. "What the hell?"

"You don't hit her. Not for anything. I warned you to back off."

"You saw her. She's strong. And the griffin is taking control."

Brian ignored his excuse. His fists were still ready. "Do you understand me?"

Tony advanced to him, his lips curled harshly. His voice had a steely quality that Brian seldom heard. He stopped out of arm's reach. "You really gonna do this? Do you really want to tangle with the big cat?"

"Are you so arrogant that you think your tiger can beat the werewolf?" Brian stood his ground. He spoke softly. He had no doubt he'd win. The half-wolf form had the claws and stamina of the tiger. It had power in its jaws and overall strength too. Something the tiger didn't have. The only thing the cat had over him was speed. He wouldn't let his friend continue to create trouble with Olivia. He had to make a stand here and now.

Tony let out an abrupt burst of laughter. "Well, it would be an interesting fight, no doubt. I think we're evenly matched, but I think we'd both die from our injuries."

His words took the wind out of Brian's sails … almost. "You need to respect my choice to be with her. Stop mocking her, stop antagonizing her, and stop counseling me about her. This is the last time I'm warning you. I mean it."

Tony took a step forward and put his hand out to shake. "You're right. I'll quit. You have my word."

Brian relaxed and uncurled his fists. He shook his friend's hand. "You should be worried. Do you think she won't remember you hitting her when she becomes a griffin? You of all people should know what they were like. You pursued them for a long time."

"I remember. I'm just hoping she's different." Tony paused and looked at Olivia's slumbering form.

"Help me get her outside," Brian said. He leaned down and gently lifted Olivia in his arms. He carried her past the bed and around the couch to the door that Tony held open. Once outside, he hesitated, looking for the best place to lay her.

"There." Tony pointed to a spot only twenty feet away. A sudden knoll in the mountain had caught a foot of glistening snow. Dark bare branches from the nearby Aspens made a canopy above it. The air was fresh and crisp; steam rose from their noses and mouths as they breathed.

Brian carried Olivia to the moonlit drift and lay her down, arranging her in a comfortable sleeping position. She'd be out for a while, thanks to Tony. He'd stay out there with her, but first he needed coffee.

When he turned back to the cabin, Tony followed, pulling his cell out of his pocket and punched his call return button. The thin light from the phone lit his face. After a brief pause, he said, "You called me."

After listening a moment, he said, "No shit! Well, that makes sense, in a twisted way." He hung up, came in the cabin and shut the door. He wagged the phone and, by way of explanation, said, "Cujo. He said Hall is tearing up Boulder and the surrounding area looking for your girl. Apparently, he lost his whole family during the war."

Brian turned to the stove and coffee pot. "You know it's still gotta be more, right? Lots of people lost their family in the war." He filled a pot with water and turned on the stove burner. From behind him came the sound of wood scraping on the floor. Tony was picking up the damaged table.

"Well, this table is shit now." The door opened, wood clunked outside, and the door shut again. Tony said, "Little boy Hall took it really hard. He's half a mental case over it. Later, during the trauma after the war, he married and had a little girl. She and the mother were killed by one of the last few griffins. Cujo didn't think it was either of Olivia's parents, but that wouldn't matter to Hall."

No, it certainly wouldn't. Hall would never quit. How in the hell could they protect Olivia from someone like that? They couldn't hide her forever. Sooner or later, they'd have to fight. But they'd need a plan. A really, really good plan. He spooned coffee in a cup and asked over his shoulder, "You want one?"

"Nah, I'm gonna try to sleep. You care if I take the bed? That damn couch has a broken frame. It's got a nasty sag right in the middle."

"Be my guest. I'll be outside until she wakes. Should be the rest of the night."

"I really am sorry, man."

Brian turned around at this. Tony looked the most contrite he'd ever seen him. "Water under the bridge."

191

Chapter 39

Olivia woke on her back in the snow in broad daylight. Blinded by the bright sun above and its reflection on everything around her, she blinked several times and finally flung her arm over her eyes.

"How are you feeling?" Brian's voice gently asked.

She moved her arm and saw him leaning against the cabin wall, holding a steaming cup of what smelled like coffee. His tired brown eyes regarded her from beneath half-closed lids. Tony stood inside the cabin, staring out the closed window at her. She noted the .357 tucked into his belt. He wore a frown and worry filled his face, as well it should. It could have been her imagination, but he looked paler than usual. Posh bastard. When she caught up to him, there would be a reckoning. She sat up with the intent to confront him in mind, but found she missed the cold wrapped around her, so she lay back down, packing heaps of the white crystals tightly around her. This snow stuff was wonderful.

From on her back, she said to Brian, "I'm sorry I fought you."

He gave a rueful smile and rubbed his cheek where she'd somehow managed to hit him the night before. "The griffin overtook you. You'll eventually learn to control it."

The griffin. That evil thing, again. She shivered, but not from cold. Suddenly the snow didn't seem so nice. She scrambled to her feet and came over to Brian. "Was it hard for you?"

He nodded, but declined to elucidate. It didn't bother her that he didn't want to talk about it. She already had a good idea that he'd probably killed one or more people. He handed her his cup, and she saw he'd left it black for her, not augmented with cream the way he took it. The steam rolled up into her face, moistening and heating her skin. She had a sudden urge to lie down in the snow again. "Is this overheating thing normal?"

"There's no normal, but I'd imagine you'll probably go through these sweats a few times before you actually change. I didn't, but Tony said he did."

"Great." She took a sip of coffee. "Any thoughts on how soon the next one will be?"

"Just guessing by the severity, I'd say that it'll be soon. The fever from your injuries must have either camouflaged the first few times or brought this one on sooner and harder. You should start experiencing other changes now."

"Like hearing Tony stomp around the cabin, cooking..." she sniffed, "...Pancakes, steak, and eggs."

"So, you do have the lion's abilities." He nodded, his beautiful chocolate eyes twinkling. "Hungry?"

"You have no idea."

"I think maybe I do." He tucked her hand in his arm and escorted her up the steps to her first meal as a shapeshifter.

That afternoon, Brian and Olivia squared off at a game of chess in front of the window. Tony lounged in

193

his usual place on the couch, reading. The book in his hands was the same novel she'd seen him read before; he must have been a very slow reader. If it had been her, she'd have had books lined up, a new one started every day. The cabin felt warm, perhaps too much so, and she started fussing internally. She didn't want to create a scene, but really, did they need that much heat in there? As she reached to steal Brian's knight with her rook, she noticed the sheen of sweat covering her hand. Uh-oh.

Abruptly, she stood, knocking into the table with her thigh and upsetting the board. She walked out of the cabin into the winter, Brian hot on her heels with an extra coat. They must have walked in silence for miles while she tried to marshal her seething at the memory of Tony' hitting her. It had built in her mind to an unconscionable act. She said, "It feels like a volcano lives inside me and is ready to blow at any moment. It only needs an excuse." She now understood Tony's need for the security of the gun.

She seemed to be burning up. The heat wouldn't leave her body. She even stuffed snow down her shirt, but it didn't help. She turned to ask Brian if he had any ideas, when that volcano deep inside welled up as if spewing lava in slow motion. Her body grew and stretched. She felt dizzy and disoriented. A blinding lance of pain speared through her every cell and she cried out. Brian stepped back and, for the first time, he looked up at her.

Olivia stood stock still, unsure of exactly what was happening. Slowly, she turned her head and saw that she was indeed growing bigger. Much bigger. Her shoulders, or whatever they were called, reached Brian's full size when he was wolf, about eight feet. Neatly tucked wings were developing above her arms. Behind that, the golden-brown feathers sprouted, trimming down in size until becoming fur of the same color. Long

194

lean haunches led to a swishing lion's tail with a black tuft on the end. Turning her gaze downward, she noted her arms becoming bird legs with sharp talons. Lion's paws for her feet grew huge claws of their own. Her eyesight sharpened. She saw a girl enter a house, miles away. She heard her, too, calling to her mother.

She felt … supreme. She fervently hoped her new sensory abilities wouldn't disappear when she went back to human form. Neither Brian's nor Tony's did.

The griffin's emotions and instincts boiled in her blood. At last, she understood. Like what Brian had said about legends, the griffin had been misrepresented. They weren't evil. They just had a very low tolerance for being wronged, like Tony had done by hitting her. And they were badass enough they didn't have to put up with it either. Though, she imagined it would be easy to overdo retribution. Meting out their particular brand of justice could easily be seen as evil. That would be her battle against the griffin: teaching it patience. Tony, therefore, would be the proving point in that.

Olivia glanced at Brian. His jaw dropped and he stared at her open-mouthed. She guessed she looked impressive as hell. She stretched her wings, allowing him time to move out of the way, and gave them an experimental flap. They seemed strong and capable. She could fly! She flapped them a few times and exhilaration filled her. Human reasoning faded and the animal took control. No longer did she belong to the land of two-legged men. She belonged to the sky. She let out a piercing cry.

"Olivia." She heard Brian's voice, but didn't care to respond. He said, "Be careful, Olivia. The animal will take control the second you let it. Keep a tight rein on it."

Why should she listen to him? She was supreme. She wanted to explore this body, take it to the clouds and see what it could do. Taking a step, she first discovered she needed to learn how to walk with four legs; she tumbled to the ground in an ungraceful heap. Try as she might, she couldn't coordinate four legs well enough to get up off the frozen earth. Her now backward knees didn't work like she thought they should.

She opened her mouth to ask Brian how to change back to human form, but only soft cries came out. Damn. First drawback to being a shifter. She clacked her beak in frustration.

As if he understood her bird language, he said, "You'll be griffin for a while. At least until you somewhat control it."

She humphed. Why hadn't they told her this before?

Brian came close to help her get up. His nearness sent her into a tizzy. Brian had told her neither he nor Tony could tell shifters while in human form because there were so many odors that humans carried. But she could. Perhaps it was the seclusion from most human activity, or the fresh mountain air, but she could smell it. The wolf scent permeated every pore of his body. Apparently, her creature didn't like werewolves in such close proximity. Too bad. The griffin was going to have to overcome its natural antipathy. She fought hard to keep from biting and slashing at him. She regretted not telling him how she'd fallen in love with him. In case this whole griffin versus wolf thing didn't work out, they'd at least be able to part knowing they had meant something to each other.

Once Olivia was standing on all fours, she tried moving again, hesitantly lifting one leg, moving it and then another. Her body stretched and then contracted. She moved like an inchworm. She tried lifting the front feet off the ground and walking on the back two only. That went well, but didn't last long. It didn't seem like what she was made to do. Brian mimed how to walk on

196

four legs, moving on all fours in a diagonal pattern at almost the same time. She tried imagining she was human and crawling. That seemed to help.

As she got the hang of the walking thing, they turned for home. What she really wanted to do was fly, but she reasoned she should learn the baby steps first. Tony waited for them on the steps to the cabin, his blue eyes judging what she had become. He looked really worried. Again, she noted the gun in his beltline. At last he said, "Welcome to your new world, Griffin." Then he went back into the cabin. Whoop-dee-do.

A moment later, he reappeared with several different bowls. "I'm not sure what griffins eat so be patient until we figure it out. You should probably try the meat first." Funny he should use that word: patient. She chuckled, but it came out as a rolling trill in her throat. Odd. She wondered what other sounds would be normal for her. As far as she knew, golden eagles weren't very talkative, and were pretty much limited to the cries such as the one she'd given Brian earlier. Lions, on the other hand, were quite vocal.

Strolling over to the dishes, she inspected each one, finally settling on a fish appetizer followed by raw beef and then a broiled steak. The rice with veggies smelled good, but didn't interest her. She was definitely a carnivore. Half-eagle, half-lion, how could she not be?

An elongated yawn rumbled up from her chest, but came out a high-pitched roar that echoed off the cabin and down into the valley. Tony smiled and said, "I'll bet that starts the neighbors talking."

Brian laughed. He agreed. "Or keeps them up at night."

Olivia turned in a circle three times and lay down, tucking her feet beneath her wings. Brian stepped close, and she noticed that the griffin didn't fuss as much at his latent wolf smell this time. That boded well for their

197

relationship. Laying his hand on her head, he said, "When you wake up, the creature will have you. Remember, you have to be in control."

She bobbed her head in a nod and chattered at him. Whatever happened, they would face it together. She had no trouble drifting off and was soon asleep.

Chapter 40

Carl Hall sat in his truck and waited. The large
building in front of him had almost every light burning
in every room. Like his own worthless son, Brett, the
occupants were wasteful kids. The girl, Melita, sashayed
across the yard of the orphanage, her blonde curls
bouncing with each step. She climbed in beside him.
The cab filled with the exotic scent of her perfume and
old smoke from a previous wood fire.

"You called me. Said you know something," he
growled.

She fiddled with her neckline, running her fingers
up and down the V-neck of her sunny yellow top. The
evening was still warm, no need for a coat. "What will
you do for me?" She gave a shy smile.

He didn't know what she thought of him and didn't
much care. But her obvious sexual innuendo was too
well-practiced. "Such as?"

"I want out of here. I'm sick of looking after these
brats. Give me a job at your construction site."

He reached over and followed his finger behind hers up and down her bright yellow neckline. "I'll take care of you. Don't worry."

She frowned and dropped her hand. Was she afraid? Or simply withdrawing from the game? He removed his hand as well. She said, "Olivia is in a valley below Lake John and just above the North Fork North Platte Falls. You know where I mean?"

"I do. You're certain?"

She nodded. "Absolutely."

He reached around her waist then and pulled her hips to him. He could take her right here and now. He fantasized about it. About how tight she'd be around him. He was already so hard, it would only take a few thrusts before he came.

Fear crossed her face, but she didn't fight him. She was cool, as only someone with a secret weapon could be. He laughed. "What's wrong? I thought you wanted me to take care of you."

"Not like this." Anger filled her amber eyes.

He stared down at her and let go. "You use your body to make people do what you want. You make promises with your actions that you don't intend to keep. Someday, someone will take you at your word. Now get out." He leaned across her and opened the passenger's side door.

She scrambled backward to a sitting position, making no move to leave. "You promised you'd take care of me."

"Honey, I gave you the best advice you've ever had. If that's not taking care of you, I don't know what is."

In a flash, she changed to a sleek golden cobra. He'd been expecting something like that and was just as quick. His hand shot out and gripped her beneath the head, holding the cobra hood closed. He squeezed with the power of the grizzly within him.

It wouldn't have bothered a real snake. Squeezing was a hard way to kill one. But, Melita wasn't a normal cobra. She was a shifter, like him, and as such, her internal anatomy was just different enough that the pressure on her neck would cut off her air supply.

He grinned as her long rope-like body twisted and thrashed until it eventually ceased to move and she lay dead in his grasp. With a powerful shove, he threw the giant cobra out the open door.

Let the authorities have a heyday with that. He laughed as he drove away.

Chapter 41

When Olivia woke, it was full daylight once again.
The sun showed that about one-fourth of the daylight
hours had passed already. The crisp blue sky had no
clouds and it beckoned her. The smell of a nearby
werewolf alarmed her, though she couldn't see it, and
she lunged to her feet. Flapping her wings, she got
maybe five feet off the ground before she dropped down
again. Faced with that failure, she hissed and stalked
into the woods. The human that smelled of wolf
followed. In an instant, she whirled and snapped.

He'd been ready and easily sidestepped her,
reproving her with the tone of his voice. "Olivia."

That brought the griffin up short and allowed her to
clear her mind of it. Brian. She hung her head and gave
a soft trill. How could she let him know how sorry she
was? He stroked her face, moving his hand across her
beak. She looked in his eyes. He was unafraid of her.
She trilled softly again and laid her head on his
shoulder. She'd had enough of this new existence and
wanted to go back to being human and in his arms.

And then she was. As simple as that. One minute the beast, the next woman. Brian took off his black parka and wrapped it around her naked body, holding her tight against him. He whispered in her ear, "Glad to have you back."

"I'm sorry I snapped at you. I feel as if I'm two beings."

"You will until you learn to keep her under control. Then, like a horse and rider, you become one unit moving together."

She leaned back, reveling in the fact that he towered over her again, and looked up into his eyes. She would put this off no longer. Without hesitation, she said, "I love you."

Wonder filled his face. His eyes grew round, and he searched her face as if looking for confirmation. He softly asked, "You love me?"

"Yeah. I do."

He hugged her even tighter against him. After a long moment, he said, "I have a confession: I've loved you since the first time I saw you." He brought his lips down on hers in a fierce brand of ownership, his teeth pressing hard against her, bruising her lips. His tongue danced like a flame in her mouth and the fire burned through her, grabbing her and tugging her heart to meet his.

He broke away and grinned widely. Snatching her hand, he pulled her deeper into the trees. They ran like naughty teenagers, giddy and laughing, until they reached a rock slab jutting out of the snow. Aspens, Ponderosas, and other pines formed a natural curtain around it. Long bare branches overhung his and her chosen nesting place, enveloping them in their own world. They peeled off their clothes. Olivia had the advantage with only a coat to remove. While he worked his shirt off over his head, she reached for him, running

203

her hands over his sinewy body, tracing the curves of his muscles and the ridges of his scars.

She felt no cold, only the rush of heat that came with passion. Her hands dropped to his belt, and she had it half undone by the time his fingers joined hers in a frantic flurry. He shucked his jeans, and she pressed hard against him, sandwiching his erection between their heated skin. Her lips and tongue busied themselves with his in deep exploration. She couldn't get enough of his kisses; she wanted to drink him in.

In one move, he wrapped his hands around the curve of her bottom and lifted her, sliding her against his chest, nipping and licking her nipples. She locked her legs around his waist. He lowered her a fraction at a time onto his engorged shaft. The movement was slow, and she found herself fighting him, squirming, trying to take in more of him than he allowed. In frustration, she reached up and grasped a thick branch. She pushed herself down, forcing him deep within. A low groan broke from the core of him, mingling with hers.

He raised her and, as he let her slide down again, she arched her back, giving him full access. The head of his shaft pushed all the way to her deepest recesses. Again, he lifted her and let her fall onto the full length of him. Each time he pulled out, her body cringed at the loss of him, but every time she fell against him, her body rejoiced at the fullness, the completion of their union. Sparks traveled her nerves. The world around them seemed to swing drunkenly back and forth with every stroke. She reached for anything to help her ground herself, to keep from getting lost in the approaching tidal wave. She fastened her hands onto his shoulders, digging her fingers into his hard muscle.

He pulled Olivia upright against him, his breath hot and ragged in her ear. He turned his head and fastened his mouth onto hers. No longer did he let her fall against

204

him. Now he pulled her down with force, causing the bone of her pelvis to collide with his, only to lift her and slide her down again. His tongue mimicked the movement of their bodies.

The orgasmic wave broke within Brian. Shudders flooded his body and his thick, quivering moan formed against her mouth. A split second later, as the heat of his climax drenched the walls inside her, her own orgasm crested and boiled through her body. Her breath caught in her throat. She bucked against him, no longer in control. Surges of spine-tingling pleasure tumbled through her every nerve ending. Her body clenched his shaft, the spasms inside her seeking to pull him even deeper.

They clung to each other until the waves of passion subsided. Brian slowly lowered them, together, to the rock slab. Still within her, he lay back and held her against his chest. He needn't have worried about the cold of the boulder affecting her; she was still anything but chilled. The heat within her could have melted the polar ice cap.

A deep resounding groan came from within Brian as Olivia eased her hips back and forth along his. Her fingers brushed across his chest, and she licked his nipple, circling it with her tongue before taking it into her mouth and sucking on it. He said, "Woman, you're going to be the death of me."

"What a way to go though." She sat up, still moving her hips. He closed his eyes and frowned with pleasure. She asked, "Do you suppose shapeshifters are naturally more sexual than the average human?"

He opened his eyes again, stroking her body with his gaze, the lust in them so strong she shivered. "Wolves are."

"Good to know." Olivia grinned and ground her hips against him. He rewarded her with a sharp intake of breath. She began an even rhythm, pushing off with her knees to lift her up his shaft, then lowering herself at a slow measured pace. Her hands massaged his chest. She watched his face, the tight grimace of building pleasure, the shallow quickening breaths through a pursed mouth, his tongue that darted out to lick his lips. He stretched his neck and arched his back, lifting his hips, rocking against hers.

She leaned down to kiss him, to add her tongue to the fire building within him. She licked his neck and then blew chilled wind on the wet skin. She took tiny bits of flesh in her teeth and nipped him.

His hands moved her body in an ever-increasing tempo. Small sparks tingled across her nerve endings. Every cell in her body felt electrified as the tension increased.

She leaned back, forcing him against the front of her inner wall, pressure mounting within her. A tight ball of energy that had been slowly building suddenly expanded into a stellar explosion that blasted through her and tore a wild moan from her lips. A second cry joined hers as Brian's body jolted beneath her, lost in its own climax. Surge after surge of pleasure pulsed through her, matching his, until they were spent.

He pulled her to lie against his body. He reached a hand to her face and turned it to him. "As I said, you're going to be the death of me."

Chapter 42

They lay dozing in the sun until the air cooled with the ebbing day. Then they dressed and walked toward the cabin. Brian began schooling Olivia right away. When they reached a clearing, he stood and rubbed his beard. Where to begin? "Everything you do from here on matters. You have to learn to do things right and for the right reasons. Your griffin is like a newborn. All the instincts are there: how to walk, how to fly, how to fight. You aren't coordinated enough to do any of it well yet. Like when you couldn't walk. You'll get the hang of everything quickly enough. We all do." He smiled wryly.

Continuing, he said, "I'm not going to school you in mundane things. What I want to show you is that you, more than almost any other shifter, have a full arsenal at your disposal. That's the biggest reason why griffins are known to be so fierce. "You already know you can change fully to your creature, or you can change one part of you. For now, change all the way. Desire the creature, and you'll become it. Move slowly, it'll hurt a whole lot less."

"How do I change the speed?"

"Just think 'slower' or 'faster.'"

She first glanced in the direction of the cabin, though they were far from it and Tony. Unbuttoning Brian's coat, she let it drop to the ground. The sight of her smooth bare skin stirred his loins. He wanted to take her to the ground again and make love to her right there. He held himself in check. Priorities. She needed to learn to fight before Hall found them again.

She began to shift. The bones in her legs and arms lengthened and thickened to nearly twice their normal size.

She winced and the pace of her transformation visibly decelerated. Majestic wings grew from her shoulders. They took Brian's breath away. They reached a span of at least seventeen feet. Truth be told, he was more than a little jealous of them. He'd always wanted to fly.

When she'd finished changing, she sat with a thump. He still found it odd that, as tall as he was, he had to look up at her. He began, "Okay. Let's get started. Pick up something with your bird claws."

Olivia reached for a smooth rock the size of a cat's head, using her talons as fingers, but it slipped between them and scuttled across the frozen ground. She tried again, grasping at the stone with it pressed against what would be her palm if it were a human hand. No luck. He said nothing. She was clever, she'd figure it out.

On her third try, she scooped beneath the rock, cradling it in her talons. She held it out for him to see.

He clapped his hands. "Now, go grip that small tree over there." He pointed to a deciduous tree with a trunk the diameter of a large cabbage. "Break it."

Her brown eyes looked questioningly at him, but she wrapped her claws around it. She squeezed. Nothing happened. After a few moments, she adjusted her grip. This time, he saw that she not only squeezed, but she applied torque as well. The tree broke with a resounding snap. He nodded. Smart girl.

When she looked at him, her eyes glittered. It was infectious and he couldn't help but grin in return.

"Well, let's not kill another tree. Sink your claws into that one. Then pull out and rip it as deep as you can. Be careful pulling out though. I don't want you to lose one of your fingers."

Olivia swung her clawed hand at the tree he'd indicated. It landed with a thunk, like a knife stabbing a watermelon. Her talons buried themselves almost three-fourths of the way. She wriggled back and forth until they loosened, and then she removed them from the tree.

Rearing her eagle hand back again, she raked the bark of the tree, leaving gouges over three inches deep. She whirled toward him and bowed her beak to the ground.

He laughed, but those claws actually scared him. She could gut someone without even thinking about it. It was a good thing, but also a little daunting. He was used to being one of the baddest animals out there. How long would it be until she realized she didn't need him to protect her anymore? Would she still want him then? How unconditional was her love?

She cocked her head to the side, watching him.

He'd been caught thinking. He brought his mind back to task. "You're one dangerous gal. Just remember that. You can hurt people without meaning to. You've seen what you can do with your bird claws. Now take your lion claws and rake it."

It wasn't as easy for Olivia. At first, she tried to just rip her claws down the bark, but the force only pushed her away. She thought to hold the tree. That brought some small success. Though, the tears on the bark were only an inch deep.

"Think cat." That was the only hint he was going to give her. She had to learn this on her own. Any technique he could teach her wouldn't be as effective as what she taught herself. As if sudden inspiration struck her, she lunged at the trunk, gripping it with her eagle claws. Pulling herself off the ground, she brought her lion feet up between her talons and shredded the bark all the way down. The resulting grooves were over two-and-a-half inches deep in some places.

"Good. Let's see what you can do with your beak. Try biting through the trunk."

Obediently, Olivia turned her head to the side and bit.

He knew she wouldn't be able to bite all the way through, but she needed to see how much force she could exert. After a moment, he said, "Okay. That's good. Let go and take a look at the marks. You should be able to crush a man's head with your beak."

She backed away. Instead of open gashes, the trunk was compressed in two even halves; shreds and splinters radiated away from them. Apparently satisfied, she turned to him and let loose with a long string of chirrups and trills.

He laughed at her. "I have no idea what you just said."

Olivia opened her wings to their full span with a snap. He wondered how long she'd been waiting to do that and, he had to admit, it was pretty impressive. What she wanted was plenty obvious. She wanted to fly.

"Flying is something you're going to have to figure out on your own. But I'll teach you how to club people with your wings. I'd imagine you can knock someone unconscious that way. Maybe even kill them.

210

Unfortunately, that hurts you as well, so you'll use your wings as a last option. Every day, we'll practice these things and more. We'll build your skill and stamina. I'll figure out something soft to protect your wings when you club. You can change back to your human self now."

Chapter 43

Brian pushed her to practice everything until it became second nature. She understood he had to make sure she was ready for whatever might come their way. She learned how to catch melons in her claws, gripping with the front set and ripping the fruits open with the hind set. She worked on attacking with her beak and avoiding those attacking her. She padded her wings with pillows, and she learned how to club people with them. They still hadn't approached flying a bit, and she chafed at that.

Shifting back to human wasn't so easy for her. All the things the griffin could do delighted her. Despite her initial success at a quick transformation, she spent that night curled up outside the cabin door, pouting.

Always, Tony stayed in the cabin. He'd stepped into the role of cook and provider. Whatever they needed, he fetched. Other than that, he stayed away from her and was always careful to have the .357 with him.

On the fifth day, Brian locked eyes with her and pulled off his clothes, slowly shifting all the way into

212

wolf. Immediately, the griffin bristled at the hated animal's presence, hissing and clacking its beak. Olivia felt like she was suddenly two individuals: herself and the griffin. And the animal definitely wanted its own way. She worked hard at keeping it contained, but she fought a losing battle. Before the griffin had a chance to overrun her, she tried a different tactic: turning, she ran a few steps, then lunged into the air. She flapped her wings, catching as much air under them as she could, and lifted ten, fifteen, and then twenty-five feet. It was difficult flying; the lion half of her just hung there, pulling her toward the ground. She angled her wings farther back and suddenly it was all okay. Catching a draft and floating upward, she adjusted her wings and body as the current shifted.

She was flying!

It felt like heaven. She was, indeed, the supreme creature on the globe. Maybe two miles out, she wrested all control from the griffin and turned toward the cabin where Brian waited. He'd shifted back to human form, wore a robe, and stood with his hand shading his eyes, watching her. She angled in close. Now, how did she propose to land? Maybe she'd soar in and run with the momentum once she touched ground. As she prepared to begin, she stole a glance at Brian. To her dismay, he abandoned the robe and again shifted to his wolf.

Fury from the griffin bolted through her. The beast ripped out of her grasp, let out a shrill cry, and beat its wings ferociously, gaining altitude again. The creature spun tightly and headed away from the cabin. Olivia fought her with everything she had. She laughed at herself, thinking how comfortable she'd gotten with the idea of being a dual-minded creature. She gave up and let the griffin fly. There was no way she was regaining control any time soon.

The creature flew a long way and she learned a lot, feeling the griffin move its wings. She learned to bank tightly, dive, let the wind lift her, and how to slow. Gradually, she felt the griffin relax, and she gently turned for home as the sun was setting. Even for an animal her size, it took over an hour to get there. It was nearly dark. As she neared, she again saw Brian, once more human and robed, waiting for her. But, as he pulled off his covering, Olivia was ready this time. She didn't want to fight the griffin. Brian hadn't shifted yet, and he was waiting for her to come closer. Instead, she changed to human form and plummeted toward the ground, trusting Brian would catch her.

He didn't fail. Any other man wouldn't have had the strength, but her Brian had a bad ass werewolf and all its strength inside him. What kind of hero would he be if he let her fall to her death? She landed in his arms and he staggered a bit, but he stopped her from falling all the way through. He set her on her feet, shaking his head, confusion and worry in his gaze. "What were you thinking?" He began dressing and handed her some clothes.

"I was thinking I wanted to sleep in our bed tonight next to you, not perched on some rocky outcropping miles from here."

He ruffled her hair and smiled. "We have a lot of work to do to get the griffin willing to at least tolerate the wolf. And then, there's the werewolf. Not to mention the tiger."

"And if we can't?" She voiced the worry that had nagged her ever since the first time she woke as a griffin and the wolf scent had upset her so.

"We will. We have to." He said it because he believed it. One look in his eyes and she believed it could happen too.

214

Chapter 44

The flat gray of the sky looked pregnant with impending snow. Even the air had a crisp, wet smell to it. The pines, which usually whispered with the slightest breeze, were silent, as if in anticipation.

Brian hefted a watermelon the size of two basketballs put together. Olivia was flying somewhere nearby. It was the sixth day of her training, eight days since she'd become griffin, and eighteen days since the incident at her apartment. A light rain fell from a cool gray cloud cover. His breath came in vapor clouds.

With all his strength, he tossed the melon as high as he could into the air. Olivia dove and snatched it, her long scythe-shaped talons skewering it neatly. She brought one hind leg forward and ripped it open with her lion's claw. Chunks of pink flesh and green rind fell to the earth.

"Nice!" said Tony with a dark scowl. He'd been standing by the cabin steps, watching. But now he retreated into the cabin, combing watermelon from his black hair with his fingers.

Brian grinned and gave Olivia a thumbs-up on her next pass. "Come down and we'll work on the wolf thing," he called.

She looped in a tight arc and lined up, lowering herself and barely skimming over the tops of the deciduous aspens, the firs, and ponderosas. Just as she prepared to land, she seemed to change her mind and took off.

Her second attempt brought her closer to the ground, but again, she hesitated and then climbed into the air. He hoped she wouldn't try what she had done the day before, and fall from the sky as a human for him to catch. He readied himself, just in case.

On the third try, she actually touched ground and then fell into a rolling tumble, stopping against a swell in the slope of the mountain.

Brian ran to her, his mouth dry. If anything happened to her...

She righted herself before he reached her.

He asked, "Are you all right?"

Olivia nodded, her heavy eagle beak nearly touching her chest.

"That was quite some landing," he said. "I don't think you want to do that all the time though. Maybe some research on how eagles and hawks fly and land is needed. Shall we try the wolf?"

She trilled and nodded again.

Brian backed away, putting a good fifty feet between them. He undressed, keeping an eye on her. If she couldn't control that griffin, then this could the most dangerous place for him to be. She could either fly away as she had the first time, or she would attack. And, while he would defend himself from her, he didn't relish the thought. He could offend her as Tony had or, worse yet, he could hurt her.

His shift into wolf wasn't as slow as the day before. He needed to be ready if she came at him. The rain plastered his fur to his skin and he growled softly. As a wolf, he liked swimming, but not rain.

Olivia stood her ground, though she snaked her neck forward and hissed at him. She clacked her beak and paced back and forth at the edge of the clearing, her wings lifted away from her sides aggressively. It was something birds sometimes did to make themselves look bigger. She didn't need help in that department. But, it told him something about her. She was having trouble not giving in to the griffin's instincts.

Still, it pleased him that she controlled the griffin well enough that she didn't leave or attack. He wagged his tail to show her that this impressed the hell out of him. He stretched onto his belly, lying on the ground with his head high, so as to appear less threatening, but not submissive. They were a team. Neither was alpha.

When she settled in one spot, he sat. She hissed, but didn't move.

Tony came to the door of the cabin with two thick, raw steaks. "Isn't this handy? It makes cooking lunch easy." He came down the steps and dropped the T-bone in front of Brian, patting him on the head. "A bone for a good doggy."

Brian growled a mock warning, but immediately set into the meat. He was famished.

Olivia stood as Tony approached. About fifteen feet from her, he stopped and tossed a thick sirloin toward her. She snatched it neatly with her beak as it arced toward her, swallowing it in three bites.

"No more until after training." He shook his finger at her and then retreated to the safety of the steps. Speaking to both of them, he sat and said, "As you were."

217

Brian watched Olivia and she watched him. She settled lower to the ground, almost nesting, and didn't move when he padded closer. He growled and whined, barked and howled. The most he could get out of her was a single hiss. Then she turned her head away. He braced himself, walked right up to her, and touched her on the wing with his nose. She ground her beak back and forth, but kept her gaze averted. He pranced and cavorted beside her, but still couldn't get any more of a rise in her temper. It seemed she had the griffin well in hand.

Backing away again, he shifted to his half-way creature: the werewolf.

She came unglued.

Screaming shrilly, her beak jutting forward, she stalked him. She held herself low, her back in a flat plane. It was clear Olivia had lost control and the griffin was loose. In a mighty jump, she landed only a few feet from him. Then she launched into the air and was gone.

Brian changed back to man and joined his friend on the steps, taking the offered robe. He felt drained.

"Well, that last bit went well," Tony said dryly. He glanced at Brian, "Shaking much?"

Chapter 45

It wasn't easy to get the griffin to settle down when Brian's werewolf was near. Olivia and Brian worked tirelessly at it. When they reached the point of toleration, they decided to shift focus and introduce the Bengal tiger. It had been almost nine days since she'd become the griffin for the first time.

Tony exited the cabin, grinning and wearing a silk robe like a prize fighter. Olivia brought out the griffin. Standing close and looking up at her, as he was, she thought she saw a glimmer of hesitation in his eyes. Still, he ripped off his robe and pounced into his creature. He growled, snarled, and hissed. He roared. He stalked right up to her and swatted her on the beak. To no avail. Though she still clacked her beak, she turned her head away, ignoring him. She was still occasionally angry with him for hitting her, but after the werewolf, the tiger seemed boring.

His snarls turned to cursing as he shifted to man and disappeared into the forest.

After she transformed back to herself, she said, "Tony needs a girlfriend. He needs to be the center of someone's attention."

Brian nodded thoughtfully. He scooped her up and whispered, "He needs lots of women for that. But not me; I only need my one. Let me show you." Then he carried her into the bedroom and thrilled her with how badly he needed his one woman. Their lovemaking, as it always had been thus far, was wild and untamed. Passion moved them. They made love through the evening, while Tony was gone. When he stomped into the clearing, they were both quite satisfied and had just gotten up, showered, and were sitting on the front steps, drinking hot cocoa.

Tony was barefoot, but dressed in jeans and an oversized pink sweatshirt.

"Nice duds." Brian laughed. "Some lady take advantage of the weather to hang laundry on a line?"

Tony didn't answer. He stopped and looked from one to the other of them. "While you two were doing your usual, playing house, I was busy working."

It was exactly the wrong thing to say, given the anger toward him that still burned within her. In a snap, Olivia shifted to the griffin. The pain was the worst thing she'd ever felt in her whole life. It was somewhere between being dropped into the sun and having her bones ripped out of her body lengthwise. The change nearly blinded her, but she lunged at him anyway.

To his credit, he stood his ground, though he started the change to Bengal and then stopped midway. They stood face to face, separated by no more than five inches, beak to nose. His breath came quick and shallow, almost in a pant. Hers was sure and steady; she wanted to kill this man. At the very least, she wanted to maim him. She repeatedly clacked her beak in aggravation.

220

One move, one excuse, real or imagined and Tony's life would be over.

She saw Brian, still in man form, out of the corner of her eye, moving out from behind her to get a better view. Brian. She again heard in her mind the echo of his constant reminder that everything she did mattered. She tipped her jaw to the left, shifted out of the creature, snatched up one of the always available robes, and walked away.

"I'm sorry," she said over her shoulder as she entered the forest. She don't know how far she walked. Honestly, she was a bit more than upset. She'd wanted to kill Tony. She almost had. Over nothing. Just some words misspoken and that knockout punch the night before her first change. Truth be told, that had probably saved his and Brian's lives. If she had been allowed to change in that tiny cabin, there was no telling what she would have done.

She was the most miserable wretch on the face of the planet that night.

Chapter 46

Brian stood near the cabin and watched Olivia walk into the woods and disappear behind a large grouping of blue spruce. She jerked on the robe and settled it on her shoulders. He didn't follow. He wanted to though. Seeing her hurt that way nearly tore him in two. But, this wasn't his mess to clean up.

Tony's voice came from the left of him. "Well, shit! Before you kill me, Brian, let me see if I can fix things with her." He entered the woods, following Olivia.

"You'd damn well better," Brian called after him. He hung on the cusp of joining them. But no, this was something Tony had to do himself. His friend had been true to his word, keeping his asshole comments to himself when around Olivia, until today. He deserved the chance to make amends. In every relationship, there was bound to be some disagreement.

He smiled with pride. He'd been relatively sure Olivia had wanted to kill Tony. But she hadn't. She'd contained the griffin with ease. Though, he was sure, to her, it had seemed like a huge battle. That she could do it so soon after becoming the creature was amazing. It was a testament to her strength. And that strength was what he'd seen when she was fighting for her life in her apartment that first night. It would be very important as they faced Hall and his men. Everything she did from here on mattered.

He wandered around the clearing and picked up pieces of Olivia's clothing. Then he flicked on the external light of the cabin and sat on the steps with a drawing pad and pencil.

Chapter 47

Olivia found a boulder overlooking a valley below. With the griffin's sight, she could see every detail as if it was daylight. Window-lit cabins with wood smoke rolling from their chimneys dotted the perimeter of a small lake. She could smell the smoke, even from this distance.

It had now been nineteen days total since the attack in her apartment. The life before that had been nothing but a dream. This was the real world, and it was full of shifters and exciting adventures. Yet, she longed for the quiet of a life like the people in the homes below her had. The time she'd spent alone with Brian in their first cabin had been heaven for her. She wondered if they would ever have that again.

To her surprise, it was Tony who found her, not Brian. He motioned for her to scoot over and sat beside her. They were silent for a long time. Eventually, she spoke. "Tony, I don't know what to say. I'm so sorry." She wished he could see how sick she felt about it.

"It took me months to learn to handle the tiger like you just did with your creature. It was impressive, to say the least. Was it difficult, talking her down?"

Olivia shook her head, though she still couldn't look him in the eyes. "No. She stopped herself and didn't fight moving back to human. It was almost seamless."

"So, you have her then. She's you now. And you're her. Sometimes it takes something like what happened to get a good grip on the beast."

"I guess."

"I know I'm an asshole most of the time, but it was just plain stupid of me to say what I did. I'm well aware of how griffins think." He paused, "And now, I'll confess something to you that may make you hate me again."

"I think I already know. You fought against the griffins in the war, right?" She'd already figured this out. His animosity seemed too deep for it to be caused by anything she'd done.

"It actually is worse than that."

She turned to face him and spoke softly. "After the war?"

He stared off into the dark. She wondered what he saw out there with his tiger vision or if he was peering at something internal. He looked ashamed. "The griffins, your kind, were out of control during the war. They slaughtered every last dragon and many, many others. Some kept on killing, as if they had to take revenge. Since knowing you, I've learned how differently griffins look at the world. I understand now how they would have felt back then. But I didn't at the time. I saw them as evil."

He glanced down at his hands, as if seeing blood there. "I led the hunt for them. We exterminated hundreds of your people. Finally, I had enough. I was

225

sick from killing. I couldn't eat or sleep. I quit, but many others kept on until there were no more. I had nothing to do with killing your parents, and that's the honest truth. But, I'm not excusing myself from the rest. I did it. And you have no idea how sorry I really am."

She wanted to hate him for all he'd done to her people, but she couldn't. She'd already guessed some of it. It was odd, but, being a griffin, she understood how her kind could very, very easily be misread. She could find no anger anywhere within her. She leaned her shoulder against his. "What a world we live in."

After a moment, she added, "That took a lot, confessing that to me. You must trust me."

"I do." She felt him nod through the motion of his shoulder. He asked, "Are we good?"

"I think so."

"Good. I'm tired of carrying this damn pistol around. Let's get back to the cabin. Brian's beside himself with worry. He's a bit like a mother hen, that one." He cuffed her arm and pulled her to her feet. Side-by-side they walked home. They talked of inconsequential things until they entered the clearing by their cabin.

Brian stood from his seat on the steps. Near where he'd been sitting, she noted his ever-present drawing pad and pencil. Even though the light above the stoop was dim, she could see his gaze go from her to Tony and back. He must have been satisfied by what he saw because he smiled. "All better now."

Beside her, Tony laughed. He turned to her and said, "See what I mean? Mother Hen."

When they joined Brian, he shook Tony's hand and hugged her tight. He gathered his sketch things and set them aside. She noticed he now spent more time drawing her with wings than without. They seemed to be something for him to envy.

226

They sat on the steps, with her between them. Brian said, "Let's talk about Hall. Let's work out a plan."

They talked until they devised a plan that needed a small valley with a road, something they could box in if need be. Over the next ridge, Tony had earlier found a narrow flat glade with rough cliff walls, pines, and no cabins. The valley's skinny river emptied with a steep drop into a deep chasm. The January thaw hit Colorado, driving temperatures into the mid to upper fifties. The snow melted and the river thawed. A few birds actually sang in the trees.

That very next morning, Tony went back to Boulder to let their location be known to a few loudmouths while Brian and Olivia strung up an old tarp as a makeshift tent in the center of the valley and changed homes.

The minute Tony was out of eyesight, she and Brian wrapped themselves around each other, pulling off all their clothes, not quite making it into the makeshift tent. Their private times together had been few and far between. Not only was it Tony's presence that had kept them apart, but also the training where she spent every waking hour. She had so much to learn and so little time.

Their lovemaking was slow and gentle, not like it had been before. Even at the first cabin, when they'd had the most time together, their passion had overrun any tenderness they wanted to share. It was different here, laying in the middle of nowhere. They were truly alone, with only the morning sun and a few birds to watch.

Brian ran his fingers through her hair, down the side of her face to her cheek. He did this again and again, staring into her eyes. He nibbled and licked her lips in a constant motion. His other hand stroked her side, from mid-thigh to ribs.

Her hands weren't idle, either. They caressed his broad back, from shoulder to hip. They played in the hollows of his buttocks and traced the deep crevice between them. Her tongue darted out, tasting his. She held his gaze and kept her nose gently against his, breathing his air even as he breathed hers. The experience was like a bath in fine wine, intoxicating and overwhelming.

She pushed against his shoulder to roll him off her and onto his back, but he would have none of it. Instead, he took her hand in his and stretched it above her. He captured her other hand and joined it with the first.

His tongue was like a fire, lapping her skin. He trapped her nipples, one-by-one, in his mouth, rolling his tongue around the dark areola, sucking and gently pulling on the nipple itself with his teeth. His free hand continued the slow stroke up and down one side of her front now, but he used his nails instead of the flat of his hand. Each time he brought his hand low, he drove it between her legs, rubbing his fingers against her swollen clit. He kept a constant rhythm starting from her mound, sliding up her body with his nails to tweak and massage her breasts.

Her body started its own rhythm in time with his, undulating like a liquid seeking the workings of his hand. Her legs, of their own, spread and pushed her hips to meet his hand each time he returned it to her wet mound. Need swallowed her. She wanted him inside her: his erection, his hand, whatever she could get of him. All, if she could.

She whimpered as he again pulled his hand away without entering her.

Abruptly he let go of her hands and brought his face to hers. "Tell me what you want."

She opened her eyes to look into his. "You. I want you." She felt his erection against her sex, hard and hot. Her body arched against it.

"You have me. What do you want me to do?" His eyes sparkled, holding her gaze.

"I want you inside me. No. Wait." There was something more that she'd wanted for a while now. "I want to taste you. To hold you in my mouth."

He kissed her deeply and eased off of her to lie back on the ground. His engorged shaft stood upright from his body, waiting for her.

She didn't begin with any preliminaries. She lowered herself between his legs and took his shaft in her hands. So soft and silky smooth! So thick and long! Rubbing her cheek against it, she inhaled his male musk deeply. Her tongue flicked out, tasting, testing the head. Little drops of lubricant beaded to the surface, and she lapped them up. Stroking his shaft with her tongue, she followed the thick dorsal cord all the way to the base and the nest of his pubic hair. The strength of his musk was dizzying there.

His sac lay before her like a secret pouch, and she cupped it in one hand, gently massaging it with her fingers. Returning her attention to his erection, she again followed that dorsal cord to the head and let her tongue circle the cap, flicking back and forth across the ridge and the crease down the center.

As if from a great distance, Brian moaned. His hands tangled in her hair and pushed her where he wanted her. She opened her mouth and took him inside, sucking and rubbing her tongue over the area where the dorsal cord joined the cap. He was so big, she knew she'd never get him all the way in her mouth. But that was okay. She kept one hand on his sac and wrapped the other around his shaft, using it as an extension of her mouth. As she sucked and lapped, she rhythmically

229

moved up and down his erection, taking in as much as she could. Brian's hips rose to meet her.

All at once, he sat up and pulled her away. "Stop. I'm so near, but I want to come inside you." He rolled her to her back, positioned himself, and pushed her legs open with his knees. He rubbed the head of his member between the lips of her cleft, wetting it. With a slow, smooth press, he buried himself within her. Sparks of pleasure ran from the base of her spine to her brain, and she arched her back to meet him.

He pulled almost all the way out and thrust back in. He paused. "Don't. Move."

Olivia's eyes were closed and she rubbed her face against his neck. "Not moving," she whispered.

After a moment, he retreated and then drove in again. This time he didn't stop. Each thrust sent a cascade of sparks throughout her. She wrapped her legs around his waist, giving him deeper access. "Don't stop."

"I don't plan on it," he hissed through clenched teeth.

The sparks inside her coalesced for a split second and then suddenly exploded. They blinded her to everything but the exquisite pleasure-pain. Dimly, she was aware of two voices crying out, of strong arms crushing her against a hard shuddering body. They lay still for a long while, wallowing in the sweet bliss that followed. He moved to get off her, but she held him. "Don't."

"I'm not too heavy?"

She laughed. She was a griffin, after all. That strength carried through to this body. There wasn't much that was too heavy for her anymore. After a few seconds, he laughed too. "I guess not."

She looked deep into his eyes. "I love you."

"And I love you." He smiled. "But you don't really need me anymore."

There was something in the way he said it that caught her attention. His eyes had a sad, fearful look to them. She said, "I'll always need you. You complete me."

He crushed her to him, and she thought she saw the glimmer of tears before he buried his face against her neck.

Chapter 48

It took three days for Tony to return. Brian reveled in his time alone with Olivia. For the most part, he kept her busy in the tent with him, making love. In between bouts of passion, they attended to a few chores. He built a woodpile while she kept a fire pit burning. They threw wet rags on a laundry line and let them dry stiff. Brian sprinkled water on the tent roof so it would sun-bleach a little. When the water dried, he tossed some dust up there for good measure. He coached Olivia in her practice and helped her score the earth with deep gouges. To an observer in a hurry, the tent would pass for a two-week-old residence. To Brian, it felt like heaven on earth.

Eventually, Tony's truck traveled down their road, gravel popping under his tires. When he climbed out, he wore no coat and his shirt sleeves were rolled up. It seemed to be a new woman-charmer look for him. "Word is they're gathering together. There are quite a few from other families. They should be here within a few hours."

Brian turned to Olivia. "Okay. A few last comments. Everything you do has a consequence. Especially because you're a griffin. Don't run on just instinct. Think. Make choices. Everything matters. Also, capitalize on the reputation of the griffin. Don't let them push you around."

She nodded. Her position was to stay put near the tent as bait, naturally. She hoped to reason with these bear people. Not that Brian expected it to work. He decided to stay with her, deviating from their initial plan. He couldn't be talked into a more advantageous position; he wanted to be close by her for when she needed him. Shaking his head, Tony took a position on the ridge above with a telescoping rifle. As a tiger, he could jump directly down the side of the cliff and be at the tent in an instant.

The bears and their entourage didn't even try to hide their approach. Trucks rumbled down the dirt track, kicking up bits of rock and mud. It sounded like an army approaching, but it was only three vehicles: a silver Ford and two black Chevys. There were eight or ten burly guys in the back of each. Most were dressed in flannel shirts. Brian wondered if they, like Tony, thought it made them look tougher. The lead truck, one of the black Chevys, stopped about fifty feet from the campfire where he and Olivia sat waiting.

The other trucks halted farther back, and the big rugged men got out. They spread in a semi-circle around the tent. He didn't see any guns, which didn't really surprise him. Like most shifters, these guys seemed to believe their brute strength gave them the greater advantage and would solve everything. Olivia had Tony's .357 tucked into the left front of her belt, in plain sight. It was a quicker cross draw right next to her hand than fighting to pull the pistol from behind her back.

Carl Hall walked toward them with a younger man, his son, Brett. The elder Hall was tall and broad of face and body with scarce hair and thick forearms. Brian had never seen him up close before this. Based on his 400 years, this man looked closer to 1000 or just a touch over. Hall said something to his son, who stopped.

Brian and Olivia stood and made sure the pistol was visible. It caused Hall a little hesitation, and he progressed slower.

Without preamble, he began. "Have you changed?"

Brian let Olivia run the show. The whole thing was about her, after all. She nodded. "But, I'm not like those before me. I've mastered it."

"It can't be mastered." He stopped—waiting to see her next move, Brian guessed.

"See that man on the ridge with the rifle?" She pointed at Tony. "If I couldn't handle this beast, he'd be dead now. I'm saying it because it's true. I'm not that type of griffin."

"There's only one type of griffin. And it's best off dead." He started to change to bear. His snout elongated a little, his face broadened even more and his clothes tightened with bulging muscle. Brian let loose with a deep snarling growl, and Olivia dropped her hand to the butt of her weapon. Slowly, Hall's man form emerged from the bear again.

She said, "It seems to me you're the dangerous one. There's no good outcome here. I'm a crack shot, as is the man above. I guarantee you're going to end up dead. So is that young fellow back there. Think hard on your course of action here. I just want to be left to live my life in solitude."

"For now. But what happens when you come into town for supplies? Or if you want some city life? You're a danger to us all. And, by the way, you aren't the only ones with guns." As if on cue, three of Hall's men

234

revealed shotguns that they'd tried unsuccessfully to keep hidden behind their backs.

"Fine, but like I said, you and that boy behind you will end up dead. And I bet he has plans of raising a family someday." Olivia pulled the gun and trained it on the kid. Brian grinned.

The broad man in front of them shrugged. "What do I care? He's an idiot."

"You may believe that, but I've noticed you keep him close to you. Now why do you suppose you do that?"

Hall roared his anger. His face filled with his desire to change fully into bear warring with his desire to protect his boy. Tony's rifle went off with a sharp crack from the ridge and a spray of dirt and rock scattered at the younger Hall's feet. The three men with shotguns snapped their weapons to their shoulders. In an instant, the leader whirled with his hands in the air, staving off any gunfire.

When Hall had his group under his control again, he turned back to Olivia. "Remember our conversation. We're not the only shifters who want you dead. Almost everyone does. We'll all be watching you, Griffin. None closer than I. Someday, I'll be back and you'll be extinct."

With that, he pivoted sharply and strode back to his black truck, circling his hand above him, telling his men to leave. He climbed in his vehicle, slammed the door, and drove away with his men. Brian and Olivia stared after them. Their little meet-and-greet plan had gone well. Relief welled within him. He'd been expecting a fight of some kind.

Olivia rolled her eyes and dropped her voice to its deepest range. "'I'll be watching you. The only good griffin is a dead one.'" She laughed at her paraphrase, but it filled Brian with worry.

235

He said, "He's right. It'll never be over. Bears see themselves as the saviors of the shifter world. Throughout many legends, they're known as symbols of courage and sacrifice. And fear is a powerful motivator, especially to those types. Plus, he's got a personal vendetta against griffins. And you're the only one in his sights."

She sighed and said, "Unless we send a clear message. You know, 'This valley is my territory, and I won't bother you if you stay away from here.'"

He shrugged. That was something Brian didn't really believe could solve anything. If he was right, then there would be no end to Hall's persecution of Olivia… ever. They stared at the retreating trucks.

Tony jogged up to them. "I heard that. Fighting should be a last resort. Fear is a powerful motivator, and they're filled with it. Any violence here is a path that leads only to more bad things happening. Let's try to think of something else."

Just as he finished his statement, the three of them heard the sound at the same time. A truck door had shut somewhere in the direction Hall's group had gone. He must have changed his mind. That could only mean that shapeshifters prepared to attack.

Chapter 49

As the woods ahead of them filled with shapeshifters, Tony said, "Pick your positions."

Brian nodded to the left. Olivia didn't answer, her choice of sky obvious. She changed to the other her. The now familiar bone ache of pain gripped her, and she slowed her transformation. Her new and, so far, favorite sweatshirt ripped into pieces and fell to the ground around her feet. Brian had already become the wolf. His always beautiful eyes looked golden in the noonday light. He nuzzled her, took the .357 in his mouth, and then glided into the depths of the trees on the left side of the valley. The white tiger was gone, taking to the shadows on the right. She launched into the air and tried not to circle Brian as he loped to an advantageous spot. He didn't need her to give away his location.

Honestly, she wasn't too worried about Tony and Brian; she figured most of the bullets and attacks would be aimed at her. But, it worried her that their adversaries had only shown three guns. They wouldn't be making such a gutsy move of backtracking for an ambush if they didn't have more firepower and more shifters than those that had been seen. It meant Olivia would have to fight in the air while dodging bullets. The upside was that the bear clan might accidentally hit some of their own people too. Or they'd be afraid to shoot for that reason.

Sure enough, from out of the trees, at least a dozen birds of prey launched at her. The griffin inside her pulled, wanting to be in control, but she'd been training in aerial combat and she was ready. She rolled and brushed off enemy talons while slashing with her beak and hind lion claws. She seemed to be pretty good at this fighting-while-flying thing. She tumbled a golden hawk, two crows, and an eagle tumbled from the sky. That left a moment of empty space around her. Even as shots rang out from below, she tucked her wings and plummeted. One of the bullets stung her left haunch, but the rest missed.

Swooping low like a stealth jet, she grabbed two human forms with guns, one in each bird claw. Before they could think to shoot, they met the same fate as the bird shifters. As she was circling for another descent, a squadron of birds, mostly hawks, but a few crows and one long-plumed phoenix, engaged her. They fought like most raptors: swooping and pulling away at the last minute to expose their claws. A few dove from above, pecking and seeking to force her down to the ground with their combined weight. The beautiful long-tailed phoenix came too close to Olivia's head, and she twisted sidewaysputting them belly to belly, fighting and plummeting toward the ground. The other birds saw their opening and bore down on her, several holding her wings in their beaks.

The strength of the griffin amazed her as she killed and dropped it, hoping it 'wouldn't be reborn immediately; she didn't want those claws back in the fight. Olivia contorted her body and reached for one of the birds holding her wings, a huge bald eagle that she killed, letting it fall.

They were maybe twenty feet from the ground. Two more birds bailed from the task of causing her to crash. It was the only opening she needed. She beat her wings with such ferocity that the motion loosed the remaining three crows and, as she rose, those birds were driven straight into the dirt and stone floor of the valley.

She'd had it with reacting; it was time for action. She wheeled around and took off after the last few birds. Their speed was no match for hers. They dipped, angling toward the remaining riflemen. That was fine with her— she'd just take a few of them with her too. She followed the birds closely, but stayed a bit above them, sheltering herself from the guns below. A large caliber rifle boomed and one bird she'd been shadowing, some kind of fisher hawk, crumpled and dropped.

Chapter 50

Brian loped in an arc around the left flank of Hall's men. He currently ran in his wolf form, but, once the fighting started, he'd bounce back and forth from this one to the werewolf as needed. He stayed close to the rock face of the cliff Tony had stood on earlier with the rifle. Between it and the gray coloring of the aspen trunks near it, he was fairly camouflaged. The warm sun sent shadows to stripe his path, hiding his movement. He paused at a cubbyhole in the cliffside and pushed in the .357 with his long lupus mouth. Just in case.

Tony had circled to the right with the rifle. He would stash it near him for easy use in emergency. Olivia had hidden a shotgun in the tent. She probably wouldn't need a weapon though. Additionally, there were four other firearms cached around the valley. These were for last resort. If they started with them, Hall's men could keep them in a standoff forever. Thinning the ranks, therefore, was the first order of business.

Rifle fire came from the center of the valley, near the river. He changed course and moved deeper into the trees, away from the rock face and toward mid-valley. He started to see, hear, and smell other shifters. A lot of other shifters. He smelled a couple in man form too. Whether or not they were shifters remained to be seen. Brian was betting they were something big and not stealthy, making it easier to remain quiet in the human form. Perhaps a mammoth or even a sea creature of some kind. The trees were thick there, clustered in groups of dark firs, spruces, and pine interspersed with the always present aspen and a few tall, slender cottonwoods.

He came across a man with a big game rifle, creeping around a wide blue spruce. Brian attacked his adversary. The hunter's strangled cry brought two others, both bears. Even as Brian finished off the rifle-toting man, he changed into the werewolf. His long, hooked claws reached for one of the other shifters, a large black bear which he neatly killed without suffering much more than a clubbing to his shoulder.

A sleek, black panther joined the second bear, a young grizzly. Neither approached him and Brian assumed they were waiting for backup.

He closed in on the pair. The panther backed away. But the young bear stood its ground. As he and the bear grappled, the panther circled them, trying to get behind him. Brian matched the big cat, maneuvering the grizzly to stay constantly between them. The bear sought to envelope him in its arms, to crush him, but Brian stepped out of range. The creature fell away and joined two more black bears that lumbered onto the scene.

That was when the panther attacked from the side. With a bellow, Brian reached with his opposite hand and flung it at the bears. Without giving his attackers time to

241

recover, he attacked the injured bear. Within seconds, it dropped to the ground.

The panther retreated. The other bears hung back. Brian became aware of a musky reptilian smell. Keeping an eye on the cat and other newcomers, he glanced around, but saw nothing. Just then, a thick gray rope as broad as his arm dropped from the tree branches above. While he struggled to remove it, the snake wrapped around him, effectively pinning his arms to his sides, squeezing.

He had to get free! But each time he moved, the python tightened its grip. The two black bears and cat were joined by yet another grizzly. They continued to watch his struggle to free himself. He had no doubt they'd try to finish the job the snake had started. He shifted to full wolf and, for an instant, the loops of snake flesh were loose enough for him to escape them. He squirmed free to face the growing menace.

The ground around him darkened in shadow and sharp talons closed around his shoulders.

Chapter 51

A particularly large American eagle snatched up something from the ground. As it rose into the air, Olivia saw it had a dark shape squirming in its claws. She recognized the long torso, tail, and snout of a wolf. Brian. She exploded into speed, seeing red.

The three of them reached the narrow gorge that produced the bottleneck at the end of the valley. The river there was high and seething with tension from the forced containment of the water. Pieces of snow and ice clogged its movement and bobbed like ships on a storm-fed sea. She was just about on the eagle when it dropped its burden into this maelstrom. Brian disappeared into the floating ice and snow and then tumbled down the waterfall into the deep chasm and pool.

Olivia dove after him, wings tucked against her sides, neck stretched toward her love. With no hesitation, she angled toward the pool and plunged into the gelid waters, peering in the murk for Brian. She couldn't find him. He was nowhere. Perhaps she hadn't seen clearly. He could be hung up on a rock somewhere above. Frantic, she rose out of the water and flew up the outside of the falls. She stared through the curtain of water at the rock face behind, close enough to it that her wingtips grazed the frigid water. He wasn't there. Reaching the top, she was about to bank and search the surface of the falls again when she heard Tony's Bengal cry out. She hesitated. He was in trouble, whereas Brian, wherever he was, was away from the fighting for the time being. With misgivings, she turned and shot toward where she'd heard Tony. Her heart was tearing apart to leave her beloved.

Be safe, Brian.

Chapter 52

Still in wolf form, Brian plunged into the icy waters. Miniature bergs of ice bobbed against his head as he surfaced. For a brief second, he saw Olivia racing toward him, wings pinned against her sides like a rocket. Something hard hit him in the temple: an ice chunk or a tree limb. He went under. Groggily, he tried to paddle to the surface again, but the flotsam above him was too thick, too close together. His feet scraped a hard ridge of rock: the lip of the waterfall.

Then he felt the world drop from beneath him. The water fractured and he fell. It seemed like forever that he plummeted. Though he was dizzy, some part of him knew to take in a deep breath. Almost a full half of what he sucked in was water. Then he hit the pool below. Though he opened his eyes, he saw nothing but brown roiling murk. The power of the falls crushed him to the bottom and scraped him across it until he reached the perimeter of the pool. He found himself under a shelf in the rock wall there, the tidal force holding him in place. He was, in effect, in an underwater cave.

Brian's lungs felt near bursting and the water he'd inhaled burned like gasoline. The cold slowed his actions, even with his hyper-metabolism. How much longer could he last? He scrambled his wolf paws against the eroded rock that surrounded him, but found no purchase. His human form, though imbued with nearly as much strength of his other forms, was inadequate to breach the eddy that held him trapped. His werewolf form had the reach and claws to get him out. The change would exhaust the last of the oxygen in his lungs, but shifting was his only chance.

He became his in-between form and used his hooked claws to grab the edge of the shelf. The water buffeted his body like a boxer pummeling an opponent in a prize fight ring. Dizziness from lack of oxygen filled his head and his starved lungs ached. If he could just hang on until he reached the shallow end of the basin, away from the falls and the whirlpool there. Pulling with every last bit of strength he possessed, he entered the swirling vortex and scraped around the boundary of the pool. Fighting to reach the surface got him nowhere.

The blackness of unconsciousness crowded his reason. It seemed to him there was something else he had to do. Something important.

The river bed changed beneath his feet. It was softer. Sand. He'd been brought three-quarters the way around the pool and pulled by the channel down the river. Blindly, Brian reached out and hooked his werewolf claws as deep as he could into the river bed. The river tide pulled against him, but he held on. Flexing his muscles, he pulled himself toward shallower water. Again and again he drove his claws into the shifting floor and pulled himself toward land. At last, he lay on a beach, of sorts, panting and regaining his bearing.

246

As he began his shift to man, something struck his head and he lost consciousness.

Chapter 53

A large group of ten or twelve assorted changelings had the white Bengal surrounded. Olivia noted two of the bears from the night attack in the park near Brian's house. She hadn't seen Hall in bear form and wondered if he was the big grizzly nearest to Tony. A behemoth of a black bull pawed the ground, preparing for a run at the tiger. She filled the air with a shattering cry, which, given the situation, sounded scary as hell. The two grizzly bears on the near side of the tiger saw her, cringed, and fell back immediately, but the third animal, a leopard of some kind, had no clue. He held himself low to the ground, still as stone except for the twitch of his tail. All his attention was focused on Tony. She snatched him by the head as she flew past, clubbing the bear she thought might be Hall with her wing on the way. She flung the cat into the melee around the white Bengal. Turning, she aimed for a second pass over the scene. The remaining shifters had formed a tight circle as if they were intent on finishing the tiger off before she had a chance to attack again. She saw not a single bird.

As she closed the distance, Tony bunched his hind legs beneath him. He sprung high into the air, landed on her back, and dug his claws into the thick mat of feathers on her shoulders. The changelings that had surrounded him roared in frustration. Shots rang out from somewhere near, but only one clipped her wing feathers.

Tony leaned close to avoid the wind shear threatening to throw him off her. He panted and grunted with the pained effort of staying on board. Without hesitation, Olivia brought him to the falls. Truthfully, she'd expected to find Brian walking beside the river or trying to scale the chasm side. Setting Tony on the floor of the gorge, she changed out of the griffin. Her nakedness was not a concern; her thoughts were all about Brian. "He fell, but I couldn't find him." Her voice was tight, thin-lipped, and her stomach lurched at every word.

In silence, the Bengal paced the edge of the maelstrom of water, and searched the banks of the river. Olivia shifted to griffin again and dove into the pool, finding no body, no Brian, nothing. She flew into the falls, coming out between the water and the rock face of the cliff. There wasn't room here for the full extension of her wings, except if she was facing the rock or the water. So, she raised and lowered herself, moving back and forth along the wall. No Brian. She should have been happy there was no body, but her worry had changed to heartsickness. Something had happened to him. Something bad. He would have found a way to her, if he could.

She heard a cry and dashed through the curtain of water, hoping to see Tony with her beloved wolf. Instead, the cries had come from the ledge above where various shifters were trying to get down. The three birds were circling low over the white tiger emerging from the woods. She jetted toward them and they scattered, squawking in raucous defiance. She joined Tony, both of them shifting to human. He shook his head before she had a chance to ask. "He's not there."

"He has to be."

"Look." He pointed to the cliffside where some of the more agile shifters were coming down in human form. "We have to go."

"We can't leave Brian."

"He's not here."

"We have to find him!" Olivia was frantic now. She wasn't leaving her wolf behind. He could be hurt and in need of medical help.

Tony gripped her shoulders with both hands, giving her a little shake with each word. "He ... not ... here."

A panther had made it halfway down the rock face and jumped to the gorge floor. He approached, snarling; his tail whipped back and forth like a wiry pendulum.

Olivia nodded and changed to her beast. Tony chose to stay in his human form and, once he was perched on her back, she took off. Yet, she couldn't bring herself to leave. She swooped back and forth, searching the banks and peering deep into the pool for her beloved wolf. The birds pretty much left her alone. With only three left, they weren't ready to meet her claws and beak. She worked downstream, past the lower falls. Still, there was no sign of him. She soared higher and continued searching the same area, working in widening circles.

There was a possibility that one of the birds had come for Brian while she was helping Tony. They could have taken him and dropped him almost anywhere. In the distance, she spotted the American eagle with the gnawed leg and bolted after it. Tony lurched at the sudden increase in velocity. He hunkered down low and grabbed thick handfuls of her neck feathers.

The bird saw her coming and beat its wings valiantly, trying to get out of the way to no avail. The creature had lost a lot of blood and couldn't gain full speed. Olivia sailed above it and snagged it in her talons, screaming her battle cry. She bore it to a high tree deep in the valley and dropped it there.

Alighting off of Olivia to land next to the bird, Tony said to the eagle, "You better change, or she'll just get angrier."

The bird was no fool. It changed to woman. An ugly smirk played across her lips. She let her gaze rove up and down his naked muscles. "Well, aren't you quite the specimen."

Tony scowled and asked her, "Where's the man who fell?"

The smirk didn't leave. "I dropped him over the edge. That's all I know."

Tony let out a low Bengal growl and asked, "Did anyone else pick him up?"

"Not that I saw, handsome. And we pretty much all flew together." She turned a disgusted gaze upon Olivia while she spoke. Then she asked, with same that nasty twist to her lips, "What happened? Did you lose your friend?"

Olivia didn't hesitate. She flung the eagle woman from the tree and lowered herself so Tony could get on. He frowned, but didn't hesitate. She had a feeling she'd be hearing plenty from him later. He'd preach about keeping better control of the beast inside her.

The thing was, the griffin wasn't out of her control at all.

Olivia flew them back to the cabin. Though the battle wasn't finished, she had no taste left for the fight with Brian gone. Tony made no objections, either. They both altered into their normal selves and entered what had been their home for over two weeks. They stood like

251

lost children. Without Brian, the cabin was an empty shell. Tony moved first; ever practical, he dressed them both and tended their wounds. Then he went into the kitchen to cook. After that battle, their bodies needed nourishment. She watched him for a few seconds, but then turned and went outside again, changing to griffin. She heard him call her name as she flew away.

Most of the shifters had returned to the trucks Hall's men had arrived in by the time she arrived. Those that hadn't cleared the gorge, she easily dispatched. She started searching for Brian again, first in the air: back and forth, circling wider and then circling narrower. She dove deep into the pool, looking into every crevice and tidal hole. She flew behind the curtain of water that fell over the cliff. There, she changed to her primary body and climbed the rocks from one side to the other. Satisfied Brian wasn't there, she began searching the forest on foot.

There was no hollow, no tangle of roots, or depression that she didn't find. She searched all the way down the river, both banks, flying and walking. Still nothing. Tony came with food and helped her look for a few hours at a time, but ultimately he left her to the task alone. He knew, somehow, that she needed to do this by herself.

For four days, she searched, going over the area again and again. Finally, the only thing she could say with certainty was that Brian was not in the valley. She sat high on the cliff near the falls, looking down on the river gorge. She kept seeing the scene in her mind. It replayed like an old-time silent movie stuck in the projector.

Someone had to have taken him. The eagle could have lied, but Olivia had been able to account for the bird's every minute except for the brief time she'd spent rescuing Tony. Initially she'd thought that the bird

252

shifters were the only ones who could have taken him far enough and fast enough in that initial foray. She'd searched the river at least a million times. Someone else must have met them and taken Brian farther. Maybe in a truck.

Olivia heard Tony come up behind her. He sat and they stared at the water in silence. She looked into his brilliant blue tiger eyes and smiled. It was a sad smile, but it was the best she could muster. Truthfully, she was glad to have his company just then and she was trying to figure out how to tell him what she'd decided when he said, "Olivia, it's been four days now. He's gone. You need to accept that."

She shook her head. "No. Someone stole him away. He's alive. I know it."

He took her hands in his. "Please, Olivia. If they were holding him as leverage to force you to capitulate, someone would have contacted us by now. He can't be alive."

She had no argument for Tony. Weakness infused her body, and she wanted to tumble off the cliff to join her love in death, but Tony pulled her into an embrace meant to comfort her. He held onto her for a long time before he pulled her to her feet and settled a robe over her shoulders. He led her to his pickup and then to the cabin. He spoon-fed her broth and tucked her in bed. She slept for a long time.

Waking somewhere in the middle of the second long, dark night at the cabin, she reached for Brian, but found his side of the bed empty. Confused, she sat up and looked around the room. Then it hit her like a wrecking ball. Brian was gone. She delved into the pool of numbness within her, even as she thought of how he had sunk into the pool where he'd disappeared. Still, she couldn't cry or grieve. She stood and walked to the window, staring out at the tree branches scratching at the night sky. Was he up there? Was there a heaven for such as them? Did God even love them, or were they some kind of joke brought about by the Devil? A mistake? She pushed open the window in their one-room cabin with the intention of leaving. Yet, she couldn't step through. Closing it again, she turned to Tony.

He was awake, staring at the coals in the fireplace. It took him a moment, but he eventually turned his pained gaze upon her.

"I need answers," she said.

He nodded, swung off the couch, and doused the fire. "Let's go. The truck is already packed."

She looked around the room and, indeed, it was empty of all their usual clutter. The house had been just a shell since Brian … died. But now, it was a hunting cabin again, waiting for its real owner to show up. She followed Tony out the door and to the truck.

They drove to Fort Collins and turned south through Loveland, then traveled southwest from Longmont on the Diagonal, through the Gunbarrel area and farther, into Boulder. Neither of them spoke a word. Olivia sank into the unfeeling well deep inside her and stayed there for the entire trip. The sun wasn't even rising yet as they reached Boulder city limits. She said the first words of their journey, "Where do we reach Carl Hall?"

"He's a construction worker. Has his own crew working up near Chautauqua at the southern end of 10th street."

"Pricey."

"Yep. He does well."

And he'd just thrown it all away. She set her lips in grim determination.

Tony navigated the streets of Boulder until they reached a home construction site with a sign: BEAR CONSTRUCTION BY CARL HALL. Catchy name. She snorted her derision.

254

Tony agreed. "Nothing obvious about that, is there?"

They parked half a block away and waited.

Tony made a coffee and donut run at a gas station up Baseline road, and she later made a bathroom dash to the same place.

At six-fifty-five that morning, a familiar-looking pickup pulled onto the lot. Two women with richly-colored hair climbed out and unlocked a dirty trailer. Secretaries entering the office? They didn't look like anyone Olivia remembered from the valley. Had they been there? That truck certainly had. Were all of Hall's employees shifters?

She and Tony watched all day. One or the other of them snoozed or ran for food or bathroom breaks while the second kept watch. Pickups and construction vans came and went. Many had business in the office trailer. She recognized one or two of the workers from the valley, but neither Hall nor his son showed. Where were they? She was itchy to get moving.

"Where do they live?"

"In a quiet neighborhood where any intruder might be noticed," he said. That ruled out surprising them at home.

The work crew wound down for the day as did the short winter sun. Dusk brought out the men, and they were all men except for the two women in the office, which meant this crew wasn't the only group at the valley. They all climbed into their trucks and headed to their respective homes or other destinations.

Only two vehicles remained in the lot: the truck the women had arrived in and a battered blue SUV.

As Olivia reached for the door, Tony gripped her wrist. Surprised, she faced him. He said, "Olivia, I just need to know you have absolute control of that beast. That this is for answers, not revenge."

255

She nodded. "I promise I'm completely in control of the griffin. I'm here for answers." And then revenge.

That seemed to satisfy him. He let go and opened his own door. "All right, I'll barricade any back entrance and then come around to the front. We don't need anyone wandering in by accident."

"Good idea." Because if anyone wandered in, she'd have to kill them too.

Chapter 54

Brian opened his eyes to dim light filtering through cracks in the walls beside him. The walls themselves were made of tree branches piled close together to form a lean-to. His bed was nothing more than a blanket on the ground and, when he tried to move, he found that logging chains bound his arms against his naked body. More of the thick chains wrapped around his legs. No one was visible, yet he had the distinct impression he wasn't alone.

He called out, "Who's here?"

Immediately, a dark face peered around an odd conflux of branches that Brian realized must be a door.

"You're up. Good." The man moved the rest of the way into the shelter. He was short, with long, dirty blond hair. A gray bandana was wrapped around the crown of his head and dirt smudged his face. As the man came closer, Brian saw that what he'd assumed was a faded military camouflage uniform was in actuality a white jumper with painted streaks of gray and medium brown across it as camouflage.

It struck him that the man was actually a survivor nut. He'd known a couple of them from the time after the war … somewhere. "Who are you?"

His captor gave a thin smile. "Hunter."

"And I'm your prey, is that it?" Brian rattled the chains. He couldn't keep the derision from his voice.

"Not at all. You're no threat to us. You're just in the way. I'm safekeeping you until this whole mess is over."

"What mess?" He searched his memory, but found nothing that helped illuminate Hunter's words. Was this some kind of a joke?

The smile twisted into a sneer. "The Griffin War."

"The Griffin War?" What the hell? The last thing Brian remembered was sitting in his kitchen reading … something. Panic filled him, tasting sweet and desperate in his mouth. "I don't remember any griffins. And why would I? There's no such thing. They're extinct. The Griffin War was long ago."

Hunter reached over and fiddled with something on Brian's head. "You're right. There's no such thing. Just testing your memory." He sat back. "You'd better rest. You got a nasty bump on your head in your underwater adventure."

Brian frowned. Underwater…? "What the hell is going on?"

"What's the last thing you remember?"

"I was sitting in my kitchen, reading the newspaper."

"Can you tell me the date?"

The date? "December twenty-first. Wednesday."

"What about your name?"

"Brian Merullo."

Hunter nodded. "The good news is that your amnesia seems to be located in just your short-term memories."

258

"Amnesia. And that's the good news." Sarcasm dripped from his words, and Brian wondered where he'd picked it up.

"The bad news is that you've lost a hell of a lot of memories."

"Such as…?"

His captor considered for a moment, and then said, "There was a battle a little over four days ago."

"You said something about The Griffin War. What does this battle have to do with that? Who was fighting this battle?" Something pushed at Brian's mind. Something important. He reached for it, but it retreated.

"You and Silver fought against just about everyone. You were on the losing side. I had circled behind you and was coming up the valley when someone tossed you over the edge of the cliff into the pool below." He tipped his head toward his right, in the westerly direction. "I climbed down and rescued you."

"Now I'm here."

Hunter nodded. "Now you're here."

"Who were we fighting against?"

"Carl Hall and most of the families."

All of this was too much for Brian, and he rocked his head back and forth on his pillow. He needed to remember. What was so important he and Tony would risk coming up against everyone else in an open fight? No matter what he tried, no memory jumped out at him. After a moment, he asked, "So, you work for Hall?"

The man nodded again, the filthy strings of his hair bobbing. "I do."

"Go get him. I want to talk to him."

Hunter stood and moved toward the door. "No can do. He doesn't know you're here."

"What are you going to do with me?"

"Do? Nothing. I'll wait until things settle down and let you go." Then he left.

259

Alone again, Brian lay in the chains on his blanket. Perhaps the best way to approach his memory loss was to back up to what he remembered and try to go forward from there. He closed his eyes and envisioned the scene in the kitchen.

He'd been sitting at the center island, reading the paper. He'd made some white chili, and a bowl of it was steaming beside him on the counter. Rising, he walked to the refrigerator, and took out some sour cream and a small bowl of freshly chopped tomatoes and cilantro. He dropped a healthy spoonful of the cream into the bowl, followed by a sprinkling of the veggies. Tasting his chili, he decided he had indeed created perfection. He loved his kitchen.

That, of course, was when Tony had called. No preamble, no niceties. His friend started in. "We have a problem."

"No. I'm eating supper. You have a problem." He continued to eat while he listened.

He heard an exaggerated sigh. "Brian. My problem is your problem too."

"Oh? How's that?"

"Cujo heard a rumor that Carl Hall and his men are threatening to kill someone, but we can't find out anything."

Brian set down his spoon. "Well now. That certainly is a problem."

"Right. Our problem."

"Yes it is." He'd nodded to himself, worried. "Where are you? I'll meet you."

The memory ended there. No matter how Brian tried, he couldn't get the memory to extend beyond that point. He had no idea where he'd met Tony or who Hall and his men had been after. But he was willing to bet that the battle Hunter had referred to had been the outcome of that initial conversation.

260

Why had Hunter mentioned The Griffin War? What did that have to do with this? He gently tested the chains. There was a little room, but not enough to wriggle free. The wolf was smaller of limb than he was as a man. If he rolled to his side and then shifted, he just might be able to escape. He'd have to make it fast: the werewolf was too big and would be in trouble in bonds so tight. The chains rattled.

Hunter's head appeared from behind the door. He watched silently.

Brian said, "Can't sleep. Never been good at it on my back. Just trying to change position."

For a moment, the military man said nothing. Then, "Get used to it."

Whatever. Brian wasn't about to apologize for trying to relieve some of his pain. That "something" again pushed at his mind. He couldn't put his finger on what it was, couldn't remember it, but it was important. For a while, he'd thought it might be some kind of trouble for Tony. That didn't ring true, however. Tony wouldn't let himself get into a situation he couldn't flee, if needed. No. It was something else. Something more important than his best friend.

He needed to escape, to go back to where Hunter had found him. Then up that cliff he'd been thrown over. There had to be some kind of answer there.

But first, he needed a plan.

Chapter 55

When Olivia entered the office at Hall's construction site, only one of the women sat in the front room. The nameplate on her desk identified her as Tanya Hall. Family business. She was busy typing on her computer. She looked up with a friendly smile. The expression changed to terror the moment she recognized Olivia. So, this woman had been at the valley. Olivia snapped her hand into the eagle claw, snatched the woman's throat and shoved her back against the wall, still in her chair. She tried to change into a grizzly, but Olivia tightened the grip, cutting off her air. She leaned in, whispering hoarsely, "What did you do with the wolf's body?"

Confusion crossed the bear woman's face. "Wolf's body?" She could barely speak from the pressure Olivia had on her throat. A sound came from down the hall somewhere. Another woman and a man were talking softly. The woman stopped speaking and her footsteps approached the front room. Olivia repositioned herself so she could watch this new intruder. This new woman caught sight of them and her mouth opened into a giant O, but she said nothing to stop Olivia, nor to warn the male left behind in what was most probably a second office. Instead, her clothes ripped at the seams and she shifted into a hissing komodo dragon that hadn't been at the party in the valley.

"You don't want to do that." Olivia tightened her grip on Tanya's throat and nodded toward a soft chair at the far end of the desk, by a water cooler. "Sit there." The komodo became a naked woman again and obeyed without hesitation, watching them.

Olivia moved Tanya to get a better look at the komodo woman's face. She spoke into Tanya's ear. "What did you do with him after he was dropped?"

Again, the confusion. "Nothing. I was in the fight with the tiger."

Olivia actually found herself believing this woman, but she again tightened her grip on the woman's throat until her breath turned raspy. She turned her attention to the second woman. "Did you?"

"Did I what?" The second woman's face filled with confusion.

Tanya whispered, "She wasn't there."

"And why was that?"

She teared. "We couldn't trust her or her boyfriend to take their part."

The second woman's face flamed and she looked away, saying, "We warned you and Carl." Really loyal, that one.

"Where is Carl?"

Tanya said nothing, so Olivia turned her attention to the other woman. She bit her lip, but after a moment said, "Dandoritto's."

Olivia nodded. She knew the place. She let go of Tanya and stood. Then she said, "You should have listened to your friend." She changed both hands to the

263

eagle claws and within a split-second she'd killed them both.

She met the man halfway down the hall. "Were you at the valley?"

It took him a few seconds before he could manage a shake of his head. He'd proven worthless to her as well. She killed him. .

Oddly, Tony was waiting in the truck for her. It actually surprised her. She figured he'd seen what was in the office and washed his hands of her completely, or maybe was even at a phone booth making an anonymous phone call to the police. He started the truck when she got in and they drove quietly up the street. Once they reached Arapahoe, he turned left toward the Flatirons, drove past the library and Fine Park to get on Boulder Canyon Drive.

She had a feeling she was in for one of Tony's famous lectures. They drove in silence for a couple miles until they reached Four Mile Canyon and the trailer park there. He pulled to the side of the road and turned off the engine. He spoke, but didn't look at her. "You said you had the griffin under control."

"I guarantee you, I do. What I did in there was me."

He glanced at her, but looked quickly away. Pain was plain on his face. He'd lost Brian and now, it looked like he lost her too. "And did you find out where Hall is?"

"Place called Dandoritto's. It's on the Hill."

He nodded, still staring straight ahead. "You promised this wasn't about revenge."

"I made no such promise. In fact, I said nothing at all about revenge. What I told you was that I was there for answers. Which I was. Which I got."

"Brian wouldn't have wanted this."

"I don't doubt that. But I'm not him, and I needed it."

264

He was silent for a long time. Then, "He was my best friend. I loved him like a brother, but I can't go down this road with you."

"Then this is where we part ways." Olivia got out of the truck. Before she could lean in and say anything else, he fired up and left without even looking her way. She should have been angry. The griffin should have bristled at the betrayal, but well, she figured she'd betrayed him first and she pretty much deserved being abandoned. Still, he hadn't even looked at her while he kissed off their friendship.

She stood in the road for a few more minutes, then decided that, covered with blood as she was, she should probably get out of sight. Tony was most probably going directly to Hall, and if she wanted to stay in the loop, she needed to get there before him. She changed, feeling the bulky muscle build as her bones became denser. The burn of wings scored her shoulder blades and she sprouted a tail. Her clothes ripped and fell to the ground. Rising to the sky as the griffin, she flew directly to the bar, passing Tony's pickup on the way. She figured the traffic in his way would give her about fifteen minutes, maybe twenty, to get her answers before he'd arrive and spoil her fun.

Chapter 56

Brian readied himself. He finally had a plan that he was pretty sure would work. If all went well, he would be free within a few minutes. Even if it got a little painful for him, it was something he could handle. He'd waited until dusk, rationalizing that it would be easier to hide in the shadows of the dark once he escaped.

He couldn't just shift and escape. His experience earlier with his chains rattling had shown the sensitivity of Hunter's hearing. He didn't need to be fighting his captor while at the same time trying to free himself. First, he'd take care of Hunter.

Raising his upper body as high as he could, given the thick logging chains that wrapped around him, he held himself up by the strength of his abdominal muscles. He screwed his face into what he hoped looked like extreme pain and called out, "Hey! Hunter. Come here." He cracked his voice, and let it fade at the end.

A split second later, his captor poked his head through the doorway. "What do you need? Don't tell me you gotta piss. If you do, you'll just have to wet your diapers. I'm not helping you with that."

"You got anything for a headache?" He barely moved his lips, letting his words slur, like any migraine sufferer.

"Nope." The head disappeared.

"This damn thing hurts worse and worse. I'm getting dizzy."

There was no movement from outside the shelter. Brian hadn't really figured Hunter would be that easy to fool. Time for more drastic measures.

He retched, twisting his head and shoulders to the side. Once. Twice. Three times, trying to bring something up. He had a strong constitution, but sometimes that was a disadvantage. Like now.

As if by magic, Hunter appeared beside him, probably worried he'd choke on his vomit.

"Man, I gotta tell you, this hurts bad." Brian groaned. He retched again as if to throw up on the man. Looking at Hunter, he said weakly, "Help me."

He leaned toward the wall, making like he was trying to turn that direction.

Hunter reached over and put his hand on Brian's shoulder, supporting him and helping him turn. He leaned in to add support.

It was all the opening Brian needed. He changed most of the way to wolf, leaving his arms human and shrugging them loose from the suddenly slack chains. At the same time, the bandage that had been around Hunter's head slipped down, momentarily blinding him until it fell to the floor.

Hunter was caught flat by the sudden shift. But even as he fell closer to Brian, he was grabbing for the skinning knife he kept on his belt. He shifted at the same time.

267

Brian, however, had anticipated that he might go for the weapon. It was either that or shift. It really depended on Hunter's alternate form.

Since Brian had left his hands as a man's, he wrestled away the knife, even as his arms were forced apart by the changing mass of the shifting man. Whatever he was, it was big, and getting bigger. It made no sense to Brian that the man should want the knife and shift. Then, the unmistakable odor of ape filled the tree branch lean-to. One of the only creatures who could handle a knife. His werewolf would be the other.

He wrapped his arms tightly around the ape's throat, exerting pressure. He growled a warning. Hunter's breath rasped through his mouth, yet he didn't stop shifting. Either the man was stupid or he truly believed he would win any fight.

Brian wasn't waiting to find out which it was. He didn't want to kill his captor, just make him pass out. He tightened his arms and held on with all the force he had. He was in a corner of the shelter, and if he let go of Hunter and tried to escape the chains the rest of the way he'd be in range of those ape claws. So, he held on, always forcing the ape to stay in front of him.

Hunter slowed and ceased his movements. Brian kept his grip for another few minutes to make sure the ape was really unconscious. Then he let go and wriggled out of the chains, changing his arms now to a werewolf's too.

He stared down at the giant, light brown body and the long, bare face. A baboon. It was the fiercest of the apes, but Hunter was way bigger. He was the size of a huge silver-back gorilla.

In a fair fight, the wolf would have lost. The werewolf might have made an even match. Might have. But it could have as easily gone the other way. He shivered.

He sniffed at the wounds inflicted by Hunter. A few were deep, but not disabling. He'd live.

And right now, he had something important to find out. Like why he and Tony had been in the valley. And who they'd been protecting.

Chapter 57

Olivia landed beside Dandoritto's in a dim alley filled with trash. The odor of refried beans, rancid grease, and burnt cheese bore down on her and she almost choked. She decided the best option she had was a frontal approach, which would catch them off-guard. With that plan in mind, she rounded the corner. The big bouncer's eager gaze glued to her approach in her birthday suit. Without a pause, she put her claw through his chest and stole his boots, belt, and coat. She left his pants behind, given his size. She didn't want to look like a homeless waif. Instead, she cinched his oversized ranch coat with his belt, like she would a dress, and cuffed the sleeves. His boots were a bit big, so she scuffed the ground when she walked. She wouldn't be using them long anyway. Taking a deep breath, she opened the door.

It looked like any other college town bar. The seedy jalapeño decor was meant to entice jailbait girls to party and drink too much alcohol. The place smelled like perfume and old sweat near the door-side dance floor.

Jalapeños hung from the warehouse ceiling. More jalapeños filled the tabletops and bar.

She scuffed toward the group of eight or nine construction workers gathered in the back around a pool table, swaying her hips like a girl on the make. She kept her head low; she didn't want anyone to spook until the last minute. A runty fellow with a blonde girl in tow was headed toward the door. Olivia had seen him at the valley, but not her. She was an innocent and had no place in what was about to happen. Olivia stepped between them and, placing her hands on his chest, she said in her cutest southern drawl, "Where you goin' cowboy? The party's just gettin' started. Tell this tramp to go home. I can take care of you."

As the cursing girl stormed out, Olivia steered the fellow back toward the way he'd come, to the green corner with the beefy construction workers. She kept her head tilted so he couldn't see her features completely. He didn't fight. In fact, his attention was focused on the deep cut of her oversized coat. Good boy. She heard one of the boys in the back mutter in a graveled voice, "Look at this cherry comin' here." The sound of his voice echoed off the walls and seemed to fill the tiny bar.

She smiled. She was close enough now to smell the piss, stale beer, and vomit from the bathrooms. Or maybe the stench came from the stains along the baseboards and wood floor. She stopped and lifted her head and glared from man to man. A few blank eyes looked back, but most slowly dawned into angry recognition.

The cowboy she'd been pushing started hard and backed away as fast as his feet could go. His pale eyes widened, and he almost fell in his rush to get free from her. "Shit! Shit!" Five men shifted to animal, and she noted the panther was there as well as more than a few bears. Carl Hall and his son, Brett, stayed as men. Most of the workers, animal and not, took a fighting stance. A couple broke pool cues for weapons. Snarls echoed from the walls. The bartender moved to the near end of the bar. Olivia saw no shifter women.

She raised her hands to ward off any combat. That would come later. "Calm down. I have questions."

Carl Hall jutted his chin aggressively at her and asked, "Questions? What do you want?" Brett and some of the workers edged to the right side, trying to outflank her. Others, including the panther, worked around the other side of her, but she stepped against the wall. This promised to be a good fight. Her hands tingled in anticipation.

"I want to know what happened to the wolf your crew dropped over the side of the ravine. We can't find his body." Her voice took a harsh turn at that last word, and she knew they'd heard it do so. The connection would soon be made that they weren't getting out in one piece. They'd attack.

Hall shrugged. "He's dead. What does it matter?"

Way wrong answer. Brett had worked his way close enough that she grabbed him and changed her arms to bird talons. She gasped at the spasm of searing pain that lanced through her bones. It wasn't the first time she'd changed that fast, nor the first time it had hurt that much, but she doubted she'd ever get used to the pain, as Brian had said she would.

"It matters." Even as she said it, she again saw Brian that first day in the hospital, his face close to her stomach, saying those very same words. He'd said them again and again while training her. He'd even said them the day of the fight in the valley. The memories almost undid her. Despair washed over her. She savagely shook her head to clear it and lowered her voice. "What did you do with the wolf?"

272

Hall stared at her. "This isn't the way to get answers."

"Sure it is. Just ask Tanya and her coworkers. They gave me answers. They told me where to find you." Carl's mouth dropped into a grim upside down V, but still he said nothing. She tugged Brett closer.

Carl Hall's big square face paled at the threat to his son. He held up his hands, warding off her anger. "Stop! We don't know anything about the wolf. Arlene dropped him off the ledge. If anyone did anything with the body, it was her. We didn't touch it."

Arlene had to be the American eagle.

"Arlene is dead. So is Tanya. You'd better come up with a better story than that." This was it, the moment where Olivia either chose to destroy everything or to walk away, seeking other venues for answers. Tony was willing to leave these murderous bastards alive if they left him and Olivia alone, no matter what they'd done in the past. Brian would have agreed. But she wasn't tiger or wolf. She was griffin. And she wasn't inherently evil, but, by these people trying to kill her because of the griffin's reputation for having a thirst for blood, they'd forced her to the cusp of becoming what they feared.

The memory of Brian's voice echoed in her head again. It matters.

Tears blinded her, and she knew then what he and Tony had tried to teach her. What she did mattered. She mattered. It took until now for her see that if she continued her current course of action, she would become nothing more than what these people claimed. They would be justified in their stance. As much as she wanted revenge for her lover's death, she couldn't keep killing. Yes, she was a griffin, but she didn't have to be what these people's fear decreed.

Olivia let Brett slide out of her grasp.

Hall's jubilant grin was all the warning she had.

273

Chapter 58

Brian slunk out of the shelter. The weather was decidedly cooler than when he first woke. He had no idea which way to go, but he remembered Hunter's brief nod to the west when he spoke of the battle that was supposed to have happened six days ago. Whether his captor had been telling the truth remained to be seen, but west was as good a direction to travel as any. If he missed the valley, he eventually might find a road to civilization. He may not remember anything recent, but he remembered Tony. A quick phone call to him would clear all the cobwebs out of his brain.

Assuming the battle was real and Tony had survived it.

Hunter's lean-to hadn't been at the bottom of a valley, as Brian had assumed, but actually was located on an abandoned road along the west side of a mountain. Fine red grit covered the surface of the road, interspersed with rock the same color and dark green cacti with thick yellow spines. For the first time, he considered that Hunter might not have been alone. He hadn't heard any other voices, but that didn't mean there wasn't an advanced guard.

Heading west took him up the mountain. Urgency drove him. But urgency for what? He slipped through the shadows of the cottonwoods, aspens, spruces, and firs in the waning daylight until he felt confident no one else had been watching the shelter. Then he flat out ran, but he kept watch for enemies and plotted escape avenues as he moved.

When he topped the ridge, he caught the scent of water. A lot of water. Eagerly, he loped down the east slope. It was brighter there; the setting sun fired the rocks, boulders, and trees with a reddish gold hue. The deep strum of falls reached his wolf ears. He could feel the vibrations in the rocks beneath his feet.

Would anyone be hanging around? Would Tony still be here, looking for him? He didn't see anyone, but with shapeshifters, a person could be hidden anywhere. Then again, it could all be a lie.

He reached the valley floor. Sunlight no longer reached that part of earth, and it was as dark as night. The river flowed wide and high, fat from a thaw. He sat on his haunches and thought about that. December didn't normally have a thaw. But, there was often one the second or third week of January. If the battle had been truly almost a week ago, it really was sometime in January. If it was the regular January thaw, that meant he'd lost almost a full month of memories.

What had happened during that time?

He rose and followed the river, skirting wide where it flooded its banks. He picked up a lope again. His injuries hadn't had a chance to stiffen, but they still hurt. He pushed the thought of them out of his mind. They'd have to wait. Fear for Tony and for what he'd forgotten, now more than anything, governed his speed. Something had happened. Something terrible. He could feel it

275

lurking at the edges of his thoughts. But, when he reached for it, it disappeared.

The waterfall was only twenty minutes up the river. The amount and force of water coming over the lip of the cliff above was simply staggering. Brian couldn't even begin to figure it. It thundered into the tidal pool below, drowning out all other sounds. A thick mist covered everything, almost like a gentle rain. He growled as it matted his fur.

Hunter had said he'd been thrown into the deep pool. He eyed the whirling current, thick with branches and foam. Only his werewolf could have survived that. He was damn lucky to be alive.

He gauged the cliff side and decided there was no path for him to climb up as wolf. He could do so as human or werewolf, but it was slower than going around. He stayed as the fast traveling wolf and retraced his steps until he came to a traversable path back up the mountainside.

It led him to a second vale above the falls. Here, the river was even wider and completely out of its banks. Most of the broad gorge floor looked like a river delta with stream grooves and channels that branched around newly formed islands. The individual tributaries tapered to the deep single channel as they neared the lip of the falls. Occasionally tall cottonwoods broke through the surface of the water, like sentinels or lighthouses.

He traveled the eastern edge of the valley, against the mountainside. A hint of a memory tickled his mind of another similar trip. He couldn't remember why, or when, but he thought he'd been wolf and had been carrying something in his mouth. It was possible that he might remember more if he walked that very same path. First, he would need to find a way across the water.

He continued upriver until he reached a place where the overfull water had split into two narrow channels.

He began hopping from island to island. Most were soggy, as if they'd been underwater recently.

Landing on what he thought was one such island, he sank through into the chill water. Scrambling his legs, he finally found a tangle of submerged branches below. They shifted, but held. His head was just barely above water. When he changed position to look for solid earth, his perch sank. Water filled his nose and he lost his footing. The current swept him away.

It was only by luck he'd landed in a tributary that joined quickly with the main channel. When the two met, the strength of the main channel pushed him to the side onto a small hillock. From there, he fought to gain purchase on higher ground. Finally, he pulled himself out of the water. Shaking from the effort, he lay on the rock and grit for a few moments to regain his strength. That urgent feeling that had pushed him all evening built again from somewhere in his hidden memories. Soon, he stood and continued his island hopping, more carefully this time. He quickly learned to tell the difference between fake land and bona fide earth by watching the islands for a moment. The fake islands bobbed occasionally. Such a simple way of telling, yet he'd somehow missed it because of the drive within him.

The night was full upon his little part of the earth. The sky had filled with clouds and the temperature was still steadily dropping. It smelled like snow. About halfway through his journey across the valley, and once past both deep channels, he happened to see something moving on an island down river from him. He changed direction. As he came closer, he saw it was the remnants of a tent that had been moored between two of the few stout cottonwood trees at that end of the valley.

Landing on that island, he saw a partial stone circle from a fire pit that had been washed away. The tent

277

itself was mostly gone, taken by the force of the water. Tatters were all that remained.

When he sniffed it, he smelled his own scent. So, Hunter had been telling the truth. He had been here. He moved closer to the tree on the south side of the rope securing the tent. He smelled ... Olivia.

The power of his returning memories was strong enough to make him stagger against the cottonwood's wide trunk. He slumped to the ground. Just before he passed out, he saw Olivia's beautiful face in his mind.

Chapter 59

Through her peripheral vision, Olivia had been watching the panther creep slowly along the filthy wall of the bar, pausing when she looked his way. He wasn't more than five feet from her, crouched low, tail whipping and legs bunched beneath him. When she let Brett go, she'd hoped that was the end of it. She didn't want vengeance, not anymore. She just wanted to be left alone.

At Hall's triumphant grin, a black streak launched at her. She sped through the rest of the transformation into her griffin form and met the panther head on, gasping at the torture of the change. The pain clouded her reasoning and, as a result, she found herself with a snarling, writhing jungle cat biting for her throat and two bears clubbing at her head. Those who had remained human stood at a distance, even the ones armed. She saw more than one pistol pointed at her. Keeping the bears between those guns and her, she grappled with the cat.

She had hold of his body with one talon, supporting her upper body with her other eagle leg and staying low to protect her underbelly. One of the bears leaned in too far, swung too close to one of her wings. She beat her wing against his arm and he twisted around to the wall and slid to the floor, roaring in pain.

Suddenly outnumbered, the second bear stepped back and she heard one of the guns fire. The bullet tore through the panther and into Olivia's shoulder, numbing it. Feeling the panther go slack, she threw the black body toward the cluster of men with everything she had. The minute he was loose from her, she launched onto a pool table. There was barely room for her head, but it afforded her better reach, especially now that she was injured. The group of men split into three.

About half of the guys, some in the process of changing to their alternate selves, ran out the back or the front of the bar, forgetting they had guns. She saw that Carl and Brett were among them. The remaining shifters split into two groups and fought on, but it wasn't much of a match. They were unsure without their buddies to support them. Their boss had abandoned them. She had no heart for the fight, and she let them escape one-by-one. Those that didn't, she sought only to injure. Still, a few went down without their heads or intestines. She took another gunshot in the side.

When the last man slipped out the door, she shifted to human and stopped at the sink behind the bar to wash her wounds. None of her injuries seemed life-threatening, but she still couldn't move her arm and she felt a stitch in her side when she turned. She felt a bit light-headed too. She'd have to get her injuries looked after. She dried herself and searched behind the bar for what she knew must be there: a camera recorder. The camera, itself, was hidden between a couple of bottles of aged whiskey high on a shelf in front of the mirror.

Contrary to the outcome of most movie bar fights, the mirror was still intact. She grinned.

Tony would be arriving any second.

Finally, she found the recorder, pulled out the DVD, broke it into little pieces and slipped out the front door. Grabbing the shirt from the fallen bouncer, she left.

Somehow, she felt responsible for Brian's disappearance, hence his death. Maybe he'd still been alive, hung up on the rocks, when she'd abandoned him to assist Tony. She blamed Tony a little too. But not much. It really was almost entirely on her. She kept thinking that if she knew what happened, she'd be able to let go. Maybe. Still, in spite of her best efforts, there were no answers.

It was only six days after the battle and Brian's death. She'd killed so many people that she couldn't count them anymore. Even the blinding violence failed to stop the desensitization of the seething rage within her. She was becoming numb, spiraling down to what surely must be her own death. In this fog, she found herself at Brian's old house near Marquis Park. She broke a window in back and wandered his home, touching the things he loved. She stumbled on a half-completed sketch of her lying on his couch from the night he'd guarded her. Even then, he'd later told her, he'd loved her. Now she saw it. She felt the first stirrings of any emotion other than fury. The blood didn't belong here. She went upstairs, showered, stitched, and wrapped her wounds. Then she dressed in his clothes, rolling sleeves and cuffs and cinching the belt.

When she came back downstairs, the mess was almost more than she could stand and she began picking up things, setting them right. It was when she picked up the chessboard that the dam inside her broke and sobs wrenched out of her. She clutched the game pieces to

281

her chest. How could he be gone? "Brian, what will I do without you?"

She sat and cried like that for what seemed hours. Eventually, she heard Tony come quietly through the back door with a key she supposed Brian had given him sometime in their past. She somehow managed to stifle her sobs and wipe her tears away, but when she saw him, she started all over again. He came and sat beside her, holding and rocking her for she didn't know how long.

Eventually, the storm of tears subsided and he said, "I thought you might come back here."

When she didn't answer, he asked, "Did all that killing help?"

She shook her head. "I still don't know anything. I have to find out what happened."

"And kill more? Did all those deaths make you feel better? Did they fill the hole inside you?" His voice turned hard, and he sat back, away from her. "Did they bring Brian back to life?"

She turned and stared at him. She could have told him she'd only killed in self-defense at the bar and she would have let everyone escape, but it didn't matter anymore. He could think what he wanted of her: she no longer cared. Damn him for saying the only thing, short of her own death, that would stop her from seeking the answers she still needed so desperately. Now her voice took its own hard-edged turn. "No."

Brian wasn't coming back. She would be alone forever, and she couldn't stay here, in what had been the center of his life. It just hurt too much. She'd have to find somewhere else. She clutched the chess pieces in her hands and let her gaze roam the room, trying to memorize every detail. Brian's sketches filled the walls. The Guilin Mountains. China. She scrambled to her feet and headed to the back door, still clutching the chess pieces.

"Where are you going?"

"Away. Goodbye, Tony."

Chapter 60

When Brian woke, it was snowing. Fat white flakes blanketed his fur, and the night sky was thick with the falling crystals. The snow hadn't been coming down for long; none had accumulated on the ground.

He closed his eyes again and yawned. It was a deep, satisfied yawn. He remembered everything: finding Olivia in her apartment, the hospital, guarding her, and training her as a griffin. He traced Hall's continued attacks through his memory and the reasoning behind them. He found no blank spots, no empty hours.

It felt good to be whole again.

Now to find Olivia and Tony. He got to his feet, noting that his injuries had grown stiff during his sleep. They would loosen as he ran. He looked out over the valley. He didn't smell either Tony or Olivia, so they had either died and Hall cleaned them out of there, or they were alive and had left. If they had gotten away, they wouldn't have stayed in the valley. They would have gone back to the hunting cabin.

And that wa's exactly where he'd head. He began island hopping again. The water had receded, exposing the islands by about two feet on each edge.

The night was still young, and he had his memories back. He paused on a tiny grit outcropping no bigger than a surfboard. It probably hadn't been above water an hour ago. He lifted his nose high and sent a long, pleased howl into the night. It was answered almost immediately by a she-wolf high on the southern ridge behind him.

He smiled to himself and resumed his journey. After being in China, he'd spent many, many years as just wolf. He'd never taken a mate as one though. The real wolves could smell the strangeness on him and shied away. But the females had always answered his calls, until they got close. Human women also left him, whether they knew his secret or not. And as for shifters, none of them wanted a lone wolf.

Still, even the mates he had taken had never made him feel like he had when with Olivia. With her, he was invincible, yet a slave to her happiness at the same time. With her, he could be himself. Completely. He loved her no matter what she did, no matter what she became. That she was a griffin only meant they could be together for the rest of their very long lives.

The hunting cabin was just over the ridge. He chafed at his slow pace, but he didn't want to land on a floating debris pile again. The few seconds it took to watch for bobbing had saved him from a dunking a few times already.

At last he stood on the final island. Ahead of him was the edge of the valley. This one was a long jump, but he'd done a few of them already and knew he'd be fine. He watched the shoreline, but nothing moved. Just as he launched, he saw the unmistakable bobbing of a floating debris pile at the edge, right where he'd intended to land. He flattened his body, trying to get more reach, but to no avail. He landed with his hind end sinking through the flotsam. The current wasn't deep there, but it was strong and it sucked at him, tugging him into it. He leaned forward, shifted to the werewolf, and dug his claws deep into the sandy grit. Slowly, he pulled his back half out of the current and fell to the ground.

Rolling onto his back, he stared up at the sky. The falling flakes looked like stars dropping from heaven. Olivia would find that sentiment funny. She'd laugh, but would join him in the fantasy. It was one of the things he loved about her. She could set aside everything and join him no matter where his mind wandered. And as an artist, it sometimes went pretty far afield.

His wounds ached, though they were no longer stiff. He needed to be treated by a doctor soon. His arms shook, and he was exhausted. But, after he stopped shaking, he rolled to his feet and changed from the halfway form of werewolf back into a full wolf. He still had some traveling to do. He had to get to Olivia. Their cabin was over the ridge.

He ran straight up the mountainside, scrambling for toeholds with his claws. By the time he reached the top, tremors of exhaustion reclaimed his body. Only part of it was from the physical exertion of climbing, running, and island hopping. Some was from his injuries. But, the majority of it came from the mental trauma he'd been through. He needed to stop and rest. And he would. As soon as he found Olivia.

At the peak, he looked north to where the cabin was, expecting to see lights, or the truck in the drive at the very least. Instead, the cabin was dark and the parking space in front of the cabin was bare.

No!

Fear raced through him. For the first time, he faced the possibility that Olivia might be dead. But he rejected the thought as quickly as it came. That missing vehicle meant that at least one of them was still alive. It also meant they believed he had died in the fall. And no wonder: they hadn't been able to find a body nor had he contacted them.

He had to find a phone. He doubted that Tony had left anything in the cabin for him, "just in case." Bellerophon had to know what had happened. She'd be able to contact Tony.

Brian took one last glance at the place they'd lived for nearly two weeks and, though exhausted, struck off along the ridge of the mountains, still traveling as wolf. Sooner or later, he'd see an occupied house or settlement. If nothing else, Walden wasn't too far ahead of him.

He wasn't alone as he loped through the darkness. Nocturnal animals made their appearance: owls, foxes, raccoons, bats, and deer. The snow started to stick to the ground instead of melting through. At one point, he came across fresh tracks of a wolf pack on the hunt. This gave him pause. From the smell, it was a large pack, with an alpha male, several females, two subordinate males and a few half-grown cubs. He could try to find a way around them, but they would eventually change direction to run after some prey. He slowed and followed them. He didn't need to catch up to them. As he predicted, the tracks soon enough veered down the side of the mountain.

Within half an hour, he saw a cluster of lighted cabins in a glade below him. The night was young. People were about. They could help him. As wolf, he crept down to the little clearing and watched the houses from beneath the broken branches of a giant Colorado Blue Spruce. These were vacation homes. He decided that the big lodge would be his best bet. But first, to get something to cover himself.

Searching the vehicles, he found almost all of them locked. Of the open ones, none had anything he could use. However, on one lighted porch, Brian saw a beer cooler with a blanket half-draped across it. Cigarettes and a lighter sat on top of the blanket. He crept to the corner of the porch and stretched his long wolf body. Snagging the blanket with his teeth, he pulled it off the cooler. The lighter fell with a solid clunk. He snatched the blanket the rest of the way and ran for the woods. Behind him, the cabin door opened and he heard a woman's voice exclaiming to her friends about the disappearance of the blanket. The clamor of three distinct women's voices followed her onto the small porch.

It made no difference now where he asked for help. These people would learn anyway that he'd stolen their blanket. Brian shifted to man, wrapped the blanket tightly around his hips, and walked out of the trees. The blonde woman farthest from him was first to see him. Her face flushed and her eyes brightened. "Oh."

As one, they all turned.

Brian also blushed, aware of all the female eyes on him. He said, "I'm sorry to borrow your blanket. My girlfriend and I were camping. She got scared of something and took off with the truck. Unfortunately, all my clothes were in there."

"What a shame." That came from the woman nearest him; she was shorter than the rest. It seemed they couldn't take their gazes off his exposed body. The blonde near the door let her gaze travel his full length. She licked her lips. At times like this, and there were some occasionally, he usually adopted Tony's persona. He grinned and walked toward them. "Kinda embarrassing. Could I use a cell phone? I'll stay out here. You don't have to worry."

Three of the women ran into the cabin and returned with their phones. The short woman who'd been closest to him approached. "You're injured."

He'd forgotten about that. Grimacing, he said, "Old injuries from a fight. It's why my girlfriend and I decided to take a romantic camping trip."

The tall blonde handed her phone to him. "I guess you're going to break up now?"

He shook his head. "She's just scared."

As a collective, they all sighed. He dialed Bellerophon and moved away from the little group in front of the cabin.

The lawyer answered.

Brian said, "It's me."

"Brian! You are alive." The relief was clear in her voice.

"Olivia?"

"She disappeared. Brian, she's not stable; she went right out of her mind when she thought you died. You need to find her as soon as you can, before she does something to herself. Tony's been looking, but hasn't had any luck."

"Can you come get me? Bring some clothes."

"I'll send Tony."

Brian glanced at the women watching his every move. He asked them, "Where are we?"

They clamored their answers together in a variety of different directions. He held up his hand, then pointed to the blonde cell phone owner. "Where?"

She pointed at the sign over the lodge entrance. "The Heartbreak." She smiled seductively at him.

He told Bellerophon and then said, "Hurry."

289

Chapter 61

Two days after the fight at the bar, Olivia lay in a depression behind an outcropping near the crest of one of Brian's Guilin Mountains. The peaks were unmistakably those she'd seen in the drawings at his home. She'd flown there with only two rests since leaving Colorado: flying north, crossing the Bering Strait, and then swerving south to fly to China.

The peak she'd chosen was far from the touristy Li River hills with names like, "Five Fingers Hill" and "Penholder Peak." "Dragon Head Hill" would have been fitting, but it was too close to the public. Instead, she settled on one of the peaks that was farthest away, unimpressive and, therefore, largely unvisited. She wasn't even sure it had an official name. She just called it "The End." She'd arrived by night, staying close to the water, and had then swooped up the mountain at the last moment. But still, a flying creature her size would be hard to miss, even in the dark. No doubt, the legends of dragons were being reborn even as she slept.

She lived in the griffin form now. Human was something she no longer wanted or needed. She still had the chess pieces, the black king and one of its rooks. She'd them in her talons all the way and kept them nestled close. Her fierce creature heart ached from the loss of Brian and from the things she'd done. There was no remedy. Food was something she didn't consider at all. There was nothing she wanted more than a slow, painful death.

She was lying in her nest when the sound of a scuffed rock caught her attention. The noise came from around the outcropping, on the gentler side of the mountain. Access could be made on foot by humans, but not easily. It was a sharp mountain, jutting almost straight up from the ground.

Slowly, she stood to her full griffin height. She would kill this person so word of her wouldn't spread. Inhaling deeply, she made her judgment on the intruder: small, dirty, male, a child. She hesitated.

A head with Chinese features poked around the corner and then, just as quickly disappeared. Scraping across the ground, a tiny hand pushed a covered bowl into sight. When the lid came off, berries and chunks of cooked meat spilled onto the ground. Despite her decision to starve herself, her stomach roared and saliva wetted her beak at the savory aroma. Again, the child's face poked around the corner. He giggled and disappeared. Seconds later, Olivia heard scraping and the clack of rock on rock as the boy climbed down the mountain.

Disgusted by her body's betrayal, she kicked the bowl. Meat and berries flew across the clearing and the bowl clattered to the edge of the mountain and down the far side. She returned to her nest, rejoicing in the biting pain in her belly. She deserved no better.

The boy returned each of the next two days. He pushed food from around the outcropping of rock and she delivered the bowl and contents down the mountain. On the fourth day, he brought an old man with him and she wondered at the strength of someone so frail who chose such a steep climb with a pack just to sit at the edge of her crag. She also worried about rumors of her getting loose. Was this the beginning of a long parade of people? She should have killed the boy the first day she'd seen him.

Instead of placing the bowl and leaving as before, the boy set it at a distance in front of her, then retreated to sit on a short natural ledge with his ancient friend. A relative? Father? Grandpa? She rose and stalked to the bowl, determined to make her message clear, and kicked it over. Perhaps the old man would understand. Then she returned to her nest, watching to see if they'd go away. As the bowl skidded down the mountain, the old man opened his pack and handed another bowl to the boy who again brought it to the center of her clearing. In an explosion of motion and roaring, she lunged out of her home. The boy, mouth gaping in silent panic, darted back to the safety of the old man's wide open arms. She stomped on the bowl and caused fragments to go shooting across the peak. Everyone present stayed stock still, with her glaring at the two humans who met her gaze with theirs. In their eyes, she saw pity.

Olivia could stand it no more and she turned away. When she looked back, the old man had set aside the boy. He rose, removed yet another bowl and hobbled toward her. His limbs trembled as he set the bowl no more than ten feet from her, but whether they shook from age, exhaustion from the trek, or from fear, she couldn't tell. He didn't leave like the boy had. She hissed. She clacked her beak. She ruffled her feathers and spread her wings. He didn't move.

292

Anger fired through her. Why didn't these people leave her alone? How dare they intrude on her grief and then presume she'd let them live? She was a griffin, after all. She lowered her head, twisted her neck in a serpentine fashion, and opened her beak to strike. He winced, but held his ground. From the edge of the clearing, the boy let out a gasp. Then a rock, a pebble really, flew at her, winging wide and landing harmlessly a few feet away. She stopped dead, once again remembering her vow of no more bloodshed. Annoying as these people might be, they neither deserved death nor ire. They were only trying to save her.

The trouble was, she didn't want saving.

Olivia retreated to her nest, curling so her back faced them. The only way she could give them a clearer message would be if she returned to her human form and spoke to them. And that was something she wasn't willing to do. Besides, there was a language barrier. She didn't know Chinese or any of its dialects, and she doubted these two had studied English.

Within minutes, she heard scuffing right behind her. A small, trembling hand stroked the feathers on her exposed wing. She shrugged and was rewarded by the sound of the boy scrambling backward out of her proximity. It didn't last long, however. Soon, he was back with the cursed bowl. Despite her annoyance, she was beginning to admire the bravery of this boy and the man she decided was his grandpa. The child again stroked her feathers, slowly working his way up her neck. At last, she raised her head and stared at him. Why didn't these people leave? Why did they care what happened to her?

Scooching across the rock edges of her nest, the boy delivered a chunk of meat into the corner of her mouth. She worked it with her tongue, trying to push it out, but the boy was determined and held it in with his hand. In the end, she gave up when the meat became soggy and gross, and she swallowed. Seeing him ready to repeat the process, she conceded defeat and gently took the next chunk from him. They continued in this way until the bowl was empty. Then he patted her head and rejoined his grandpa. He returned with a smooth silk blanket the color of the setting sun and gently covered her. Then, together, he and his grandpa picked up the pack and left.

For two weeks the pair came daily, placing the bowl in front of her and carefully backing away while she ate. The boy was brave, often sidling up next to her and stroking her feathers. The grandpa kept his distance. She started looking forward to their visits.

Memories of Brian became so much a part of Olivia's life, she doubted her sanity. The only time they ceased was when the boy, alone or with his grandpa, came to care for her. Only his presence kept the ghosts at bay.

Often she'd visualize when she and Brian had walked together in the woods, hand in hand, chatting about his past, the griffin, or whatever caught their interest. The heady scent of pine, snow, moist rock, and earth had intoxicated them, and the animals within, and so they'd made love right there among the trees on a smooth, warm bed of limestone slabs. Sometimes they flew high in the clouds, Brian aboard her back, cajoling her to fly higher and faster. To dive and swoop. To be battle-ready. His voice haunted her, teasing and whispering. He called her name…

But then the memories always phased into another one: Brian's drop into the gorge. She saw him fall a million times, his face either slack or contorted in terror. Sometimes, he screamed her name. Other times, it was her who dropped him. Always, she couldn't find any trace of him. And always, she and her griffin sobbed until she slept from emotional exhaustion.

Chapter 62

Brian stood and moved to the center aisle of the Chinese bus. From the seat opposite, Tony also stood and stepped in behind him. They hunched over like beggars, their heads brushing the roof. Taller than anyone else, they looked over the top of everyone standing in front and behind them. Most were native Chinese, but there were also a few foreign tourists.

It was now almost three-and-a-half weeks since the battle in the valley where everything had gone wrong. And it was over forty days since the night he'd first met Olivia, when everything had begun and become right in his life. He had to find her. China was his best hope. Specifically, this region of the Li River. He and Tony had been at it almost two weeks now, searching tiny tourist towns and the pointed karsts nearby.

He took a deep breath, immediately regretting it. What little bit of air that had been coming through the open windows while the bus traveled had stopped as the bus ceased moving. The natural stench of excrement, urine, and rotting produce filled the air.

Brian turned sideways in the aisle and looked at Tony. His friend had his thumb and forefinger pinched against the bridge of his nose. His eyes were closed and he had a pained expression on his face. "If I have to step into one more stinking—"

"Shhh! We don't need to alienate people. They have to like us. We need their help."

"Fine." He dropped his hand and turned his lips up in the kind of smile that people get when forced into civility.

The line of passengers in the center aisle began a shuffling pace toward the front exit. Brian paused to let a young Chinese woman with two toddler sons into the line ahead of him.

Tony's voice came from behind. "Can you at least tell me again the name of this town?"

"Xingping."

"And how about the total number of mountains we've searched since coming to China?"

"Again, they're called karsts. Are you forgetting this on purpose?"

"I just don't see the point in remembering something I'll never use or see again."

Brian shrugged. "You never know where life will lead you. I'm betting you never planned on being here in the first place."

"Touché." After a moment, he again asked, "So, how many?"

"Karsts."

"Right. Karsts. How many?"

"Somewhere between forty-two and forty-seven."

"Great. How many more here?"

"As many as it takes."

They fell into silence as they finally reached the door and climbed down the steps to the street. For such a small town, there was a steady flow of mostly pedestrian traffic. Brian took a deep breath of clean air. It tasted of engine fumes and filth. But it was better than the air in the bus.

Tony said, "Looks like the last three towns." They moved with the traffic toward the river.

"Xingping is smaller, not so touristy."

"How do you know Olivia will be here? For that matter, how do you know she's even in China?"

"Because I lived among these karsts along the river for a long time. They're still important to me."

"Right. I get that. But why would she be here?"

"Tony! Give it a rest. You're giving me a headache." Brian frowned. Truthfully, his friend had a point. Though he knew Olivia loved him with all her soul, would she be here? If she wasn't, he wouldn't know where to look. Where would she go if it hurt her too much to feel him close to her? If she didn't want to feel anything? He had no answers to that. She had to be here. And she had to be alive. To consider that she might have killed herself out of despair was more than he could bear. They would find her. Everything would be right again.

They walked in silence until they reached the riverfront. A wall of merchants lined the bank, hoping to sell to pedestrians and water travelers alike. Trinkets of all types glinted in the sun from tables and blankets on the ground. The few that were lucky enough to own stalls filled their upright divisions with a riot of colored scarves, blankets, shirts, necklaces, and jackets.

A tall, blonde European woman stood in front of the first stall they passed. Tony elbowed Brian in the ribs and leaned into him to speak. "Hey! You know who she reminds me of? One of those Canadian chicks at that lodge above Walden." They kept walking.

"Don't start." Brian didn't look at him. He'd never live it down. He'd never been so glad to see Tony as he'd been that night. After three hours of waiting alone with the women, he had been as nervous as popcorn in a hot frying pan. He focused on the wares of the stalls.

"What'd you get? Something like seventeen propositions and one proposal? All from four Canadian women."

"Shut up." Then, to take the sting out of his words, he glanced at his friend and smiled. "It made me feel cheap."

Tony burst out laughing. The noise was so loud and hard, people turned to stare. The attention only seemed to inflame his humor. He wrapped his hand around his stomach with one arm, laughing and wiping his eyes with his other hand. He was still chuckling when his cell phone rang.

"Silver," he answered, wiping his eyes again. After a brief pause he said in a gentle voice, "No. I'm fine. Just laughing at Brian."

Brian listened and tried to interpret the conversation, based on what he heard Tony say. It had to be Bellerophon on the other end. Tony never used that tone with anyone else. Not even any other woman. Were the two in love? The thought of it brought him a stab of worry for Olivia. All levity aside, what the lawyer had told him about her frame of mind worried him more than anything. Would she really try to kill herself? He had to find her. Where was she? He shaded his eyes and looked around the crowd, almost expecting to see her watching him.

"No, we haven't found her yet," Tony continued. Then, he said, "I don't know, some horrible little place in China."

Brian moved to the next stall, and Tony followed slowly, listening to his caller. After a moment, he said, "That's interesting." He put his hand over the phone and said to Brian, "They found Carl Hall's body. He was sitting in his truck in front of his house where he was shot. Brett is being held for his murder."

That didn't surprise Brian. A boy could only take so much abuse and that one had swallowed more than his fair share. He turned to the items the next merchant had for sale and froze. There, on a brilliant red scarf was the image of a golden griffin. He snatched it from the wall and studied it. It was a glamorized version, true, but the griffin looked like Olivia. Griffin mythology wasn't new in China, but the images had changed with time. This one was current. Without turning, he reached behind him and patted his hand on Tony. "Hang up. She's here."

"Gotta go." Then Tony stood beside him, staring at the scarf. "Are you sure? It could be a coincidence."

Brian lifted his gaze and looked around the stall. Griffins in gold graced more than half of the stall's brightly colored items. "Oh, yeah. I'm sure."

He dug in his pocket and removed some coins. Holding them out to the young woman who manned the stall, he said in Chinese, "I want this. It's beautiful. Did you paint it?"

She smiled at him and reached for the money. It was, no doubt, way more than she usually got for her scarves. She chose to answer in English. "My father paint. I sell."

"Where is he?"

She motioned to one of the sharply pointed karsts that stood back from the river. It looked like any other. "He there. With my son."

Chapter 63

Olivia was caught in a vision at Tony's lake cabin. She and Brian both leaned way out through a giant glassless window, watching the moonlight play on the water. The silver reflections swirled and twisted and became a tiger. Other ripples formed into dark, hideous shapes with gaping maws and heavy claws. The pines shadowed them, even as the snow camouflaged Tony. She hid beside her love inside a broken stump. Her heart twisted, pushing her grief to the surface. Brian pulled her to him and she inhaled his musk, soaking it in as if it was a balm.

Suddenly aware of someone in her clearing, hoping it was the boy, she snapped open her eyes. The scent from her daydream strengthened, and she wondered if she wasn't awake, but still trapped in her tortuously enjoyable vision. Two men stood in front of her: Tony and Brian.

Brian.

Only not.

He was ghost-thin. Almost like a stick. He'd shaved his beard and moustache and had cut his hair. Still, his dark brown eyes glittered and his pale skin crinkled at the corners of his mouth as he smiled.

Her mouth dried. What was this? Terror cascaded through her. She lowered her head and hissed, spreading her wings and sidestepping in a wide circle around him. He stopped and slowly raised his hand in a gesture she knew so well. That hand had once before soothed the beak of an angry griffin. She shifted to human form and snatched her blanket from her nest for a cloak. She stared at him for a moment. He lowered his hand, but said nothing.

She shook her head, trying to clear the webs of the vision, but it remained. She was convinced she'd finally gone over the edge into permanent insanity. Her voice low and cracked from disuse, she asked, "Are you a ghost?"

He smiled that unique-to-Brian smile again and shook his head. "No."

Her hand flew to her mouth. Brian? Could it be? Blinking furiously to keep tears at bay, Olivia stared at him and dropped her hand to her side, afraid to ask, afraid to hear he'd hidden away from her on purpose. But she needed that answer too. "Where were you?"

He took a step toward her. Still unconvinced of reality, she retreated. He took another slow step. "I was held captive. As soon as I escaped, I went looking for you."

"But I was gone."

He nodded, still coming her way. She let him. He said, "I figured out where you'd gone and made Tony bring me. It took us awhile to figure out exactly on which peak you'd built your nest."

"You knew I'd be here?"

"Where else?"

302

"Is this real?" Blinking didn't stop her tears anymore and they cascaded down her face.

He opened his arms. She stepped into his strong embrace, inhaling his unique male musk. It smelled like heaven. His heart beat strong against her and his breath roared in her ear. He held her for a long time, kissing her hair and rocking her. Maybe she was still dreaming, but she never wanted to wake from this.

"Brian, I've done some terrible, terrible things."

"It's in the past."

Olivia heard a soft cough and looked around Brian to see Tony beaming at them. He said, "Besides being held prisoner, he had short-term amnesia. He couldn't remember anything of what happened. He couldn't even remember that first night, at your apartment."

Brian pulled her attention back to him, with a hand on her chin. He met her gaze with his own of sincerity and tenderness. "You know, wolves mate for life."

A fire of love and desire for this man raced through her body and she smiled up at him. "I think Griffins must also. I don't want anyone else. Ever."

He lowered his lips to hers and pulled her into a deep branding kiss. Knowing how all her visions ended, she'd tried to keep her guard up, to keep from being sucked in too far, but his kiss crumbled every wall she'd erected. The aching gap in her equilibrium, her reality, slowly began to fill.

"Not to interrupt, but to interrupt anyway, what the hell is all this?" Tony bumped a bowl filled with copper and brass beads with the edge of his foot.

Brian answered for her, looking around the clearing. He chuckled. "Tribute. Our Olivia has a following."

She grimaced. "I can't keep them away. Every day, more show up."

He turned his beautiful brown-eyed gaze on her again. "Well, we can't stay here. Besides, I like a bed to sleep in."

Still not entirely sure she wasn't hallucinating, she said, "There is one person I'd like to see again before we go." If this wasn't real, she was willing to play along. Why wake? So far, this vision had been drastically different than the others. Would it end the same way?

"We passed two groups of people on the way up: two women and, a fair bit behind them, a boy and an old man."

"The second group is them."

The three of them sat down on stones at the edge of her small rock home. Brian kept hold of Olivia, as if afraid she'd leave, which was fine by her. She told both of them about her time there and the boy who had saved her. Brian described the years he'd lived in the area. Tony, while chiming in occasionally on their conversation, poked through the tribute bowls. He'd pick up a piece of something, examine it in the light and either pocket it or put it back. Most things went back to where he'd gotten it.

Growing tired of his treasure hunt, Tony wandered to the edge of the crag and stood on top of the outcropping. Eventually, he said, "The two women are approaching now. I can see the old man and the boy not too far behind them. The women must have stopped for quite a while."

He hopped down, grinning and rubbing his hands. "At last, we can get out of here. I need something to eat besides these berries." He flipped his hand toward the bowls.

Brian frowned at him, but said nothing. She just grinned. Same old Tony. Brian asked her, "What do we do? Should we hide?"

Olivia shook her head. "Just sit and wait. If they see I'm gone, they hopefully won't stay."

It was as she'd said. Brian, who spoke Chinese, explained to the two women that she'd angrily left and it didn't look as if she'd return. They were distraught, but left their gifts behind with a prayer in the hope that she'd come back. After they left, Olivia said, "I need to be griffin for the boy. It'll frighten him if I'm not here." She owed him and his grandfather one last visit with the beast.

He nodded, but didn't look pleased as she pulled away. In truth, it scared her to let go of him. Any minute now, this part of her daydream would end as they always did. She knew that the boy and his grandpa would never arrive. Instead, Brian and Tony would disappear and the horror of that fall in the ravine and the endless gulf of loneliness and guilt would start. Yet, shifting to griffin had to be done. The vision had to run its course. There was nothing she could do to stop it anyway.

Slowly, she backed away and let the griffin have her body. She didn't take her gaze off Brian as she grew and stretched into the beast. She expected this vision would change. And when it did, this time, she'd finish it, throwing herself over the edge of the mountain to die on the rocks below. She couldn't take it anymore. The hallucination this time was too perfect, too cruel, for her to continue living without Brian.

She'd just settled into her nest, still facing Brian when her dark-haired Chinese boy stepped into the clearing. Her heart stopped. The presence of the boy had always before brought clarity to her life, such as it was. With him near, the visions dissipated. But, he was here. And yet, so was Brian. Was this … could this be…?

Olivia stood abruptly, sending the boy, open-mouthed, scurrying to his grandpa. Before now, she'd always moved with great care to keep from startling

305

either of them. But now, she had to know. She stalked to Brian, still in her griffin. Cocking her head at him, she watched for signs of a glimmer or transparency. Seeing none, she lowered her head and jabbed the smooth curve of her beak against his chest. He felt solid enough.

As if he read her mind, he asked, "Still not sure I'm real, huh?"

She chattered her love to him, not caring that he didn't understand and not wanting to move away from him long enough to change to human. He smiled and raised his hand, stroking her beak. His smooth hand dissipated her fears. Dear God, it's real! Brian was real! He was alive! She lifted her head and placed it on his shoulder, rubbing her beak against his chin. While she crooned softly, he told their story in Chinese to the boy and his grandpa, Tony looking on.

When Brian finished, neither the boy nor the old man moved a muscle. If they believed the three of them were possessed demons, they didn't show it. That was good. Olivia tromped to her nest and returned with the chess pieces in her beak. She dropped them in the boy's hands and he curled his fingers over them. He looked around her at Brian, who gave him her thanks.

As the boy shifted his gaze back to her and then to the gift in his hands, she saw the sorrow there. She could tell he knew this was goodbye. While the two Chinese watched, Brian grew into the wolf, his clothes splitting and scattering to the ground in rags. Seeing his skin furrowed over his ribs hurt her. He'd been so close to death. Then Tony changed to a snarling and spitting silver Bengal, showing off. The boy backed away, eyes wide, but the grandpa reached out a shaking hand. Tony stilled as the old man stroked his white fur.

Then the three of them turned away. Brian and Tony bounded down the steep mountain like it was a playground, while she plunged off the edge of the crag, catching the air currents beneath her wings and lifting high into the sky. She looked back at the boy and his grandpa in the clearing. They stood with their eyes shaded, watching as she sailed away.

Olivia had no idea where they were going. Nor did she care much, but, as she kept Brian under her watchful eye, she knew the two of them would find a nice quiet cabin on a lake somewhere far from civilization. As for Tony, who knew what he would do.

The End

Publisher's Note

Please help this author's career by posting an honest review wherever you purchased this book.

About the Author

Wendy Koenig has been writing since she was a young child in Illinois, filling spiral notebooks with poetry and short stories. It wasn't until after a short stint in the military that she began working on novels. It was also then that she began seeking publication.

Her first piece to be printed was a short children's fiction, "Jet's Stormy Adventure," serialized in The Illinois Horse Network. She attended the University of Iowa, honing her craft in its famed summer workshops and writing programs. She graduated from the University of Maine, Presque Isle, in 2006. Her first novel was published in 2007. Since that time, she has published and co-authored numerous books.

Several of her stories have taken international awards: First Place Short Fiction and Second Place Novel in the 2005 Abilene Writers' Guild International Contest, Second Honorable Mention Novel in the 2005 CNW/FFWA International Writing Competition, and Second Honorable Mention Novel in the 2007 Frontiers in Writing International Contest.

Her short stories and poetry have appeared in multiple venues, including KidVisions eZine, Upcountry eZine, Echoes magazine, and the annual Breathe anthologies. She currently writes adult and Young Adult science fiction and action/adventure, as well as adult romance.

She currently lives in New Brunswick, Canada.

www.ingramcontent.com/pod-product-compliance
Lightning Source LLC
Chambersburg PA
CBHW071448110726
47908CB00003B/549